Child of Love

We Three Kings: Book #2

KIMBERLY RAE JORDAN

THREE**STRAND**
PRESS

A CORD OF THREE STRANDS IS NOT EASILY BROKEN.

A man, a woman & their God.
Three Strand Press publishes Christian Romance stories
that intertwine love, faith and family. Always clean.
Always heartwarming. Always uplifting.

Copyright © 2021 by **Kimberly Rae Jordan**

All rights reserved. No part of this publication may be reproduced, distributed or transmitted in any form or by any means, without prior written permission.

This is a work of fiction. Names, characters, places, and incidents are a product of the author's imagination. Locales and public names are sometimes used for atmospheric purposes. Any resemblance to actual people, living or dead, or to businesses, companies, events, institutions, or locales is completely coincidental.

Scripture taken from the New King James Version®. Copyright © 1982 by Thomas Nelson, Inc. Used by permission. All rights are reserved.

Child of Love/ Kimberly Rae Jordan. -- 1st ed.
ISBN-13: 978-1-988409-56-6

*"Though the mountains be shaken
and the hills be removed,
yet my unfailing love for you
will not be shaken
nor my covenant of peace be removed,"
says the Lord, who has compassion on you.*

Isaiah 54:10

Prologue

July

Heather King sat at the counter in the kitchen, waiting for Essie to finish what she needed to do for the afternoon and evening to come. Though Heather had offered to help, the kitchen was Essie's domain, and she didn't take kindly to people trying to intrude.

"I'm not sure Hunter is going to be able to pull this off," Heather said. "I mean, I can't believe how complicated he's made this. Why doesn't he just pop the question?"

Essie laughed. "I'm surprised he's waited this long."

"It's only been seven months," Heather reminded her. "Though I suppose he feels he's been waiting for Carissa forever."

"He knows a good thing when he sees it," Essie said.

Heather wished she could run into a man who was a good thing. She was super happy for Hunter and Carissa. But considering her oldest brother hadn't had a real interest in a serious relationship, it seemed unfair that he'd found love first.

She just wanted a man who could see her for who she was: a person who loved her family greatly. Someone who enjoyed reading books and eating chocolate. She also spent more hours than she cared to think about watching true crime shows. She loved kids, too, and absolutely doted on her soon-to-be niece—provided Carissa agreed to marry Hunter.

"Your turn will come, sweetie," Essie said. "Your mother and I are certainly praying that for you."

"Thanks." Heather had also prayed more specifically about it since Hunter and Carissa had started dating the previous Christmas. Seeing them together had just made her even more aware of the fact that she wanted a relationship, too.

"Is Hayden coming over?" Essie asked as she pulled a pan of dinner rolls from the oven.

Heather wanted to reach over and take one to slather in butter while it was still warm, but she knew she'd get her hand smacked if she did. "I don't think so."

"I suppose that's not too surprising."

Sadly, it wasn't. Hayden continued to struggle with pain from the injuries he'd suffered in the car accident that had killed their dad. They kept hoping with each surgery he had that the pain would lessen. But so far, it seemed that was not to be the case.

"I'll save him some food," Essie said. "Hunter can take it to him when he goes home later."

"I know he'll appreciate that."

"Who will appreciate what?" Heather's mom asked as she walked into the kitchen.

"Essie said she'd send food for Hayden with Hunter later."

Her mom sighed as she sat down on the stool next to Heather. "I wish he'd come for the evening, but I understand why he doesn't want to."

Heather suspected it was more than just pain keeping Hayden in his apartment.

Though he'd never said as much, she got the feeling that he thought his life might as well be over. He'd made a few comments over the past few months about no one wanting to deal with a person who was grumpy from pain and covered in scars. Heather knew there were women out there who would be willing to love him just as he was, but there was no convincing him of that.

"What time are you picking Rachel up?" her mom asked.

"Hunter asked me to swing by Carissa's around noon."

"And is Carissa wondering why she isn't just dropping Rachel by the house?"

"I asked her if I could take Rachel out. I'm sure she's assuming we're going to McDonald's and a movie."

"This is going to be so much fun," her mom exclaimed. "I sure hope she says yes."

Heather and Essie both laughed, then Heather said, "As if there's any chance she'd tell Hunter no."

"And I can't tell you how happy I am about that."

Heather was grateful that they'd never doubted Carissa's reasons for being with Hunter. There might have been some women who would have taken advantage of the situation Carissa had been in when they'd met her for the first time. But instead, Carissa had worried that they'd given her and Rachel *too* much.

"Rachel is going to lose her mind when she realizes what's going on," Heather said.

"Are you going to tell her?" Essie asked. "I mean, it'll be obvious we're planning something when she shows up and sees us decorating and stuff."

"I'm just going to tell her we're having a party."

Her mom chuckled. "As long as she's invited, I don't think she'll care too much about what the party is for."

The weather was cooperating for the celebration. The Saturday had dawned sunny, and it didn't look like that was going to change at all. Heather was thankful, since the final portion of Hunter's day included a barbecue in their backyard.

"Well, let's get going," Essie said. "Everything is ready food-wise except for cooking the meat, which George will do later."

Hunter was confident enough in Carissa's answer that he wanted to celebrate that night, keeping it just to those he felt closest to. He and Carissa's circle of friends was quite small, so that meant the gathering to celebrate this momentous occasion would also be quite small.

Still, it would be missing some very important people. In addition to their dad and Hayden not being there, Carissa's parents wouldn't be either. Heather pushed aside her grief at that thought because she knew her dad would be mad at her for being sad on what was supposed to be a day for celebration.

"Remember to be quiet," Heather told Rachel. "Your mom and Hunter will talk for a bit, then we can join them, okay?"

"I can't wait!" Rachel said in a loud whisper. "When are they coming?"

George looked down at the phone in his hand, where he was using the security cameras to monitor Hunter's progress as he drove up to the house. "In a few minutes."

The other guests were due to arrive in about forty-five minutes for the celebration. She was actually a little surprised that Hunter had kept to his schedule so well.

"They're in the house," George told them.

They were standing behind some of the large bushes that were off to the side of the deck. It hid them, but they could see through the branches, and unless Hunter and Carissa spoke in whispers, they'd be able to hear them. They'd tested that out earlier just to see.

There was also a photographer hiding behind a huge potted plant with a clear view of the arch. Hunter wanted to have photos of the occasion, and Heather couldn't blame him for that.

Heather thought the backyard looked like a dream. If the days weren't so long, they would have had a ton of fairy lights strung through the yard. But since the sun would still be shining brightly until later in the evening, they'd had to content themselves with an abundance of flowers and balloons. The focal point of the décor was the arch where Hunter planned to propose to Carissa, which was covered in white and blush pink roses and balloons with a pearlescent sheen to them.

"What is all this?" Carissa asked as the couple stepped out of the house onto the deck.

Rachel let out a little gasp but managed to keep quiet otherwise. Through the branches, Heather could see Hunter leading Carissa over to the arch.

"I'm not sure if you picked up on the theme of the stuff we did today," Hunter said.

"Well, each of them represented a date we went on."

"Yep. I picked ones that I thought you really enjoyed," Hunter said. "Though I have to say that the ride at the Mall of America remains one of my favorite things we've done together. Plus, it was our first date, which will always be special to me."

"I'm glad we went on it again today," Carissa agreed. "But you still haven't explained what all this is about. It's not my birthday."

Heather had a hard time believing that Carissa didn't even suspect what Hunter was planning. Hopefully, that didn't mean she hadn't been thinking about a future with him, too. If Hunter was the only one on the proposal page, they were getting ready to witness a very sad moment.

"I've spent the last seven months thanking God for bringing you and Rachel into my life. You've both infused joy back into our lives, reminding us that even amid sorrow, there is joy. I've loved every minute we've spent together, and more than anything else, I want to know that I get to spend the rest of my life with you."

Hunter lowered himself to one knee, still holding Carissa's hand. "Sweetheart, will you marry me?"

"Oh, Hunter," Carissa said, her voice barely loud enough for them to hear. "I would love nothing more. You've proven that what I suspected seven months ago is true. You're a loving, caring, and honorable man, and I would be so blessed to spend my life with you. I love you so much."

Hunter slid the ring onto Carissa's finger, then stood and took her into his arms. Heather was sure they were speaking to one another, but it wasn't loud enough for them to hear. As they kissed, Heather felt tears form in her eyes at how wonderful the moment was.

"Mama! Mama!" Rachel called as she darted out from behind the bush. "Does this mean Hunter's gonna be my daddy?"

When she got to them, Hunter grabbed Rachel and swung her up into his arms. The three of them stood there, arms wrapped around each other.

"I can't wait any longer," her mom said, following Rachel's lead and leaving their hiding spot.

Heather laughed, then she, Essie, and George joined the others on the deck. The photographer continued to take pictures as they hugged and congratulated Hunter and Carissa.

"I always wanted a sister," Heather said as she hugged Carissa. "And I think I've hit the jackpot with you."

Carissa smiled at her, happiness glowing in her eyes. "I feel the same way. I can't believe we get to be a real family now."

"You've felt like family since day one," Heather said to her. "Now it will just be official."

"I can't wait!"

The photographer took several posed pictures of them. Then Essie went into the house to get the meat ready for the barbecue while George fired the grill up.

As they prepared to celebrate the beginning of a new chapter for Carissa and Hunter, Heather hoped that she would have the opportunity one day to celebrate a love her own.

Chapter 1

Heather King muttered under her breath as she sat in traffic on I-394. She gripped the steering wheel tightly as the wipers tried to keep up with the snow that melted on the windshield. She would have asked George to drive her that day, but her mom had had some errands to run as well. And while Heather disliked driving when it was snowing, her mom just never drove, period.

For as long as she could remember, either her dad or George had driven her mom wherever she needed to go. Of course, now with her dad gone, it fell to George to drive her. Not that he minded. It was his job, after all.

When the weather was good, Heather didn't mind driving as much. But when it was snowing and dark, she absolutely hated it. She didn't need a shrink to tell her that part of that came from how her dad had died. The horrific multi-car pile-up that had taken her dad's life and severely injured her brother had been the result of icy roads caused by bad weather.

So now, Heather crept along the highway, even though it would take significantly longer to get home. Other cars on the road flew past her, and a couple honked at her, apparently not appreciating her safer pace. *Idiots.*

All she wanted was to get home so she could get ready for the fundraiser that evening. They had it every year in November, and she should have been home already, but she'd been held up at the office with a phone call.

It was barely five, but the sun had already set, leaving the city overshadowed by twilight. Honestly, she wouldn't have minded the early darkness or the snow if she'd been home, curled up in the solarium with a fire going in the woodstove. But driving in all that...no, thank you.

Heather inched up her speed a tiny bit, wanting to just get home. All of a sudden, she heard a bang and felt it reverberate through her car as the vehicle swerved toward the shoulder. She had to fight the instinct to slam on her brakes. Instead, she lifted her foot off the gas, keeping a tight grip on the steering wheel.

As horns blared behind her, she put her blinker on and allowed the car to move onto the shoulder, hearing a flapping sound as she did. Only as her car slowed right down did she put on the brakes and come to a stop.

With her hands still clenched around the steering wheel, she leaned forward to rest her head on it. Her heart pounded so hard in her chest she thought she'd see it if she looked down.

Tears pricked at her eyes as she swallowed hard against the tightness in her throat. Every time her dad had tried to teach her things about driving—because he wanted her to be safe on the road—she'd just brushed his concerns aside. He'd persisted, though, and something must have stuck because as soon as she'd heard the bang, his voice was in her head, walking her through what she should do.

The stupid thing was that even *he* had said it was unlikely that she'd ever experience a blowout, but that if one happened, it would most likely happen in the summer. However, here she was, sitting on the side of the road in a winter storm with a blowout.

Why did this have to be the exception to the rule that happened to her? She could have done with one that didn't put her life in danger.

Exhaling, Heather put the car in park and slumped back, tipping her head against the headrest. Her heart still pounded almost painfully in her chest, and she felt like she couldn't take a deep breath. She tried to keep her mind from dwelling on how close that call had been. If she'd swerved into the traffic instead of toward the shoulder, it could have been so much worse.

She sat there for a couple of minutes, willing her heart to slow from its panicked galloping. When she could finally take a deep breath, and her heart rate had slowed to an almost normal rate, she hit the button to put her flashers on, then reached for her phone.

As she was deciding who to call, there was a rap on her passenger side window, and her heart rate—which had only *just* settled—ratcheted up again. Holding her phone against her chest, Heather glanced over at the window to see a man peering in at her.

She debated what to do for a split second. Was she about to get killed while sitting on the side of a highway that she despised? After a moment, she slowly lowered the window a couple of inches, hoping she could get the window back up in time if he suddenly pulled a gun.

No doubt her mother would yell at her for this, and probably her brothers would as well. But if, by some chance, the man was a good Samaritan and could get her back on the road sooner rather than later, it would be a good thing.

"Looks like you blew a tire," the man said, his voice gruff over the sound of the traffic. "I can change it for you if you'd like, since it's probably gonna take awhile for a tow in this weather."

While she definitely would like, it seemed to be a toss-up whether trusting him would get her back on the road or if it would get her killed.

"Here." Two of his fingers appeared in the space of the lowered window, a business card held between them.

Heather hesitated for a moment before reaching over to take it, trying not to shiver at the cold air coming in through the open window. She turned on the overhead light and looked down at the card.

Asher Larson

Larson Automotives

The card also gave a phone number and address. She took a picture of it with her phone, then after a moment's debate, she opened up a text message to one of her brothers. She chose Hayden because Hunter was tied up with things for the fundraiser. Plus, of the two, Hayden was least likely to worry. He probably wouldn't even respond to her text.

Got a flat on 394. A guy stopped and offered to help me out. Here's his info. If I end up dead, look for him.

She really, really hoped that this guy was genuine in his desire to help her and didn't want to kill her. It wasn't that she didn't believe that there were genuinely nice people out there. It just seemed that the not-so-nice ones were who they heard about.

But her dad used to tell them that amongst the nice helpful people in the world, he also believed that God sometimes sent angels to aid them. She'd take either of those possibilities over the killer one.

Please, God, let this be someone You've sent to me.

"If you want, you can go sit in my truck with my little girl while I change your tire."

His little girl? He had a child with him? That should make him more trustworthy, right? Unless it was just a ruse to get her into his truck.

"Pop the trunk so I can get your spare," he said, seeming to take it for granted that she was going to accept his help.

And she was, wasn't she?

Yeah, she was.

She reached for the lever that would release the trunk, then turned the car off. Keeping an eye on the traffic, she opened her door just enough so that she could slip out, then she hurried to the back of the car where the man...Asher...met her.

He was a large man, standing several inches taller than her, with broad shoulders. "Come to the truck. It'll be warmer."

After a moment's hesitation, she followed him to the big truck that sat behind her car with its flashers on. On the front door was a logo for the same company that had been on the business card. That was a good sign.

The interior light was already on, so when he opened the back door of the cab, she could see the little girl that sat there. She had big blue eyes and dark brown hair and was bundled up in a worn jacket.

"Isla, this nice lady is going to sit with you while I change her tire, okay?"

The little girl nodded without hesitation, curiosity clear in her beautiful blue eyes.

"Get on in," Asher said. "I'll be back when I'm done."

Feeling more confident about her decision, Heather managed to climb up onto the seat without too much awkwardness, glad she'd worn pants to work that day instead of a skirt or dress.

Once she'd settled in the seat, Asher shut the door and walked back toward her car. He'd left his headlights on, which illuminated what he was doing. However, she didn't pay attention to him, turning instead to the little girl sitting beside her.

"What's your name?" Isla asked.

"I'm Heather."

"My name is spelled I S L A, but you say it like eye," she pointed to one of her eyes, "and la like you're singing."

Heather grinned at the little girl as she explained her name. With such a unique name, she probably had to explain it frequently. If she'd just seen it written down, Heather would have assumed it was Is-la.

"It's a beautiful name," Heather told her. "How old are you?"

"I'm seven."

Heather thought of Rachel, the little girl who was now a permanent feature in their lives since Hunter had proposed to her mom, Carissa.

"Do you have any brothers or sisters?" Heather asked, not sure what else to talk to the girl about.

Isla shook her head, causing more hair to slip free from her lopsided ponytails. "It was just Mommy and me, but then Mommy died. So now it's me and Uncle Ash."

"He's your uncle?" Heather asked, looking out the front window of the truck to where Asher... Ash... worked on the tire.

"Yep. He's my mommy's brother. When she died, he got me."

Heather hadn't expected she'd learn the story of their lives when she'd agreed to sit in Ash's truck. "Do you like living with him?"

"Oh, yes." Isla smiled broadly. "He feeds me good food, and I have a nice bed to sleep in."

Heather couldn't help but smile in return, though she had to admit a bit of curiosity given what Isla had revealed. Good food? A nice bed? It sounded as if that hadn't been something she'd had previously.

"That's good you have those things."

"Yep. Best of all, Uncle Ash doesn't hurt me."

While Heather was thrilled to hear that, the idea that someone had hurt the little girl made her feel sick. "I'm glad to hear that."

Isla tilted her head as she stared at her. "Do you have a little girl?"

"No, I don't have a daughter, but I have a niece." Technically, Rachel wasn't a niece yet. But the little girl called her Aunt Heather these days, so Heather claimed her as a niece. It would be real soon enough. "Her name is Rachel, and she's nine."

"Is she nice?"

"Yes, she is. Very nice."

"Maybe she could be my friend." Isla frowned. "I don't have many friends."

Heather wasn't sure what to say to that. Would the little girl know *why* she didn't have friends? She couldn't very well say that Rachel would be her friend when Heather wasn't sure they'd ever meet each other.

"Why don't you have many friends?" Heather couldn't keep the question from slipping out.

"I'm going to a new school, and the kids aren't very nice to me."

"I'm sorry to hear that."

The little girl's chin sank to her chest, her spark seeming to dim. "Uncle Ash says I just need to let them get to know me."

Heather was inclined to agree, but she also knew from things Rachel had said that sometimes kids were just downright cruel. "That's probably true."

"They say I'm dumb because I'm seven, but I can't read good yet."

"Do you like books?" Heather asked, thinking of the books that Rachel read voraciously.

Isla shrugged. "I like coloring books. I like to color a lot."

"Have you told Santa what you want for Christmas?" Heather asked after they'd discussed what types of pictures she enjoyed coloring.

The little girl scowled at her. "Santa isn't real."

Heather wanted to argue with her, but she wasn't going to lie. The previous year, Rachel had still believed in Santa, so finding out what she wanted from Santa had been easy.

"Do you have a Christmas tree?"

"Not yet," Isla shrugged. "Uncle Ash said maybe next week we'll get one."

Heather thought of the elaborately decorated house she was going home to. For the second year in a row, she was being reminded through a child how fortunate she truly was. For as long as she could remember, Heather had always looked forward to Christmas. She knew she could count on her mom and dad—and Santa—to make the holiday fun and exciting.

"Do you have a tree?" Isla asked.

"I live with my mom, and she loves to decorate a tree." In fact, she had several trees, but it seemed wrong to mention that when the little girl didn't even have one.

When the door next to her opened, Heather jerked around. Ash stood there, rubbing his gloved hands together.

"Tire's changed," he said. "You should be good to go, but get that other tire looked at. It may have had a defect in it for it to blow that way."

"I will." She turned back to Isla. "Thank you for keeping me company."

Isla grinned at her. "You're welcome."

Heather swung her legs around, and when Ash stepped back, she slid out onto the icy ground. She kept hold of the door until she was sure that her feet wouldn't slip right out from underneath her.

"I'll be right back, Isla," Ash said, then he closed the door.

"Thank you so much for helping me out," Heather said as they walked to the front of the truck. "I really appreciate it. How much do I owe you?"

Ash waved his hand. "No charge. Just get the tire looked at."

"I will." Heather glanced back into the truck and lifted her hand to wave at Isla before smiling one last time at Ash before heading around to slip back behind the wheel.

Once in her car, she waited for a break in the traffic before pulling out onto the road once again. She glanced into her rearview mirror to see if Ash's truck followed her, but in the wash of headlights, she couldn't tell.

Rather than focus on what was behind her, she shifted her gaze back to the road, then instructed her Bluetooth to call Hayden to let him know that she'd survived her encounter with the stranger and made the acquaintance of an adorable little girl with big blue eyes and a sad life story.

Chapter 2

Not long after the woman's car had disappeared into traffic on the highway, Ash pulled his truck up to his house. He wasn't sure what had prompted him to pull over and help the stranded motorist, except that maybe he'd needed to do something he knew he was good at.

Also, the weather and road conditions meant that there were probably a lot of calls for tow trucks, so whoever it was would have been waiting awhile. The woman had clear reservations about opening her door and given that he currently had a bit of a rough look going on, he wouldn't have been surprised if she'd passed on his offer of help.

"The lady was nice," Isla said as he unlocked the door and waited for her to go into the house ahead of him.

"What did you talk about?" Ash asked as he walked into the small kitchen after taking off their jackets and boots.

"Books." She gave him a frown before adding, "*Coloring* books. Christmas trees. Santa."

They'd covered a few topics while he'd been busy. Unfortunately, they were all rather hot-button issues. It had been years since he'd had a Christmas tree, which meant that he didn't have even a fake one in storage, and he definitely had no decorations to put on one.

His budget was currently stretched thin since he'd had nothing for a little girl when he'd gotten the call that his sister had OD'd and left a child behind. Ash didn't know why they'd called him, except that he was family, and he wasn't sure that he'd do a better job than a home with good foster parents. But he'd known there was no guarantee that she'd end up in a good home, so he'd agreed to take her.

When he'd let his parents know about Gwen's death and the fact that she had a daughter, they'd made it clear that they didn't care. Basically, they'd told him they'd mourned the loss of Gwen years ago when she'd left home and turned to drugs and alcohol.

Ash hadn't been surprised at their response, though it had annoyed him, especially since they had a granddaughter that they wanted nothing to do with. It was their loss.

Well, it was kind of his loss, too, because he didn't know how to be a parent, let alone a parent to a little girl. The kids at school were already making fun of Isla because he couldn't do her hair right, and the clothes they'd picked out didn't fit her properly and apparently weren't "cool."

The little girl was far more resilient than any seven-year-old should have to be, and he hated she was suffering because of his ineptitude.

"Are we going to get a Christmas tree?" Isla asked as she climbed up on the chair at the small table where they usually ate.

"Yes." Hopefully they could find one at a thrift store because he didn't want to have to spend money on a new one. "But first, what do you want for supper?"

Thankfully, Isla wasn't a fussy eater. That was probably because she hadn't had enough food to eat while she'd been with her mom, so she ate pretty much anything he offered her.

"Grilled cheese and tomato soup."

It hadn't taken Isla long to learn what he could cook, which really wasn't much. He could do sandwiches, spaghetti, mac and cheese, and tortillas. Sometimes he bought a rotisserie chicken and made some instant mashed potatoes. He tried to buy more fruit and vegetables for Isla, even though it put a dent in his bank account.

When it had been just him, he'd eaten a lot of canned and frozen food. Stuff he could throw together quickly at the end of the day. But now, he had to make a decent breakfast as well as put together a lunch for Isla to take to school. His budget priorities had had to shift as the demands on him had grown.

Unfortunately, his income hadn't grown to accommodate those demands, and recent events had made his current situation even more challenging.

The garage had been his dad's, and Ash had worked there since he was a teen. When his dad had wanted to retire, he'd given Ash the option to buy the business outright or to pay him a monthly payment, which they'd used to help fund their retirement down south, where it wasn't frigid for months on end.

Because he hadn't had the money to pay him outright and no bank would give him a loan, Ash had had to agree to the monthly payment. Everything would have been okay—though he certainly wouldn't have gotten rich—if only some guy with lots of money hadn't opened a garage close to his.

The flashy new place somehow managed to undercut his prices, which he couldn't figure out since he didn't think his prices were that high. Whatever the reason, his precarious financial situation had become even more fragile with their arrival.

With his dad retiring, he'd lost a set of hands, so he'd needed to hire someone. But he was, in a sense, paying his dad a salary and not getting work in return. He only had a part-time guy who helped him, and he'd been putting in long days to keep on top of the work he did get.

But he could no longer do that now that he had Isla to consider. As it was, she spent more hours a week than she should at the garage with him.

The school she went to was right down the street from his garage, so he took her to work early each morning, then he walked her to school. In the afternoon, he picked her up and brought her back to the garage until he was done for the day.

She usually spent her time at the garage coloring or watching videos on his phone. It wasn't ideal, but it was likely better than the life she'd had with her mom.

He was doing the best he could, and he only hoped that it would be enough.

"Can I help, Uncle Ash?" Isla asked.

"Yep. You can get the butter from the fridge."

He picked up the bag of bread from next to the toaster, then pulled out a cutting board and set it on the counter, telling Isla to lay out six pieces of bread. While she did as he told her, he got three cheese slices from the dwindling pack in the fridge.

She knew the drill from there. So while she put the sandwiches together, Ash dumped a can of tomato soup into a pot and added some milk.

Though he never would have said he was lonely, he had to admit that having someone else to talk to—even if it was about coloring books or kids' videos—was kinda nice. He wondered at times if Isla had been forced to be quiet when she'd lived with her mom.

When she'd first arrived, she'd watch him but would hardly say a word. But over the past few weeks, as if realizing that he would not get mad at her for talking, she'd begun to chat whenever they were together. He'd told her that she needed to be quiet at school and when he was working, but otherwise, she could talk all she wanted. And so she did.

"Do you think if I told Santa what I wanted for Christmas, he'd bring it to me?" Isla asked when they sat at the small worn table a short time later with bowls of soup and their grilled cheese sandwiches.

Ash frowned at her. "I thought you didn't believe in Santa."

"Maybe he *is* real. That lady asked me what I wanted Santa to bring me. So if she believes in him..." She shrugged.

Ash wasn't sure what to say in response. He'd asked her the same question a week ago, but she'd declared that there was no such person, so he'd let the subject drop. He'd just hoped that she wasn't announcing that at school or there might be some upset children and parents.

"Well, what are you going to tell Santa that you want for Christmas?" Ash asked.

So far, the only things he knew she really liked were coloring books, crayons, and stuffed animals, though she hadn't arrived with any of those items.

She took a bite of her sandwich, and the bump of her foot against his leg told him that she was swinging her legs as she contemplated his question. "I don't know."

He wasn't sure if that was really true, or if she was afraid to tell him. Hopefully, that wasn't the case. The last thing he wanted was for her to be scared of him. He knew he could be a bit scary because of his size—especially to someone so small—and his gruff way of speaking. He needed her to know that she never needed to fear him. That he would do everything to keep her safe.

She continued to take small bites of her sandwich and sips of her soup. Finally, she said, "What do you want from Santa for Christmas?"

Ash lifted his brows. "Me?"

"Yeah. What do you want?"

He didn't know what to say since the list of things he wished Santa could bring him wouldn't be very interesting to a child. Things like new tools and some extra cash.

"Maybe some new gloves?"

Her gaze dropped to his hands, where he held his sandwich. "Do your hands get cold?"

"Sometimes." He couldn't lie about that. His gloves were wearing thin and had torn in spots, which made them unreliable at keeping out the cold. "Maybe a new beanie."

"I'd like new gloves and a beanie too." Her brow furrowed. "But in purple. Not black like you have."

Well, now they were getting somewhere. He could maybe find her some purple gloves and a beanie. Maybe a scarf too.

Over the next couple of days, Isla continued to add to her Santa list. She didn't ask for expensive things like tablets or gaming systems. No, she'd added things like socks, shoes, and boots. Super practical items that Ash should provide for her without them being Christmas gifts.

On Monday afternoon, Ash had the hood up on a car replacing the battery when he heard the bell jangle above the door leading into the waiting/office area. He grabbed the rag sitting on the frame of the car and wiped his hands on it as he walked toward the office.

As he approached the door, he heard a woman speaking to Isla. Anytime someone showed up while Isla was at the garage, he worried that they'd report him for having her there. He wasn't sure if it was a reportable offense, but all it took was someone deciding it was, and he'd find himself under the microscope of child protection services.

"I've decided to believe in Santa," he heard Isla say, her words making him frown.

As he stepped into the room, he spotted the woman he'd helped on the highway. He could see her in a way that he hadn't been able to on Friday night. She was all polished beauty, with her dark hair hanging in loose curls over her shoulders. The dark purple coat she wore reached her ankles and looked to be wool. Add all that to the type of car she drove, and it reinforced his belief that she was a wealthy woman.

She turned to look at him, smiling as her gaze met his. "Hello."

Ash nodded in response. "What can I do for you?"

"I don't think I introduced myself on Friday night." She tugged off her glove and held out a slender hand. "I'm Heather King."

"Nice to meet you." Ash tightened his hands around the rag he held. "My hands are too dirty to be shaking with anyone."

Heather didn't lower her hand. "I'm not worried about that."

From the lift of her chin and the determined look in her eye, she wasn't going to back down. Ash sighed as he let go of the rag and reached out to grip her hand. Though the temptation was there to keep the handshake light and brief, Heather didn't let him. She gripped his hand firmly and gave it a confident shake before letting go.

"How did you find this place?" he asked as he went back to gripping the rag in his hands.

"You gave me your business card."

Right. He'd forgotten about that. He'd hoped that by giving her some information about himself, she'd be reassured that he wasn't going to attack her. She'd also taken a picture of it, and he'd assumed that she'd sent it to someone.

Not just beautiful and stubborn, but also smart. A deadly combination for someone who also had money. But he refused to be intimidated by any of that.

Chapter 3

Heather could honestly say she'd never been in a garage like Larson Automotive before because...well...she'd never been in *any* car repair garage. The waiting area was clean and uncluttered, though the scents of oil and rubber hung in the air.

When Heather had walked in, Isla had been sitting in an office chair with a phone propped on her knees, watching something. On the desk in front of her chair, there was a small juice box and a wrapper from some crackers. Her gaze had lit up when she'd seen Heather.

But now, Heather's attention was on the tall, broad-shouldered man who stood in the doorway that led from the waiting room into the garage area. Ash wore a pair of dirty, dark blue coveralls and held a stained rag in his large hands. Though he wore a backward ball cap, his hair was long enough that she could see light brown curls reaching past the collar of his coveralls. His eyes were the same blue as Isla's, making Heather think that the little girl must have inherited them from her mom.

"I wanted to thank you again for your help on Friday night," Heather said.

"You already thanked me."

Heather nodded in acknowledgment of his statement. "I also wanted to invite you and Isla to the employee children's Christmas party that my family's company puts on each year."

Ash frowned. "Wouldn't that just be open to the children of your employees?"

"It's open to them but also to anyone else we'd like to include."

He crossed his arms, a frown still on his face. "Who was the last non-employee you invited?"

Heather smiled at the memory. "That would be a woman and her daughter last year. My brother and I met them at an apartment block that was going to be torn down and leave them homeless."

Ash glanced over at Isla. The little girl sat with her arms wrapped around her legs and her chin resting on her knees as she watched them, her eyes wide. "We don't have anything to wear to a party."

"It's not a formal event," Heather explained. "Jeans and a sweater or shirt would be just fine for you. And for Isla, I actually have some things for her."

Ash scowled at that. "You bought her something?"

Heather shook her head. "My brother's fiancée has a little girl a year or so older than Isla. When Carissa mentioned she was planning to donate some clothes Rachel had outgrown, I thought I'd see if you could put them to use for Isla."

"They're not new?" Ash sounded skeptical. Like he believed Heather was trying to pull one over on him.

"Nope. But they're still in good condition because Rachel isn't very rough on her clothes. I think you'll find one or two things that Isla might like to wear for the party."

Ash crossed his arms over his chest. "You're assuming I'm going to agree."

"You're right. I am." Heather couldn't help but smile. "So, are you?"

"I'm not sure."

Thankfully, it wasn't an outright refusal. She didn't want to force the guy to say yes, but she was sure that Isla would love it, and Rachel would be nice to her.

"Well, here is the information," Heather said, holding out the card they'd given to all the employees that year with the party details on it. Ash hesitated, but then stepped closer to take it from her. "We'd love to have you come. But regardless, I'd like to leave the things for Isla."

Heather stepped aside to reveal the large, wheeled suitcase she'd brought with her. Carissa had packed the clothes in it before handing it over to Heather. Once she'd gotten over her incredulity that Heather had accepted help from a strange man on the side of the highway, the other woman had been curious about Ash and Isla, and she'd been more than willing to pass on Rachel's clothes after hearing Isla's story. What Heather knew of it, anyway.

"That looks like a lot more than an outfit or two," Ash said, his gaze focused on the suitcase.

"I don't know exactly what's inside. Carissa just said that she packed what she'd planned to donate to the thrift store." Heather stepped closer to the door so she could escape before he refused the clothes or the party invitation. "I've also written my number on the card if you have any questions. Feel free to give me a call."

Ash's expression didn't soften much until Isla slid off the chair and came around to where he stood. She took his hand and looked up at him. "Can we please go to the party, Uncle Ash?"

Heather watched as Ash stared down at his niece. "Maybe."

The smile that broke across Isla's face told Heather that she hadn't yet learned that her uncle's *maybe* was probably a *no*.

Although, what did she know? Perhaps when Ash said *maybe*, he really would give it due consideration before deciding.

She hoped that they'd agree to come because she was sure that Isla would enjoy it. Ash...probably not so much. But hopefully, seeing his niece happy would make him happy.

Ash looked up at her, pinning her with those vivid blue eyes that were even more remarkable because of the dark lashes that framed them. "I'll let you know."

Heather smiled. "Thank you again for your help on Friday night. I was supposed to go to a fundraiser with my family, and I would haven't been able to make it if not for your help."

Ash's nod was likely to be his only acknowledgment of her comments. With a final smile at Isla, Heather turned and left the garage. George had brought her since she hadn't known where she was going, and she hated having to find a place she'd never been to before. Next time, she'd have a better idea and could find it on her own.

Next time...

Was she already planning another visit to the garage? Heather supposed that she was.

"Everything okay?" George asked after she slid into the front seat next to him.

"Everything is great."

"Good." He put the car into gear, and they slowly pulled away from the garage.

Given that it was nearly five, it was dark already. She wondered how much longer they would be at the garage. Was Isla there with him every day?

She remembered some of the issues Carissa had shared that she had as a single mother, and one of those was balancing her work with Rachel's school hours. That was likely the same for Ash. He probably couldn't just operate his garage during the hours Isla was at school.

Though the garage wasn't the best environment for a child, the space where Isla had been sitting had been clean and warm. And her uncle had been within shouting distance of her. He was undoubtedly doing the best he could to parent a child that, from what Isla had said, he'd ended up with unexpectedly.

The week progressed without hearing anything from Ash, and Heather found she was disappointed by the idea that they might not come to the party that Saturday. She really hoped to see them again.

Also, she wanted to make sure she had enough time to buy Christmas presents for Isla that Santa could give her at the party. Although, she supposed she could go ahead and buy the gifts, and if they didn't show up, she could stop by the garage to drop them off.

With that in mind, after work on Thursday, she picked Rachel up, then swung by a store where she could shop for Isla. Before Ash had joined them in the office, Isla had managed to tell her she'd decided to believe in Santa, and she knew what she wanted from him. Though Heather was sure that her list was longer, Isla had listed off a few items before her uncle had appeared.

So now she was in search of a bunch of purple winter wear items. She'd brought Rachel with her to help with sizing and to get a little girl's opinion on things. She already knew that Rachel and Isla were different in some ways. Rachel loved books, but Isla didn't seem to.

"I like this one, Auntie," Rachel said, gesturing to one of the winter jackets that hung in the girl's clothing section.

"Isla likes purple. Is there one in that color?"

They looked through the racks for a purple jacket, then moved to mitts, boots, a scarf, and a beanie. All in purple. Once that was done, Rachel helped her pick out some coloring books and crayons.

Heather hadn't told Rachel much about the circumstances that Isla had come from, only that her mother had died and she was living with her uncle. Rachel understood about living with a single parent since it had been just her and her mom for a long time.

"So, will I get to meet her at the party?" Rachel asked once they had paid for their purchases—including several new books for Rachel as a thank you to the little girl for helping Heather out.

"I hope so, but I don't know for sure yet if they're coming."

Rachel held her hand as they left the store, and Heather was reminded again of how far things had come in the year since they'd first met Carissa and Rachel. She'd gone from Miss Heather to Aunt Heather, and she couldn't be happier about the change.

Heather took Rachel back to the house with her, knowing that Carissa and Hunter would be there for dinner. It wasn't unusual for the trio to join them at the house for dinner. Sometimes Hayden even showed up, but that was rarer.

She didn't know what would happen when Hunter and Carissa got married because Hunter and Hayden lived together. Though Hunter would deny it to their brother, he kept an eye on Hayden. He'd recently had another surgery and was still in pain from that.

"Did you find what you needed?" her mom asked once they were seated around the table for dinner.

"I think we did," Heather said. "Right, Rachel?"

Rachel nodded. "Lots of purple stuff for Isla."

Her mom had been less than impressed when Heather had shared what had happened on the roadside on Friday night. However, her anger at what she saw as risky behavior softened when Heather explained what Isla had told her about her mom dying and how the kids at school were mean to her.

Kids in need had always been a soft spot for her parents, and even more so in her mom's now that Heather's dad had passed away. Though her dad had often spoken of being aware of people who were less fortunate than they were financially, Heather hadn't given it as much thought as she should have in the years following her dad's death.

Meeting Carissa and Rachel had brought it forcefully to her attention, given the horrible conditions they'd been living in. There had been no denying that they had needed help, and Heather and Hunter had stepped up to try and give them that.

There had been so much joy in helping Carissa and Rachel. It wasn't that Carissa had been a bad mother. She'd just ended up in dire circumstances that had made their lives extremely difficult.

Since then, Heather had prayed each day as part of her devotions that God would open her eyes to people's needs.

Whether it had been buying boxes of chocolate from a secretary at the office, who was selling them as part of a fundraiser for her child's school or adding some of her own money to help an employee's family cover the cost of a funeral for their teenage son who'd passed away unexpectedly, there had been plenty of opportunities to help people.

This situation with Ash and Isla was interesting, since Ash had helped her out first. But perhaps it was God's way of making their paths cross because it wasn't likely they would have any other way.

She wasn't sure yet how to help the pair. Giving Isla some of Rachel's things seemed a good place to start, but she hoped that there might be other ways they could help the pair.

As she said goodbye to Rachel, Carissa, and Hunter after dinner, Heather forced herself to accept that Ash wasn't going to bring Isla to the children's party. She didn't blame him for not wanting to come, since he didn't know what he might be getting them into. However, even if they didn't show, she still planned to see them again.

When her phone rang with an unknown number just after seven that evening, Heather hesitated a moment before answering it. But since it might be Ash, she took the chance of answering it.

"Uh...may I speak to Heather?" a man's gruff voice asked.

"Speaking."

"This is Ash...Asher Larson."

"Hi, Ash," she greeted him happily. "I'm glad you called. Are you and Isla going to be able to join us on Saturday?"

"Yeah," he said, then cleared his throat. "Uh...yes, Isla would really like to go to the party."

"Excellent. All the information for it is on that card I gave you," she told him. "But call me when you get to the hotel, and I'll come meet you."

"Are you sure? You don't have other things to do for the party?"

"Nothing more than socializing. My mom and her Christmas elves take care of all the details."

"Okay. I'll call you."

Heather couldn't help smiling as she hung up the phone after they said goodnight. Rachel had had a blast when she'd come with Carissa the previous year, and Heather could only hope that Isla would have the same experience.

Chapter 4

Ash reached past the jacket he had on to tug at the neck of the green sweater he wore with a pair of dark wash jeans. It hadn't been his first choice of outfit, but it had been all he could find at the thrift store. It wasn't something he would have chosen himself. But the woman at the thrift store had insisted that if he trimmed up his beard a bit, he'd look just fine. Handsome, even.

Ash wasn't going for handsome. All he wanted was to not embarrass himself or Isla at the party. Isla had chosen an outfit from the clothes that Heather had left for her that had a decidedly Christmas theme to it.

The pants were a red, green, and black plaid, while the long-sleeve, black T-shirt had a Christmas tree with red decorations on it. She'd even found a matching headband, which meant he'd only had to brush her hair and then push it back.

There had also been a pair of black ankle boots that, even though they'd been a bit big, Isla had insisted on wearing. The black wool coat with double rows of silver buttons she wore was also a little loose but worked well with her outfit.

"Am I pretty, Uncle Ash?" she asked as they walked into the hotel where the party was being held.

"You look beautiful," he assured her. "Just like a princess."

She looked up at him as they came to a stop off to the side of the doors. "Your princess?"

He smiled down at her. "Definitely my princess."

Her hand tightened in his, and she did a little dance. Ash pulled out his phone and sent a text to Heather to let her know they were there.

It only took a couple of minutes for the woman to appear. She wore a pair of black slacks and a fluffy red sweater. Her dark hair hung in loose curls around her shoulders.

"Hi, you two," she said with a big smile. "I'm so glad you could make it."

"I've never been to a party," Isla said.

"Well, let's go see what's happening." Heather held out her hand to Isla.

Isla took it without letting go of Ash's, so the three of them made their way across the large foyer of the hotel. Heather led them down a hallway to a spacious ballroom that had been decorated for Christmas.

"Wow…" Isla breathed. "Lots of trees."

Ash had to agree that there were a lot of trees in the big room. Each was loaded with different types of decorations. Ash hadn't known that there were so many different ways to decorate a tree. Growing up, their family tree had just had an assortment of colored balls along with whatever decorations he and Gwen had made at school that year. His mom hadn't bothered to keep any from previous years.

There hadn't been many homemade decorations to add to the tree once he and Gwen had gotten to be pre-teens. He supposed that Isla would have some decorations for a tree this year. Unless they didn't make Christmas decorations at school anymore. He had no idea.

He actually had no idea how to make Christmas special for Isla. It was the main reason he'd accepted the invite to the party. If they were offering a holiday experience that he couldn't, he'd take advantage of it.

A little girl with a wide smile skipped up to them. Her gaze zeroed in on Isla, then she said, "Hi!"

Isla glanced up at Ash, clearly wary of this friendly little girl. She hadn't had great experiences with the kids at her school so far.

Heather smiled and took the girl's hand. "Isla, this is Rachel. She's my niece."

Isla's brow furrowed as she stared at the other little girl. When another woman joined them, and Heather introduced her as Rachel's mom, Isla's frown deepened.

Ash guessed that she was comparing the pretty woman with a caring smile to her own mom, who had been wasting away on drugs and often abusive because of her addictions. He was a bit surprised by the desire to gather Isla into his arms and assure her that even though she didn't have a mom like Rachel's, she still had someone who cared for her.

"Do you want to decorate a cookie?" Rachel asked.

Isla looked up at him. But even though he nodded, she didn't release her tight hold on his hand. She let go of Heather's hand and pressed against his leg.

Ash lowered himself to her level and slid his arm around her waist. "Do you want me to come with you?"

Eyes so like his blinked a couple of times, then Isla nodded. "Please."

The word was barely a whisper, but Ash heard it loud and clear. "Of course, princess."

She hooked her arm around his neck, and as Ash got to his feet, he lifted her up with him.

The woman with Heather gave Isla a gentle smile. "Let's go find some empty seats."

Ash followed the two women and the little girl as they moved further into the large room, dodging excited kids and their parents. Finally, they came to a stop at a rectangle table that had several empty chairs.

Rachel slid into one of them, then smiled up at Isla and patted the spot next to her. Ash carefully lowered Isla onto the chair, holding her steady until she was safely seated.

A young woman dressed like an elf stood on the other side of the table and greeted Rachel and Isla with a big smile. "Hi! My name is Lizzy. Are you ready to decorate some cookies?"

Rachel nodded vigorously. Isla looked at Rachel, then nodded as well, though nowhere near as enthusiastically. Ash wasn't sure that his niece had any clue what they were doing since he doubted his sister had done anything like that with her.

"What sort of cookie would you like?" Lizzy the elf asked. "We have stars, bells, trees, and stockings."

"I'd like a tree," Rachel said.

Heather settled onto the seat next to Isla and said, "I think I'd like a bell. What would you like, Isla?"

"A bell?"

"Sure!" Lizzy the elf had more enthusiasm for cookies than Ash had for... well... anything. "Two bells and a tree coming right up!"

Ash stayed behind Isla's chair. They were both totally out of their depth in this fancy room with an overabundance of Christmas trees. Once Isla seemed more at ease, Ash looked around the room.

He hadn't known what to expect, but it surprised him a bit that he wasn't the only man there. In fact, there seemed to be a near-even split of men and women present in the room.

As he watched, a tall man who had similar coloring to Heather approached them, a smile growing on his face when his gaze landed on the woman standing behind Rachel's chair.

"Hello, darling," he said as he bent to kiss her. "I see we're decorating cookies once again this year."

"Brace yourself for another sugar overload," the woman said with a laugh.

The man looked at Heather, then at Isla, before his gaze lifted to meet Ash's. "Hi. I'm Hunter King."

Ash shook the man's hand when he offered it. "Ash Larson."

"This is his niece, Isla," the woman said, resting her hand briefly on the back of Isla's chair. "I'm Carissa, by the way."

"Nice to meet you," Ash said with a nod.

"I understand we have you to thank for rescuing Heather on the highway the other night."

Ash crossed his arms, uncomfortable with the man's thanks. "I'm just glad I was able to help."

Hunter smiled. "Well, we really appreciate you helping her out. She doesn't like driving much, and that incident isn't likely to help."

"I thanked Ash already, Hunter," Heather said, glancing up at Hunter. "You don't need to go spilling all my weaknesses."

"It's my job as your brother," Hunter said with a shrug.

Heather rolled her eyes before turning her attention back to the cookie in front of her. "No, it's not."

"Hey, you two," a woman said. "No fighting."

This woman was middle-aged, with a friendly smile and eyes like Heather's and Hunter's. She held out her hand to Ash. "I'm Eliza King. These two belong to me."

Ash shook her hand, wondering how a split decision to help someone had landed him there. "Nice to meet you. I'm Ash Larson, and this is Isla."

"It's lovely to meet you both." Eliza smiled at Isla when she looked up at her.

"Look at my cookie, Grandma," Rachel said, holding up a cookie with lots of green icing and an abundance of sprinkles.

"That looks very nice," Eliza said as she bent closer to the little girl. "Who are you going to give it to?"

"Hunter!"

Heather and Carissa laughed while Hunter grimaced. "I think you should let Aunt Heather have it."

Rachel shook her head. "She has her own."

"Your mom?" Hunter suggested.

"Nope. It's for you."

Rachel focused again on her cookie as Hunter shifted closer to Ash. "These cookies can end up being super... super... *super* sweet. So brace yourself."

"Do you want my cookie, Uncle Ash?" Isla asked as she looked up at him. "Or can I have it?"

"You can have it, princess. Since you're doing all the work to make it pretty."

She beamed at him before going back to her decorating.

"Lucky man," Hunter murmured. "You dodged that bullet."

Ash nodded like he agreed, deciding that Hunter didn't need to know that it would be a long time before he'd take food from Isla. Her history of having little to no food would make it difficult for Ash to ever take food from her—even if she offered it.

When Isla and Rachel finished their cookies, Rachel handed hers over to Hunter, then she took Isla's hand and led her to another table. Ash trailed behind them with Hunter at his side. While Hunter ate Rachel's cookie, Ash carried Isla's in a small plastic bag.

It looked like their Christmas tree would have its first decoration since this next table held all the things to make them. He would have to get a tree sooner rather than later. Ash was sure that Isla would want to hang her decoration up as soon as she could.

"Has Isla been with you for a while?" Hunter asked.

Ash glanced away from where Isla was bent over her decoration, making liberal use of glitter and glue. "Since the end of September. My sister overdosed."

"I'm sorry to hear that," Hunter said, his brow furrowed. "Were you close?"

"Not recently." Ash wasn't keen on revealing much about his messed-up family to someone who seemed to have a loving, supportive one.

"Was she your only sibling?"

Ash nodded. "Is Heather yours?"

Hunter shook his head. "We have a brother, Hayden. We're triplets."

Ash's eyes widened. "Wow."

"Yep. I have a feeling that's what my parents said when they found out they were having three babies instead of just one."

"Is your brother here?"

"No." Hunter frowned. "Hayden was injured in a car accident. The same accident that killed our dad, as well as Carissa's parents."

"They were in the same accident?"

"It was that big pileup five years ago."

Ash remembered when that had happened. It had seemed especially tragic because it had happened not long before Thanksgiving.

"Was your brother badly injured?"

"His legs were crushed, among other things, and he's had to have a lot of surgeries. Unfortunately, he's still in a lot of pain most days." Hunter hesitated. "Christmas isn't his favorite holiday."

Ash could only imagine. It wasn't his favorite holiday either, though he hadn't had an experience like Hayden had. That year was tough, what with his sister's death and Isla adjusting to a new life. Still, he felt an obligation to at least acknowledge the holiday for Isla's sake.

She'd missed out on a lot of Christmases already, so Ash was determined to give her a celebration that year, even if only on a small scale. Now, thanks to Heather, Isla was experiencing a part of Christmas that Ash wouldn't have been able to give her.

And even though he wished he could be anywhere but the fancy ballroom, he wouldn't let his discomfort rob Isla of the experience. He had a lot to learn about being a parent. But one thing he knew already, from having been a child, was that meeting her basic needs and keeping her safe was just the starting point. His goal was to do what he could to bring a smile to her face each day.

However, this day, it was other people and experiences he had nothing to do with that brought smiles to her face. And maybe she'd made a new friend.

Ash looked at the little girl sitting next to Isla. She seemed gentle and caring, which was exactly what Isla needed in a friend. Also, Rachel didn't seem to care that Isla was wearing her hand-me-downs and that they hung on Isla's small-for-her-age frame.

"I think she's having fun," Heather said as she came to stand next to him, her arm brushing against his. "At least, I hope she is."

Ash watched Isla for another moment before turning his attention to Heather. "Yes. I think she is. This is all new for her."

"Then I'm glad that you could make it. Last year, Rachel and Carissa came for the first time, and Rachel was thrilled that she could come again this year."

"I appreciate her being friendly to Isla. Not every kid she's come in contact with lately has been that way."

Heather frowned. "Isla mentioned that. It's so frustrating when kids can't just be nice to each other."

Ash shrugged. "Not much I can do about it, unfortunately. I've tried to speak to the school, but they seem to feel that it doesn't qualify as bullying. And maybe it doesn't. But after all Isla has been through, it just seems overly mean."

Heather rested her hand on his arm for a moment. "Well, I'm sure Rachel would love to be her friend."

Though Ash wasn't sure how that would work, he didn't brush Heather's suggestion aside. From the look of things, Isla might ask to hang around with Rachel after that day.

When Isla shifted around in her seat to show him the paper star she'd decorated with glitter. Ash dropped to his haunches and listened as she talked to him about what she'd put on it.

Setting the star back down on the table, Isla slid off her chair, then wrapped her thin arms around Ash's neck, squeezing tight.

"Thank you for bringing me," she whispered in his ear. "I love this."

Unexpected emotion squeezed Ash's chest, robbing him of breath for a moment. "You're welcome, princess."

He knew then that he'd do anything he could to bring her the happiness she'd missed out on so far in her short life. Though he'd never imagined being a parent, his heart swelled with affection for the little girl who'd unexpectedly landed in his life such a short time ago.

Chapter 5

Heather watched Ash hug Isla, her heart warming at the sight. Ash was a rough man with a gruff exterior, and she could tell he wasn't comfortable there. With scruff that looked just a bit past a five o'clock shadow and his light brown hair hanging in long, loose curls, he lacked the polish of Hunter. Heather didn't know if the style was purposeful or if he just hadn't had the time to get a haircut, but something told her it was probably the latter.

She'd felt the calloused skin on his hands, and even now, she could see stains on his fingers. Despite their presence, she knew his hands were clean. Her dad had always said that a man who did manual labor would have hands that showed his hard work, and Heather could see that was true of Ash.

In the short time she'd known him, Heather had caught glimpses of Ash's soft heart for his niece behind his hardened exterior, and she very much admired that.

"Would you like to make another decoration, Isla?" Heather asked as the little girl loosened her hold on Ash's neck. "You can make as many as you'd like."

Isla nodded and slid back into the chair. The young woman supervising the table helped her get set up with another decoration. This one was a white plaster candy cane that could be colored and had a gold string strung through a hole in the top. The little girl bent over it with markers, carefully coloring it. Heather smiled as she thought of the things Santa had for Isla later.

Ash hovered near Isla, never venturing far from her. He stood with his hands in his pockets, responding whenever anyone spoke to him but not initiating any conversation. He was definitely a man of few words. Or maybe it was just that he wasn't comfortable with them yet.

Yet...

Heather pondered the word as she greeted some of the employees who hung around the decorating table watching their children. Even though she just wanted to stick close to Isla and Ash, she knew that she also had to speak with others there, since it was her family putting the party on.

But even as she spoke to different people, her thoughts kept going to Ash and Isla. Would there be a way—or even a reason—to keep them in her life beyond this day? Would they have a place to go that Christmas?

The previous Christmas, they'd still been struggling to embrace the joy of Christmas since her dad's death four years earlier. This year, it was a little easier to feel that joy and happiness as Christmas approached. Not that they didn't still miss their dad. But since Christmas had been his favorite time of year, it felt wrong to not celebrate it the way he would have wanted them to.

Meeting Carissa and Rachel had played a significant role in helping them turn the corner from overwhelming grief and loss to joy once again. She couldn't imagine life without them now, and Heather couldn't wait for the wedding that would legally bind Carissa and Rachel to their family.

"That is so pretty," Rachel said as she leaned to look at what Isla was doing.

Isla glanced at Rachel, then up at Ash, before looking back at the other little girl. "I like to color. It's my favorite thing."

Rachel smiled at her. "You're really good at it."

"Thank you," Isla said softly.

Once the girls were done with their decorations, they were put into small bags for them to carry.

"Why don't we get some food?" Heather suggested.

Ash looked like he was going to argue, but at Isla's excited reaction, he just nodded. Rachel came with them to fill plates from a large assortment of finger foods. They found seats at one of the round tables on the opposite side of the room from the activity tables.

"Are you busy at the garage these days?" Heather asked Ash, wanting to learn a bit more about him.

Ash shrugged as he picked up one of the sausage rolls. "Off and on."

"Does Isla hang out at the garage with you a lot?"

As he chewed the bite he'd taken, he regarded her with his remarkable blue eyes. It seemed like he wasn't sure that he actually wanted to answer that question. Heather didn't want him to think she was judging him.

"I know that it can be hard for single parents," Heather said. "Carissa is a single mom, and she's told me about how hard it was for her to juggle her job and Rachel's school hours. You're fortunate to be able to have Isla with you when she's not in school."

Ash's expression cleared a bit, but it seemed like he still didn't trust her completely. "I prefer to keep her close by. Her life before she came to me wasn't great, and I want to make sure that she's safe."

Heather nodded. "That's completely understandable. I know you don't know me from Adam, but if you ever need any help with Isla, I'd be happy to give you a hand."

Ash's brows rose at her offer. "Uh...sure."

"Do you have family that could help you?"

He shook his head. "My folks don't live around here. They retired and moved to Florida."

"Wanted to get away from the cold, huh?"

"I guess so. Can't really blame them for that." From the tone of his voice as he said that, however, it sounded like there were other things he blamed them for.

"Growing up, I always assumed I'd move away from here as soon as I could because I didn't like the cold, but here I am. Still here, all these years later."

"This has always been home, and with the business, I can't really go anywhere else."

"I get that," Heather said. "I don't think I could move away from my family or my job here now."

"Can I have more juice?" Isla asked.

Ash hesitated for a moment.

"I'll take her to get more," Heather said. "Rachel, do you want more too?"

When Rachel nodded, Heather got up and shepherded the two girls over to the table where the punch bowls were. There was another elf there with a ladle in his hand. He carefully refilled the cups Rachel and Isla held out to him.

After thanking him, they walked back to the table, holding their cups carefully in both hands. Carissa and Hunter had joined them at the table and were talking to Ash. Heather looked around for her mom, wanting to make sure that she didn't need any help.

It wasn't as if her mom did everything by herself. She had an entire staff of elves helping her, but Heather still wanted to make sure that her mom was okay.

She spotted her over by the part of the ballroom where Santa would soon set up. Heather glanced at Hunter, and when he nodded, she knew he'd take care of Ash and Isla while she went to their mom.

"Everything good to go?" Heather asked when she joined her mom and a handful of young people dressed up as elves to help Santa with the presents.

Her mom smiled, her eyes sparkling with excitement. That look had slowly become more frequent over the past year, even though there had been a minor setback in August when their family dog had passed away from old age. Heather had worried it would be a devastating blow. But even though it had been hard for her mom, it hadn't come out of the blue, so they'd all had a chance to say goodbye, which seemed to make a difference.

Seeing their mom happy—along with Carissa and Rachel's presence in their lives—had helped to draw that happiness out in Heather and Hunter, too. Even Hayden had shown moments of happiness...or maybe it was moments of less sadness.

"Like last year, we'll have Rachel and Isla go at the end."

Heather knew that this year, they'd agreed to keep Rachel within the limit they used for most of the employees' children. There were a few other employees that they'd become aware of being in difficult financial straits recently, so their children would get a bit extra. As would Isla.

She'd been happy to see that Isla had chosen an outfit from the clothes she'd dropped off. Though she would have liked to buy her a bunch of new clothes, even with the limited amount of time she'd spent with Ash and Isla, she'd been certain Ash would have balked at that.

Not wanting to miss Rachel and Isla's reaction to Santa's arrival, Heather headed back to their table. She'd just made it when one of the elves asked over the sound system if the kids were ready. The screams and clapping were near deafening, but Isla appeared confused as she reached for Ash.

Without hesitating, he picked her up. The little girl wrapped her arm around Ash's neck as she looked around, obviously trying to figure out what was going on. Ash's height helped to lift her above many of the people there so she could see when Santa appeared at the door.

His ho-ho-ho boomed loudly as he made his way from the large doors of the room to the oversized red velvet chair that waited for him at the other end. He had a big sack slung over his shoulder that looked heavy but wasn't since it contained only empty boxes. The actual gifts were already in sacks around his chair, waiting to be handed out to the children.

The kids that had been there in previous years were more than happy to line up with their parents to get their gifts. The newer kids were a little slower to join the line. Rachel hung back, and Ash didn't move from where he stood with Isla.

Once several kids had already seen Santa, Heather held out her hand to Rachel, then looked at Ash. "Come get in line with us."

His brow furrowed as he frowned. "I'm not sure…"

"Don't worry," she said with a wink. "Santa has a gift for each of the kids."

"Even me?" Isla asked.

Heather nodded. "Even you."

Though he was still scowling, Ash fell into step with Heather. He didn't put Isla down, and the little girl kept her gaze on Santa.

"Do you think he got me what I asked for in my letter?" Rachel asked, dancing from one foot to the other.

"He might have," Heather said. "But he'll probably save a few things to bring you on Christmas Eve."

"Ooooh, right."

"I didn't write him a letter," Isla said, a frown drawing her brows together. "How will he have something for me?"

Ash looked at Heather with an arched brow. Clearly, he wasn't touching that question with a ten-foot pole. But that was fine, because she had an answer for Isla.

"I think he knows what you'd like," Heather told her. "But if you still want to write him a letter, I can make sure he gets it."

That response caused Ash's eyes to widen, then narrow as his frown deepened.

"I can't write very well," Isla said, her shoulders slumping.

Rachel reached up to touch Isla's knee. "I'll help you."

Heather was so proud of Rachel and her generous heart. They'd seen a bit of that the previous year when she'd asked for a new laptop and a husband for her mom. Heather smiled at the memory because, in the end, Carissa had ended up with both. Well, not quite a husband yet, but soon.

As the line dwindled, Isla chewed on her lower lip, clearly nervous, while Rachel danced with excitement. When it was just the four of them in the line, Heather urged Rachel to go first.

She didn't hesitate even a second, happily skipping to where Santa sat. The man, who was an employee with grandchildren of his own, lifted Rachel to sit on the cushioned arm of his chair with the help of one of the elves. The two engaged in an animated conversation, and then Rachel slid off the chair and took the bag the elf held out for her.

"Let's go chat with Santa," Heather said once it was clear Rachel was done.

She didn't tell Ash to set Isla down, and he didn't look like he wanted to do that, anyway. Instead, the three of them walked to where Santa sat, a broad grin on his face.

"Hello, Santa," Heather said. "This is Isla, and this is her first time meeting you."

Being the wise Santa he was, the man seemed to understand without Heather having to say it that Isla was nervous.

"Well, Isla, it's a pleasure to meet you." Rather than ask her to sit with him, Santa leaned forward. "Are you excited about Christmas?"

Ash lowered himself down to one knee, setting Isla on his other one, bringing her closer to Santa. He kept his arm around her, though, and Heather appreciated Ash's desire to protect his niece from anything she might fear, even the jolly old man.

"I guess."

Santa glanced at Heather then and apparently recalled their conversation earlier in the day. "Are you learning some songs at school for Christmas?"

Isla nodded. "*Jingle Bells.*"

"Oh, I like that one," Santa said. "Any other ones?"

"*Santa Claus is Coming to Town.*"

That made the man laugh. "Well, I think I'm here already, don't you?"

Isla nodded. "But the kids probably won't believe me."

"That's okay," Santa said. "You and I know that I was here today, but I'll be back for Christmas."

"Why are you here now?" Isla asked, her question making Heather smile.

"They asked me to make a special appearance for this party, and I always say yes."

"So you'll still be back at Christmas?"

"You won't see me, but I'll be around." He leaned forward a bit. "I have to wait for the children to go to sleep before I can come on Christmas Eve, so make sure you go to bed when your uncle tells you to."

"I will," Isla said with a vigorous nod. "Promise."

"Excellent." Santa gestured to the elf who was hovering nearby with a bag in her hand. "Now I have a little something for you today."

Isla's eyes widened as the elf handed over the colorful gift bag. "That's for me?"

"It certainly is. Ho, ho, ho. Merry Christmas!"

Isla took the bag, clutching the handle as Ash pushed back up to his feet again.

"Thank you, Santa," Isla said.

"You're welcome."

Ash watched the interaction closely, his expression revealing nothing of how he felt about what was going on. She hoped he didn't regret coming there that day. That was the last thing Heather wanted. She'd just hoped to give Isla a memorable Christmas moment, given what the little girl had revealed about recent events in her life.

Chapter 6

Ash carried Isla to the table where they'd eaten and sat back down, keeping Isla on his lap. The closer they'd gotten to the front of the line and to Santa, the more he'd felt her little body tremble. He hadn't been sure if it was from fear or excitement. Thankfully, neither Heather nor Santa had tried to force Isla to go closer to the bearded man than she was comfortable with.

It had actually gone better than he'd imagined, and shortly into the conversation with Santa, Isla had stopped shaking. That she'd faced something that clearly caused her some distress made Ash both proud and angry.

No one so young should have to feel that they had to hide their fear and face down something that scared them. Still, he was proud that Isla had turned to him, trusting that he would keep her safe, even though she was scared. He hoped she'd always feel that way about him.

"Can I open it?" Isla asked, still holding onto the handle of the bag.

Ash noticed that Rachel was opening her bag, which was smaller than the one Isla had been handed. When he glanced at Heather, she said, "It's up to you."

"Sure, princess. You can open it."

She didn't need to be told twice. He helped hold it as she pulled out red tissue paper in search of what was inside. The first thing she pulled out was a beautiful stuffed bear.

Isla immediately hugged it. "It's so soft!"

She then handed it to him and peered into the bag again. Next, she pulled out a matching set of gloves, scarf, and beanie. All in purple. Isla's smile was huge as she rubbed her cheek against them.

"They're pretty," she said, holding them up so he could see. "And sparkly."

He didn't think he would have picked out something so girly, but he was going to have to learn how to find the sparkly stuff, since Isla clearly liked it.

The next items she pulled out delighted her even more. With a big smile on her thin face, she showed him an assortment of coloring books and a large box of crayons and markers.

Though Ash wished he could afford to buy her all those things, he was grateful that someone had. And it sort of made it easier to have Isla think it came from Santa rather than Heather, even though Ash was certain the wealthy woman had been responsible for picking out all the items.

Apparently, whatever conversation the two had held in the truck while he'd changed Heather's tire had covered a lot of ground. It mystified him a bit because from what he'd seen so far, Isla didn't warm up to people that quickly.

"Do you like your things?" Rachel asked Isla. She had a small stack of books on the table in front of her.

"Yes!" Isla said with a big smile.

From the sparkle in Rachel's eyes, Ash wondered if she had helped Heather pick out the items. It would make sense. A little girl would have a good idea of what another little girl would like.

He was glad they hadn't included any books because Isla didn't like them much. There was usually half an hour or more each evening devoted to her reading efforts. Unfortunately, more often than not, tears were shed because she knew she couldn't do what the teacher wanted her to.

Ash didn't know how to help her. He couldn't remember a time when he couldn't read. School had come easy for him, but it seemed that Isla was more like her mom. Gwen had struggled a lot with school, and Ash had memories of fights between her and their mom as she'd struggled with her homework.

It had bugged Gwen to no end that Ash breezed through his schoolwork, and he'd even ended up skipping ahead a grade. So, while they'd been two years apart in age, they'd only been a year apart at school. She'd hated that so much.

He wished he could make things easier for Isla, but all he could do was encourage her to try harder. If things didn't improve soon, he might have to look into finding a tutor for her, though his budget couldn't really stretch to that. He'd figure it out, though. He had no choice.

As Isla chatted with Rachel, Ash encouraged her to keep eating the food she'd taken. If she could fill up now on food she liked, she might not protest too much over whatever they ended up with for supper later.

"I heard you have a garage," Hunter said as he settled on the chair beside Ash's.

He looked at the polished man for a moment before nodding, but he didn't say anything more.

"Do you take on apprentices?"

"Apprentices?" Ash wasn't even sure how he would have gone about doing that, even if he'd wanted to. "No."

"Would you be interested?"

Ash shrugged. "Never really thought about it."

Hunter angled his chair a bit so that he faced Ash more directly. "Our company has been looking for more ways to give back to the community by creating opportunities for people to develop a career or even have a chance to brush up on skills that might have gone rusty."

Ash mulled over his words for a moment. "Are you talking about teens or adults?"

"Both, actually. I'd like to give teens who are interested in mechanics the opportunity to do some hands-on learning. However, I'd also like to give adults who may have slipped through the cracks the chance at a job."

He'd definitely learned hands-on with his dad, but he'd also had to take training in order to deal with the more advanced aspects of repairing cars. That would be true of what was required for anyone wanting a career in automotive repair. When he mentioned that to Hunter, the man nodded.

"I can see how that might be an issue." His brow furrowed. "Would you be able to give them some basic training? Oil changes and such?"

"Possibly," Ash said. "But unfortunately, I wouldn't have much time to train someone. I need to be able to take care of my customers."

"Of course, and I certainly wouldn't expect you to do this without compensation. We'd pay you for your time and the use of your garage. We'd even provide cars, if needed, for them to practice on."

Ash was a bit flummoxed by what Hunter was suggesting. It wasn't that he was so busy that he couldn't find the time to train people, but he had to be available if work came in. He couldn't afford to turn customers away.

"I'm not sure how it would work."

"And here isn't really the place to discuss it," Hunter said with a grimace. "I realize that. But would you be willing to meet with me to discuss how it might work from a practical standpoint?"

Did he want to partner with the wealthy family? He wasn't sure, but he also wasn't sure that he wanted to dismiss it outright because an additional source of income right then might be a good idea. What would be the harm in hearing the man out?

"Sure," he said with a shrug. "I would just need to make sure that I have flexibility when it comes to Isla's school schedule."

"Of course," Hunter agreed readily. "I know from Carissa how challenging things can be as a single parent. Isla would always come first."

Ash was glad to hear that, but he was still waiting for the catch. Surely there was one. He couldn't believe that this was being offered out of the goodness of Hunter King's heart.

Was it their way of thanking him for helping Heather? If so, she was even more important than he'd realized.

"He's going to be my daddy." Rachel's words had Ash glancing at the little girl and then back to Hunter, who was now smiling with affection at Rachel. "Last year, I asked Santa for a husband for my mama."

"Santa brought him?" Isla asked with a healthy dose of skepticism, although it was also mixed in with some awe.

Hunter chuckled at Isla's question. "No. Santa didn't bring me. We met last Christmas, and then Rachel's mom and I fell in love. We're going to be getting married soon."

"So he'll be my daddy," Rachel said again, clearly thrilled at the idea.

Isla leaned against Ash. "Uncle Ash is like a daddy. I love him."

Warmth spiraled through Ash at the words she'd never said to him before. They'd never really discussed his role in her life beyond being her uncle. It made him feel like he must be doing something right, even as he struggled to figure out how to parent this amazing little girl.

He leaned over and pressed a kiss to the top of her head. "Love you too, princess."

Words of love hadn't been something he'd grown up with. For some reason, his parents weren't given to voicing their feelings for each other or their children. There had been a few times as an adult when he'd wondered if they'd ever really loved him and Gwen.

Since Isla had arrived, he'd thought more about it. In his mind, it was important that Isla never have to wonder if she was loved. It would require him to put effort into being different from his parents and the example they'd set, but he was determined to do it.

He needed to make sure that Isla always felt secure in her place in his life. He wasn't used to putting anyone else first, but he was going to try his best to do that with Isla. Coming to the party was a step in that direction. If it had just been what he wanted, they wouldn't be there.

Isla beamed up at him, and Ash knew that he'd do anything to keep that look on her face. Her smiles had been few and far between at the start. But like a flower, she'd slowly begun opening up, though she didn't talk at all about the life she'd had before coming to live with him.

"I can see that Isla's got you wrapped around her little finger, just like Rachel has me," Hunter said with a grin, clearly not having an issue with that.

Ash didn't have an issue with it either. He couldn't give Isla a lot of things, and since she'd come to live with him, what she'd seemed to want more than anything was his attention and his love. And food.

"My life has definitely undergone some changes since her arrival," Ash said. "But it's all been good."

Well, mostly good. He still needed to figure out how to do her hair and cook healthier food.

Hunter's expression turned contemplative. "Did they give you a hassle being a single man?"

Ash thought back to the moment he'd been contacted about Gwen's death. Given the trajectory of her life when she'd left home, the news hadn't been totally unexpected.

The news that she had a daughter, however, had been shocking and distressing. And his distress had only increased as he'd picked up on certain things...like her relationship with food.

"Not really. They did a background check on me, and I also had home visits and interviews." Which he'd had to work around his hours at the garage in the few weeks since they had placed Isla with him. It had all been condensed into a short period of time. "But from what I understand, that's all pretty normal."

"I'm glad it wasn't an issue for you."

Ash focused on Isla, where she was now eating more of the food that had been on her plate, her Santa gifts back in the bag. He looked up from Isla and found Heather watching him. His gaze held hers for a moment before he focused on Isla again.

Though he didn't really care what Heather thought of him, he couldn't help but wonder. He knew the life he and Isla lived was probably foreign to someone as rich as her, but Heather didn't seem to judge him for it. No one he'd interacted with that day seemed to, which puzzled Ash.

He glanced around the room, noticing that the crowd was thinning. People were putting on their jackets and gathering up their things before heading for the large doors leading out of the room.

Isla probably wanted to stay as long as possible, and Ash wasn't of a mind to hurry her along. This was probably going to be the highlight of her Christmas, so he'd let her stay as long as they were allowed.

Hunter got up when his mom came to the table, then excused himself and headed off with her. Heather took the seat her brother had vacated, smiling at Ash as she did.

"Have you enjoyed yourself?" she asked as she crossed her legs.

Ash lifted a brow at her question. "I suppose I have. As long as Isla is enjoying herself, I'm happy."

Heather's smile grew at that, showing a hint of a dimple in one cheek. Though he'd tried not to notice, it was hard to ignore how beautiful the woman was. He didn't interact with many women anymore unless they brought their cars to the garage or worked at Isla's school.

When he'd been in his early twenties, he'd dated a lot more. But back then, the responsibility of the garage hadn't rested on his shoulders. He'd gone to work, collected his paycheck, and then had time to hang out with friends and go on dates. Now—especially since Isla had come—his priorities had changed, and dating was nowhere near the top of his list. Though he had to admit that he sometimes wished he'd had a girlfriend or wife to help with Isla.

"I'm so glad you could both come today."

"Thank you for inviting us." He glanced at Isla to make sure she wasn't paying attention. "And thank you for helping Santa out with the gift."

Her eyes sparkled. "Being Santa's helper is a lot of fun."

"You certainly go all out for the kids."

Heather nodded, then gestured at the room. "My dad started doing this each Christmas. He loved kids and Christmas, so having something that brought those two things together was right up his alley. We continue on with it in his memory."

"Was he Santa?" Ash asked, suspecting that he might have been, given what Heather had said.

"He definitely was. It was a highlight for him to see the kids get so excited when they met Santa." Her smile softened a bit as she looked at the girls. "He would have loved to meet Isla and try his best to convince her that Santa was real."

"I think maybe she's come around," Ash said. "Thanks to you."

Chapter 7

Heather went through the file that lay on her desk, trying to focus on the information that had been gathered regarding an upgrade to the childcare facilities they provided in the company. HR had put together a report on their current situation and what they proposed for upgrades.

While Hunter had his plate full overseeing the many divisions of the company, Heather's focus was on their employees, which meant working alongside HR to ensure they provided the best working environment for them. It was yet another thing their dad had insisted on that they'd done their best to carry on with in his absence.

A rap on her door had her looking up to see Hunter coming into her office. He dropped into the chair in front of her desk.

"What's up?" Heather asked.

Hunter didn't usually come to her office. If he needed something, he would just pick up the phone and call her.

"I'm heading to Ash's garage. I thought maybe you'd like to come with me."

Heather lifted her brows at his words. "Why would you think that?"

He laughed and shook his head. "Let's see... We'll go with... Isla will probably be there, and it might be useful to have her entertained while I talk to Ash."

"Oh. Well, of course."

"Of course." Hunter got back to his feet and headed for the door. "I'll meet you at the car in ten minutes."

Heather wasn't sure if Hunter saw that she was a bit fascinated by the pair or if he thought she was just drawn to Isla the way she'd been drawn to Rachel. It was true that the little girl had touched something within her, but also true was that she saw qualities in Ash that she really admired.

He'd helped her out when he didn't have to. When it probably would have been easier for him *not* to, especially since he'd had Isla with him. Since then, she'd seen how he was trying his best for the little girl he was now responsible for.

Her dad had always said that his family was the most important thing in his world and that he'd gladly give up everything in order to take care of them. She knew from what he'd told them over the years that wealth hadn't been the goal he'd set out with when he'd started the company. He'd just wanted to be able to take care of his family.

That it had done so well had been an unexpected blessing. Because of that, he'd done what he could to help take care of other families by providing a company that supported employees in such a way that they could take care of their families. Heather was sure that was why God had blessed the company.

With time ticking, she flipped the file closed and slid it into her bag, along with her laptop. She'd tackle it again once she got home later.

After pulling on her coat and swapping out her shoes for her boots, she made her way down to the basement garage where Hunter's car was. She had to admit that she was glad that Hunter had come up with a reason for them to visit the pair, since she hadn't been sure what sort of excuse she could use that Ash would accept.

Hunter was waiting in the car when she got there, and soon they were on their way to the garage.

"Do you know where you're going?" Heather asked as Hunter exited the underground garage onto the street that ran in front of their office building.

"Yep. Already punched the address into the GPS."

"Do you think Ash is going to take you up on what you're offering?" Heather asked.

When Hunter had run the idea by her initially, she hadn't been sure that Ash would see it as beneficial for his garage.

"No idea. He's a hard one to read, but I think there's a chance that he'll see that it's a good thing."

"Are you using the same tactic as you did with Carissa?"

"What's that?" Hunter asked.

"How it would be a good thing for Isla?"

Hunter chuckled. "That really did work for Carissa, though she did know what I was doing. I'm just glad she didn't hold that manipulation against me."

"Falling in love with you might have helped that."

"Well, it's hard to do something similar with Ash since it won't directly benefit Isla the way the things we did for Carissa benefitted Rachel."

"I wish there was more we could do for them," Heather said. "But something tells me that Ash has too much pride to allow that."

"Seriously though, do you think he and Isla are okay? Carissa had been a single mom for a long time, and it was a challenge a lot of the time. From the sound of things, Ash hasn't been a single dad for very long, and to a little girl, at that. I'd be lost in those circumstances."

"I don't know how they're doing. Isla has mentioned that she's been teased at school, and it sounds like she's been struggling with stuff like reading. I wouldn't be surprised if she hadn't been in school much before coming to live with Ash."

"How do you help someone who likely won't accept help?" Hunter asked. "I don't want to make Ash feel like he's not doing a good job."

Heather had no answer for that. She had a feeling that their family's wealth would always stand between them and Ash. It had been a challenge for Carissa. But in the end, her love for Rachel and for Hunter had allowed her to move past what might be considered their different stations in life.

"Why do you feel the need to help Ash?" Heather asked, curious about how he viewed Ash. She wanted to be sure that nothing Hunter did made Ash feel like they looked down on him. "Did you just make this proposal up?"

Hunter glanced over at her. "No. I didn't make it up."

With everything already on Hunter's plate, she was a bit surprised he'd taken on something else. But as Hunter explained his thought process in coming up with the proposal for Ash, she could hear his passion for the project.

"He might be leery of working with you," Heather said, wishing that wasn't the case but understanding why. "He doesn't know us from Adam."

"I get that," Hunter agreed. "But how can he get to know us if we don't spend some time with him?"

Heather couldn't fault his logic, and honestly, she trusted that Hunter had done his due diligence regarding this. He wasn't someone who did things off-the-cuff. Well, except when it came to Carissa and Rachel. He had dived in headfirst to take care of them the previous year.

When the GPS directed them through the final turns to their destination, Heather found herself with a flutter of nerves in her stomach. She wanted this to go well for so many reasons.

The sun had already set, so the garage's lights were on, spilling warmth through the windows. They walked together to the door leading into the office area.

Isla was once again sitting at the desk, but this time she had a paper in front of her, along with the crayons Santa had given her. She looked up when they walked in, her eyes brightening as she smiled at them.

"Hi, Isla," Heather said. "How're you doing?"

"Not good," she replied with a frown. "I'm doing homework, and I don't like it."

Before Heather could say anything, Ash appeared, wiping his hands on a blue rag. Again, he wore stained coveralls, and his hat was on backward. It seemed to be his uniform, and Heather didn't think it was a bad one. She never would have thought she'd be attracted to a rough-around-the-edges sort of man, but here she was.

"Hi, Ash," Hunter said. "Thanks for making time for us."

Ash's gaze met Heather's, and he gave her a nod. She smiled in return, and for a moment, Ash's attention stayed on her. But then he blinked and turned his focus onto Hunter.

"So, what can I do for you?" Ash asked.

"How about you show me around?" Hunter suggested. "And I'll tell you more about what I've been thinking."

"Sure." Ash nodded to the doorway behind him. "It'll be a pretty quick tour."

Though Heather would have liked to hear the conversation between the two men, she decided that she'd keep Isla company instead. The little girl needed her attention more than anything Hunter and Ash were discussing. Hunter would catch her up on the details later.

"What are you working on, sweetheart?" Heather asked as she went to the desk.

Isla peered up at her with wide eyes. "Am I your sweetheart?"

Oh. She hadn't thought much about using the endearment. It was one she used for Rachel, too. "You are definitely a sweetheart."

"My teacher said I'm stubborn and difficult."

Heather felt anger flare inside her. "What?"

Isla shrugged as she looked down at her paper. "I try to do what she says, but it's hard sometimes."

"Well, why don't you show me what you're working on?" Heather pulled a chair around the desk to sit beside Isla, looking down at the paper she'd been working on. It seemed that she was having trouble keeping her letters in the lines. Heather couldn't remember too clearly, but she thought that she'd been able to write her name by the time she went to kindergarten.

"What grade are you in, sweetheart?"

"I was supposed to be in grade two, but they put me in grade one."

That info seemed to reinforce what Heather had thought about Isla's school experience before coming to live with Ash. "What is your favorite subject?"

"Art. I like to color."

Heather remembered that from their previous conversations, which had led to the coloring books, crayons, and markers in her Santa bag. "Do you like to draw circles and lines?"

"Sometimes," she said.

"Letters are just swirls and lines." Heather picked up a crayon and looked around for a printer. Spotting one in the corner, she grabbed some paper from it. "Here, let me write my name."

Isla leaned forward to watch as Heather printed out her name. "You have a long name."

"Yep. I do. You're lucky that yours is shorter."

"I don't like to do this," Isla said with a long sigh. "But I have to."

"How about you write your name while I write mine? What's your first letter?"

For the next few minutes, Heather encouraged Isla through each letter. The little girl's feet swung as she wrote, every once in a while hitting one of the legs of the chair she sat on.

"Very nice," Heather encouraged after Isla had finished one line of her name. "Let's do another one. Do you want a different color?"

After swapping out her red crayon for a blue one, Isla began to carefully write out her name again. It felt a bit like she was writing lines for having done something wrong, but Heather also knew that it was only through repetition that Isla would learn to write her name easily. All she could do was offer her encouragement and praise for doing so well.

The little girl was so eager to please that it made Heather's heart hurt. The idea that a teacher would tell her she was stubborn and difficult was maddening.

"Did you tell Uncle Ash what the teacher said?" Heather asked.

Isla bit her lip as she focused on writing her name, then she shook her head.

"Why not, sweetheart?"

The little girl frowned. "Didn't want to make him mad."

"I don't think he'd be mad at you."

But maybe Isla wouldn't know that. Maybe they hadn't been together long enough for her to know how Ash would react. Maybe she'd had experience with people who got mad at her.

Heather was almost one hundred percent certain that Ash wouldn't get mad. Or at least he wouldn't get mad at Isla. Now the teacher? Yeah, Ash might get mad at him or her.

It was so frustrating because Heather knew for a *fact* that there were wonderful teachers out there who would help children who were struggling. Rachel had had a wonderful teacher the previous year that she'd told Heather about on a regular basis. Rachel had been so sad when she'd finished the school year, knowing that she was leaving her favorite teacher behind.

That was the type of teacher Isla needed. But how was she supposed to get a different teacher when Isla was probably going to the school closest to where they lived? Convenience was most likely a factor for them.

"I'm done," Isla announced and slid the paper toward Heather.

Heather picked up the paper, noting that the last few lines were neater than the ones at the top of the page. All she'd needed was some encouragement and guidance.

"You did a great job," Heather told her, leaning over to give her a hug. "Do you have more homework?"

Isla slumped back against the office chair, a scowl on her face. She crossed her arms and pressed her chin to her chest. "I have to read."

"Well, get your book, and let's read."

Isla glanced at her. "You'll help me?"

Though Heather had no idea what that might entail, she nodded. Isla looked into the backpack that lay open on the desk. She pulled out a large plastic Ziploc bag and handed it to Heather. She opened the bag and pulled out the book and a paper, reading the instructions on the top of it. After that, she felt a little more equipped to tackle this with Isla.

"What story are we reading?"

Isla pointed at the bookmark that was stuck between pages near the start of the book. Heather opened the book, skimming over the short words written in large font.

"Okay, sweetheart." Heather held the book out to Isla. "Let's read your story."

Chapter 8

Ash wasn't sure what he'd expected when Hunter had asked to meet with him at the garage, but clearly, the man had a plan. Whether he was on board with that plan, Ash didn't know yet. His recent interactions with rich men and their businesses had not been positive.

However, Hunter was sure doing his best to convince him of how beneficial his plan would be. He even had a folder that contained all the information he'd shared with him.

"There's no rush for you to get back to me about this, but call if you have any questions." Hunter handed over the folder. "I think this could be beneficial for you and helpful for others."

From what he'd heard so far, Ash was inclined to agree, but he wouldn't say anything until he'd read through it all a few times. Given his precarious financial position, he couldn't afford to make decisions without giving them serious consideration.

Well, except for Isla. Taking her in had been a decision he'd made without much thought. As soon as he'd been told about her and about what had happened with Gwen, he'd said he'd take her. Thankfully, it was a rash decision that he hadn't come to regret.

Speaking of... As he and Hunter moved in the direction of the waiting room, he could hear Isla talking. Or rather, reading.

Ash grimaced. Reading was the worst part of their day. Each night, they struggled through it, which usually resulted in tears for Isla. He'd tried asking her teacher for some help, but the woman had told him to just get Isla to practice more.

"You did great, sweetheart," Heather said. "Now on to the next page."

Standing beside Hunter, Ash watched Heather and Isla, who sat close together, their heads bent over Isla's book. Hunter glanced at Ash and smiled, but he didn't say anything, clearly understanding that this was important.

Ash knew the story well since Isla had been practicing it for a week already. It sounded like they were on the last page.

When she got to the end of the story, Heather held up her hand. "You did an amazing job!"

Isla smacked Heather's hand, a beaming smile on her face. "Really?"

"Yep. You got almost all the words by yourself, which is amazing."

"I've read it so much," Isla said with a big sigh. "I want a new story."

"When do you get a new one?"

"I have to get all the words right when I read to the teacher."

"You're nearly there. I bet you get a new story soon."

Ash hoped so because he was as sick of the story as Isla was. When Heather glanced over, her eyes widened briefly.

"Done with your chat?" she asked as she sat back in her chair. "We've just been doing some homework."

"Look, Uncle Ash." Isla got down from her chair and approached him with the paper she'd been working on when Heather and Hunter had arrived. "I did my name good."

Ash lowered himself to one knee, wrapping his arm around her as he looked down at the paper. He could see that it had gotten better by the end of the page and suspected that Heather had something to do with that.

"You did a great job, princess."

She grinned at him, then hooked her arm around his neck, pressing her cheek against his. It was a position she seemed to like. Ash stood, lifting her up easily as he did so.

He looked at Heather and found her watching them, a gentle expression on her face. Why this woman had taken an interest in their lives, Ash didn't know. Were they simply a charity case to her and Hunter? That seemed like the most likely explanation. It was probably the reason she'd given Isla a huge suitcase of clothes and the things from Santa.

Everything in him balked at being viewed as needing charity. He worked hard at his garage, and though he wasn't rich, he usually could make ends meet. The rival garage and Isla's arrival had tightened things up, however, and he'd be the first to admit that he knew nothing about what a little girl might need.

If it weren't for Isla, he'd probably brush aside any offers of help. But he couldn't afford to do that when it came to his niece. He needed to put aside his pride for her sake. She was the most important person in his life now.

Heather smiled, her gaze going to Isla. "She did a great job reading too."

"Thank you for helping her out," Ash said. "Homework isn't a lot of fun for her."

"From what I remember, homework wasn't a lot of fun for me either," Heather admitted. "Rachel doesn't seem to mind hers, though."

"That really depends on the homework," Hunter said. "She is absolutely not a fan of math. Usually, I end up having to help her with that since math comes easier to me than Carissa."

Ash felt a bit envious of Carissa in that moment. Having someone to help shoulder the burden of parenting would be great. But he wasn't going to get into a relationship just so he'd have help with Isla. That wouldn't be a good foundation for a long-term relationship.

"I only like art homework," Isla said. "I just want to color."

"Our fridge is proof of that." Ash bounced Isla a little. "We've hung lots of your pictures up there."

Isla nodded with a proud look on her face. "Lots of them."

"Maybe you could draw a picture for me," Heather said.

Ash frowned, wondering how wise it was to continue to allow Heather to spend time with Isla. So far, though, Isla had only benefitted from her interactions with the woman. The problem would come when Heather moved on from them. Isla had already suffered neglect and loss, and he didn't want her to suffer more.

"Yes! Next time I see you, I'll have a picture for you."

"Well, for now, we have to go," Hunter said, then looked at Ash. "Let me know if you have any questions about my proposal."

Ash nodded. "I will."

"Thanks for hearing me out." Hunter turned to Heather. "Ready to go?"

Heather nodded, then picked up her coat and slipped it on. "We'll see you soon."

Ash didn't bother to ask when that might be. They'd show up when they showed up.

Isla waved and called out a goodbye as the pair left the building. Heather glanced back with a smile and a wave of her own.

Once they were gone, Ash set Isla back down. "I'm just going to close things up so we can go home."

Isla knew the drill. So while he was busy doing that, she put her things into her backpack. By the time he was ready to set the alarm on the building, she had her jacket and boots on.

It was snowing as they left, and Isla squealed in delight. The snow didn't hold the same appeal for Ash because he knew that if it was significant, he'd be out shoveling it before work the next morning.

It had been many years since he'd found any joy in the snow, but he had to admit that sometimes Isla's excitement was infectious. Since they had work and school the next day, however, they wouldn't be able to enjoy that particular snowfall.

Back home, Ash made them some supper, for once not having to hassle Isla to do her homework. She'd already done the two things she'd been assigned. Heather's help that day had eased the stress their evenings usually held.

It was almost unfair that not only was she wealthy and beautiful, but she also seemed to be genuinely nice. Ash was only human, and there were parts of her that drew him to her. Not the least of which was how she interacted with Isla. Every time she was with her, he could see that Heather was focused on Isla. Not just tolerating her, but seeming to enjoy the time she spent with her.

Ash wasn't sure he'd ever had anyone show quite so much kindness to someone he cared about. It pained him to admit, but he was fairly certain that even Gwen hadn't treated Isla with that much kindness. He'd never seen the two of them interact, but from things Isla had said, it seemed that she'd suffered from a lack of love and care.

"When will we see Heather again?" Isla asked as she ate the spaghetti Ash had managed to throw together.

"I don't know. She has a job, so it might be a few days." Or more.

"She called me sweetheart." Isla stared at him, her brow furrowed. "Do you think she likes me?"

The insecurity that had her asking that question broke Ash's heart. And he really hoped that he wasn't wrong when he said, "Yes. She likes you."

Isla's expression eased into a smile. "I like her too. She's pretty and smells nice."

Ash hadn't gotten close enough to know how Heather smelled, and any perfume that might have lingered in the air after she left had been swallowed up in the overwhelming smell of oil and rubber. But his eyesight was just fine, so he couldn't deny that she was pretty.

It had been a very long time since a woman had dominated his thoughts the way Heather was beginning to. He didn't want that, though. Of all the women to be attracted to, it annoyed him that it was someone rich. As far as he was concerned, the wealthy had too much power over those with less. And he hadn't spent enough time with the Kings to know if they were really any different.

He just had to keep that in mind during any interactions with her. He had enough on his plate to deal with already. Spending too much time thinking about Heather would just add more complications to his life, which was the last thing he needed.

Now that she'd given Isla some clothes and gifts from Santa, maybe Heather would be done with them. It was going to happen eventually anyway, so it was better to have it happen before Isla got any more attached.

A couple of days later, it became apparent that Heather wasn't going to stay away for long. She seemed to have figured out the best time to come to the garage for when Isla would be there. That, of course, thrilled Isla to no end.

Her presence allowed him to get a bit more work done because he wasn't having to constantly check on Isla. But not only that, having most of Isla's homework done before they got home would mean their evening would be less stressful.

That day, Isla had another paper of words that she needed to write, plus a new story to read. It was great that she'd moved on because it meant she'd read the previous story to her teacher's rather exacting standards. However, the first day with a new story was always a trial for both of them as Isla tried to figure out the words, and Ash had to resist just telling her what they were.

Though that might help her get through the story in the short term, it wouldn't benefit her in the long run, so he had to bite his tongue when she struggled with words. He wasn't sure if Heather struggled with that as well. But from what he could hear from where he was working on cleaning some parts on the workbench right outside the office door, she wasn't just jumping in with the words.

When she'd arrived, she'd said hi to him, but then sat down with Isla at the desk and talked to her about her day. Ash hadn't been sure what to make of it.

Was she just coming to help Isla with her homework? Did she think he wasn't doing a good job of things? She might be right about that, but he was trying his best to juggle all the new things that had come with accepting Isla into his life.

The thing was, while he knew that what he could give Isla was far and away better than what her mom had been able—or willing—to give her, he also knew that she could also have so much better than him. Having Heather come around was a reminder of that.

Part of him wanted to tell Heather to leave them alone. To just let them live their lives as best they could without her interference. However, even the limited time she'd spent with Isla was already improving their lives more than Ash could have imagined possible.

"Heather, would you show Uncle Ash how to fix my hair?"

Isla's question had Ash pausing, the parts he'd been cleaning on the workbench forgotten as he waited for Heather's answer.

"Of course," Heather replied. "If he wants me to show him some things, I can do that. Next time I come, I'll bring some hair stuff like what Rachel uses."

"Thank you so much," Isla said, her voice filled with excitement.

Ash sighed as he looked back at the parts on the workbench. He'd never aspired to be a hairstylist, but it looked like he was going to learn how to do Isla's hair.

Chapter 9

Heather pulled her car into the garage's small parking lot, then picked up the two bags she'd brought with her and got out of the car. The lights in the building cast a warm glow into the late afternoon twilight, and she hurried to the door, eager to escape the winter temperatures.

Once in the warmth of the office area, she blew out a breath and stamped her boots on the mat to rid them of the snow from outside.

Isla grinned at her from behind the desk. "Hi, Heather!"

"Hi, sweetheart," Heather said as she set her bags on a nearby chair. After taking off her coat, she hung it on a hanger on a small rack near the door. "How are you?"

"I'm good."

Heather went to the entrance of the work area of the garage and spotted Ash walking toward her. "Hi, Ash."

The man gave a nod—which Heather was coming to realize was his version of a greeting. "Hey there. What's up?"

"I thought I'd come by and help Isla with her homework, and if you have the time, I can show you some hair stuff."

"Sure. I'll just finish with this and get cleaned up."

"Sounds good." Heather would have liked to watch him work for a bit, but she turned and went to the desk where Isla sat. "What are you working on today?"

As she sat down beside the little girl, Isla recounted what she had to do. It wasn't much different from the previous times she'd helped her, only this time she also had a math sheet. Isla tackled her writing and the math worksheet, with Heather only having to give minimal guidance, but she sighed heavily when it came time for reading.

"I don't like to read," Isla said. "Why do I have to read?"

"Reading is important, sweetheart. It will help you with lots of things."

Isla scrunched up her nose. "Like what?"

Heather tried to think of things that might appeal to her. "Do you like coloring unicorns?"

Isla nodded. "I make them really pretty."

"Did you know that there are unicorn stories?"

"Really?" Isla didn't look entirely convinced that there was any such thing.

"Yep. Rachel loves to read unicorn stories. Do you want me to see if I can find a unicorn book for you to read?"

Isla bit the end of the pencil she held. Apparently, she suspected that there was a trap to Heather's question. "Maybe?"

Before Heather could respond, Ash walked in. He no longer wore the coveralls that he'd had on earlier, and he looked like he'd cleaned up a bit. The man was definitely attractive with his tall, muscular build and striking, light blue eyes. He didn't have a polished look like Hunter did, but Heather found she liked that.

"Ready for some hair care tips?" she asked.

Ash grimaced. "I suppose so."

"It's really not that bad," Heather said as she went to get the bags she'd brought with her. "Hunter has even learned to help Rachel with her hair."

The man still didn't look convinced, but he approached the desk where Isla sat, clearly willing to tackle it, regardless.

"Because I didn't know what all you already had, I picked up a few things that you can keep after I show you how to use them."

She set out the things that Carissa had told her might be helpful. Glancing at Ash and Isla, she found them regarding the items with wide eyes.

"Little girls need all that stuff?" Ash asked. "Clearly, I've been doing it wrong."

"Not wrong," Heather hurried to assure him. "You don't need to use it all, but some of these things will make doing her hair easier. What do you find the hardest?"

"Honestly?" Ash sighed. "All of it."

"I don't like when I have tangles," Isla volunteered. "It hurts to get them out."

Heather picked up one of the bottles as well as the detangling brush she'd bought. "Then these will help."

She told them how to use the hair product, and then, after removing the elastics that were currently holding Isla's hair in lopsided ponytails, she brushed through it with the detangling brush.

"That doesn't hurt much," Isla said with a smile.

"That's great." Heather handed the brush to Ash. "The best way to deal with really tangled hair is to work from the bottom up. You can grip a handful like this so that if you hit a tangle, the way you're holding it will keep it from tugging at her scalp."

Ash's brow furrowed for a moment, then he nodded. "Makes sense."

Heather felt a rush of warmth that she was able to offer him some help. "Do you have a blow dryer?"

"Yeah, but it's nothing fancy."

"You don't need fancy as long as it works." She pulled out another brush. "You can use this once you've detangled her hair to help blow dry her hair."

"Another brush?"

Heather laughed. "A person can have several brushes—all with different uses. But in this case, I just brought along a couple as well as some combs."

After they were done with the brushes, she pulled out a rat tail comb and showed him how he could use that to make a straight part from the crown to the nape. Then she pulled each side into a ponytail, using the brush to make it smooth.

"Also, these elastics would probably hold her hair better," Heather said as she held up the pack she'd picked up. "I've also brought some headbands if there are days you want to leave her hair down, or you can just make one ponytail in the back."

Isla was a dream to work on, sitting still while Heather walked Ash through each of her suggestions so that he could see how she did things. Clearly, the little girl was desperate to have better hair.

"Why don't you try?" Heather suggested as she released Isla's hair to allow it to fall down around her shoulders. "Then, if you get stuck, I can show you how to get unstuck."

Ash hesitated, then took the brush Heather had been using. He reached for Isla's hair, then pulled his hand back and said, "My hands are clean. They're just... uh... stained."

"I know that," Heather said, resting her hand briefly on his arm. "It's fine."

"Isla seems to like ponytails the best," Ash said.

It took him a couple of tries, but eventually, he seemed to get the hang of parting the hair and then smoothing it into nearly level ponytails.

"Can I see, Uncle Ash?" Isla asked when she figured out he was done.

"I don't have a mirror here, princess."

"Let me take a picture," Heather suggested, picking her phone up from where she'd left it on the desk. She took a couple of pictures. One from the back and one from the front. Then she handed the phone to Isla so that she could see what she looked like.

"Uncle Ash!" Isla exclaimed. "You did such a great job. I love them."

The biggest smile she'd seen yet crossed Ash's face. Though it didn't hang around long, she didn't doubt his happiness at Isla's excitement. That she'd played a small part in their shared joy made her happy, too.

"I'll definitely need more practice," Ash said. "But this is good. Thank you."

Heather smiled at him. "You're very welcome."

"Can we do braids next?" Isla asked. "Some girls in my class have pretty braids."

"If your uncle doesn't mind me coming around again, I can do that."

Isla looked up at Ash. "I want braids."

"I know you do," Ash told her with a small smile. "You've told me that plenty of times."

"Well, I'd be happy to come back and show you how to do braids," Heather said. "It can be a bit complicated at first, but I think you'd pick it up quickly."

Ash pulled his hat off and ran his hand through his own hair before replacing it. "I never dreamed I'd need to know stuff like this."

"I hate to break it to you, but the things you'll need to know for parenting a girl are just beginning."

Ash sighed. "I figured as much."

"But for all that you might not know, I can see that you know the most important thing for her," Heather tried to reassure him. "And that's that you love her."

"I do," he said. "I had never really thought much of having kids of my own, but I can't imagine my life without her now."

"You get to keep me, right?" Isla said.

"I do. And that makes me very happy."

Isla lifted her arms, and Ash bent to pick her up, wrapping her in his embrace. Heather smiled at the pair, once again finding Ash's devotion to his niece to be a very attractive quality in the man.

That should have been a good reason to keep her distance from the pair, because she had a feeling that Ash wasn't drawn to her the way she was to him. And not just to him, but to Isla, too.

Ash turned his attention to her. "If you have some more time to spare, I'd appreciate the help in learning how to braid her hair."

Even if she hadn't had time to spare, she would have agreed to help him out. "I'd be happy to come back." Heather hesitated. "Also, I wanted to invite the two of you to the Children's Christmas program at our church this Sunday evening."

Ash frowned for a moment. "I'm not sure."

"Just think about it," Heather said, not wanting him to refuse her outright. "You can let me know later this week. You have my number."

"Okay."

"Well, I'm sure you're anxious to get home, so I'd better head out." She told him what homework they'd done so he could sign off on anything that he needed to.

"What about all this stuff?" Ash gestured to the hair stuff on the desk.

"Oh, that's for Isla. I figured it would be easier for me to pick up what she needed since I have a bit more experience with it."

Ash looked like he was going to argue, but then he glanced at Isla, who was beaming. "Thank you. For everything."

"You are very welcome." She gave Isla a hug but resisted doing the same with Ash, though part of her thought that maybe he could benefit from a hug as much as Isla could. "I'll talk to you later."

The cold that greeted her sent shivers through her as she hurried across the parking lot to the car. After climbing behind the wheel, she started it up and stared at the garage as she rubbed her hands together, waiting for the car to warm up a bit.

Thankfully, her car heated up quickly, and soon she was leaving the parking lot, though she did it with great reluctance.

As she drove home, Heather tried to figure out what to do about Ash and Isla. They were a very welcome addition in her life—starting from the night he'd helped her—but what she didn't know was if she was as equally welcome in theirs. Well, Isla likely was happy with her presence in their lives. The unknown was how Ash felt about it.

Heather wanted him to be happy that he'd stopped by the side of the road to help her, but she wasn't sure that he was. She didn't want Ash to view her as someone to merely tolerate, but it wasn't like she could force him to be happy about her coming around. And she didn't want him to think she was trying to buy his affection.

The things she bought for them were purchased not because she wanted to flaunt her wealth, or because she thought Ash couldn't provide for Isla. She bought them because doing it brought her joy. Unfortunately, she knew Ash might not view it that way.

Maybe she needed to have a conversation with Carissa about how she'd felt when they'd done things for her and Rachel.

Was it any surprise that some of the same things that had drawn Hunter to Carissa were drawing her to Ash? Their dad had always stressed how important certain qualities were in people. Things like being hardworking, determined, honest, and loving.

It was his exposure to those things through his mom that had made them so important to her dad. He'd looked for those qualities in a wife, and he'd worked hard to instill them in her, Hunter, and Hayden.

It made sense that they would also want those qualities in anyone they would consider for future partners. But it was more than just that, though.

Heather had met plenty of men with some or all of those qualities, but she hadn't been drawn to them the way she was to Ash. It pained her to think that perhaps Ash looked at her but didn't see any qualities he was attracted to.

By the time she got home, Heather was decidedly less happy. The joy she'd felt being around Ash and Isla had faded to melancholy. She felt a bit helpless when it came to her emotions, and she wondered if there was any hope of being more than just a passing figure in their lives.

Would she only have them in her life for a season? The Christmas season?

Chapter 10

Ash's head jerked up when he heard the bell jangle over the door in the waiting area. Before he could even move, he heard Heather's voice as she greeted Isla. His heart thumped hard in his chest at the sound, and he wasn't sure that he liked that he was responding that way to just the sound of her voice.

Her arrival didn't take him by surprise since she'd texted to ask him if it would be convenient for her to come back that afternoon to teach him how to braid Isla's hair. Ash wished he could have said no. But knowing how disappointed Isla would be if he did, Ash told her it was fine.

And now here she was, and Ash couldn't deny that there was a part of him that was glad. For Isla's sake... That was *definitely* why he was glad.

He wandered over to the doorway, keeping his steps slow so as not to appear too eager to greet her. By the time he stepped into the office, she already had her coat off and was listening as Isla excitedly recounted her day.

"No one teased me about my hair!" Isla exclaimed as she came around the desk. "Uncle Ash did such a great job."

"I'm so glad to hear that, sweetheart." Heather gave Isla a hug. "Your uncle is amazing to learn this stuff for you."

"He loves me," Isla said, joy in her voice.

Ash's heart clenched at her words. It was true. He did. Who would have thought that him learning how to do her hair would be so important to her? His hair had never been that important to him. But since Isla's had been a source of teasing at school, it stood to reason that hers would be.

Heather glanced up and spotted him standing there. Straightening, she gave him a smile that wasn't quite as bright as it had been in the past. He wondered what had happened to dim it.

"Hi there," she said. "I figured I'd come a bit early and help Isla with her homework."

Ash felt relief at her words, knowing it would be one less stress when they got home later.

"I sure appreciate your help with that," Ash said. "It seems that you make it more fun for Isla than I do."

"I don't mind helping." Heather smiled at Isla, then looked back at Ash. "I enjoy it."

Well, that made one of them. He didn't think that even Heather could make Isla enjoy it, but at least she was happier to work on it with the woman. That was enough for Ash to welcome Heather back.

"When you're done work, we can do some braiding," Heather said. "If you still want to learn."

Ash glanced at Isla and saw the pleading look on her face. "I do."

"Don't worry, you won't be on braiding duty forever. Isla will eventually learn to braid her own hair. I did."

He was glad to hear that. "Maybe I'll learn to braid my hair too."

Heather's smile grew at that. "You could, though it's easier on longer hair."

"You could grow your hair like mine," Isla said.

Ash chuckled at that. "I'm not sure that would be too practical for me."

"I could braid your hair once I learn how," Isla offered.

"I think we've got some time before that," Ash said. "Why don't you focus on your homework for now?"

Though Isla frowned, she went back to her seat at the desk, and Heather followed her. She glanced at him as she sat down beside Isla.

Something in her gaze that day differed from previous visits, but Ash couldn't quite put his finger on what it was. She seemed a bit more reserved. He might wonder what caused it, but he'd never ask.

"I'll see you in a bit," he said, then returned to his work in the garage.

Knowing that Heather was coming, he'd purposely finished up any car work earlier. Not wanting to still be dirty when she arrived, Ash had scrubbed his hands harder than usual, then turned his attention to the inventory in his shop. It was something he needed to do anyway, and the bonus was that it wouldn't get him dirty again.

As he continued with his work, he heard Heather gently coaxing Isla through her homework. He felt guilty about allowing Heather to do what was really his responsibility. However, sharing the task seemed to benefit Isla. And since Heather seemed more than willing to help them out, he tried to squash the guilt and just embrace the help.

When he heard Isla exclaim with happiness that she was finished with her reading, Ash made his way to the office. She grinned at him as he joined them.

"I read the story without Heather's help," Isla told him. "She said I did good."

Heather had an affectionate look on her face as she slipped her arm around Isla's slender shoulders and gave her a hug. "You did great, sweetheart."

"I'll read it to you later," Isla said.

The offer surprised Ash, since Isla avoided reading at all costs. "I look forward to that."

"Should we get on with the braiding lesson?" Heather asked as she got up to retrieve her bag from the chair near the door. "This may take a little while."

Ash felt like perhaps that was an understatement. He hadn't braided anything in his life, and his few attempts to follow a YouTube tutorial had left him with a mess and an upset little girl.

"It might be easier for you to braid her hair wet until you get the hang of it," Heather said as she set her bag on the desk and pulled out a few things.

"I'm all for things that will make it easier."

Heather got Isla's chair situated so that they were both standing behind it. When she waved him closer, Ash hesitated, then stepped to her side. He was acutely aware of his worn clothes and stained hands next to her refined appearance. He felt like he needed to explain again that his hands were clean, but he held the words in, even though he felt like he was getting Heather dirty just by standing next to her.

"The most popular braid is the French braid," Heather said. "But I'm going to start you out with a simpler one."

"I appreciate that," Ash told her.

She looked over and gave him a smile. "First, we'll pull her hair up into two ponytails."

Ash took the comb and separated the hair the way she'd shown him during their first lesson. She chatted with Isla about what she'd been doing at school while he did that, which helped Ash relax. When he had both ponytails done, he regarded them with a frown since they weren't perfectly level.

"Looks good," Heather said. "Now, we'll braid each one."

Heather moved closer to him, her arm brushing his as she took the hair on one side in her hand. He would have stepped away to give her space, but he wouldn't have been able to see what she was doing if he did.

As she worked through the braid, Ash tried not to be distracted by her nearness or the light scent of her perfume that seemed so out of place in his garage. When she finished that one, they moved to the other side.

"Divide it into three sections," Heather said, obviously assuming that seeing her do it once was enough for him to grasp what needed to be done.

He didn't want to disappoint her or Isla by not picking up on it, so he did as she said. His pulse kicked up when her hands settled lightly over his at one point, showing him how to get into the rhythm of layering the sections of hair over each other.

Ash wasn't sure that his brain would remember this lesson or if his thoughts would be of the gentle touch of Heather's hands on his. Her skin was so soft against his more calloused hands.

"That looks great," Heather told him with a smile when he finally made it to the end of the braid and finished it off with the elastic she handed him. "You did a great job, Ash."

"Now, if I can just remember how to do it when you aren't around to tell me."

"Do you want to try it again?" Heather asked. "This time without my help?"

Ash hesitated, not wanting to take up any more of her time, but he ended up nodding. He told himself it was because he wanted to get this right for Isla.

She undid the braids of both ponytails, then brushed the hair out before turning the task over to him. Though she didn't do more than offer encouragement, she stayed close to Ash as he worked.

"You picked up on that very quickly," she said when he finished the second braid.

They were by no means perfect, and he wasn't sure Isla would want to go to school with her hair like that. But hopefully, after a bit more practice, his braids would have the smooth look that Heather's had.

Once again, Heather took pictures of the braids so that Isla could see what they looked like.

"They're nice," Isla said, though there was a thread of disappointment in her voice. "But some girls have braids that are flat on their head."

"Those are French braids," Heather told her. "And I'll teach your uncle how to do those eventually, but he needs to practice these more first. If you want, I can French braid your hair now, and if it's not too messed up in the morning, you could wear them to school."

Isla nodded, apparently eager to accept Heather's offer. "I want that."

"You can watch me do this, Ash, so you know what's coming."

Ash didn't need a second invitation to stick close, even as he lectured himself about it. Heather was obviously a pro at that type of braiding because her fingers moved quickly, creating a braid that lay flat against Isla's head. He could see why that would appeal to the little girl. It was a more mature style than the braids he'd done.

"I'm not sure I'll ever be able to do that," Ash said when Heather was finished.

"I know it looks complicated, but I think you'll get the hang of it with some practice."

Ash didn't share her confidence. With his larger hands, he wasn't sure he could do something as intricate as the braid Heather had woven.

"I like it," Isla announced after seeing more pictures.

"It should still be okay in the morning," Heather said. "It's braided tightly enough."

Ash hoped that was the case because he had a feeling Isla was going to be wearing the braids whether or not they looked okay. After Heather had cleaned up the stuff she'd brought, she pulled a couple of books out of her bag.

"I know reading isn't your favorite thing, but I thought you might like these books." Heather held them out to Isla. "They're stories about unicorns, and you can color the pictures."

Isla took them from Heather after a glance in his direction. Ash wasn't sure if she thought he would tell her she couldn't have them, but at his nod, she looked back at the books.

"Maybe the next time I come, you can show me how you've colored the pictures, and we can read the story together."

That got a smile from Isla, but all that Ash's stupid brain picked up on was Heather's plan to come back again.

Heather turned her attention to him. "Have you thought more about the Christmas program?"

He'd like to say that he'd thought a lot about whether they should go. But that really hadn't been the case. The debate had raged for all of about five minutes because he knew Isla would enjoy it, and for that reason alone—yeah, right!—he'd decided to attend.

"I think we'll go," Ash said.

She hesitated for a moment, then said, "Would you and Isla like to join us for dinner beforehand? My mom asked me to invite you."

Ash's brows lifted at that. "Your mom?"

"Yes. She enjoyed meeting you both, and she'd like to see Isla again."

Ash had no idea how to respond to that. His own mother hadn't wanted to see Isla. Why would someone like Mrs. King?

"Will Rachel be there?" Isla asked. "I like her."

"Yep. Rachel will be there with her mom. Hunter will be there too, as well as our brother Hayden. Maybe."

"Maybe?" Ash asked.

Heather sighed. "It will all depend on how Hayden's feeling. If he's having a good day, he'll join us. If not…"

Remembering what Hunter had told him about the car accident that had taken their dad, Ash realized that even though it seemed as if the King family had everything, they'd also suffered tremendous loss and were still dealing with what had torn their family apart. That knowledge helped him feel like perhaps they were more alike than he'd originally thought.

Still, he wasn't sure that he and Isla were up for eating dinner at a wealthy family's table. Were there manners that they'd need to know? When they ate at home, it was pretty simple. Usually, one plate or bowl and whatever utensil was necessary to eat the meal he'd prepared.

As if reading his mind, Heather said, "It won't be anything too fancy. Hayden will ask what's for dinner, and if it's something with a name that needs translation, he won't come."

"What if it's Italian?" Ash asked.

Heather laughed as she waved her hand. "Oh, if it's Italian, he'll definitely be there. His favorite dish as a kid was spaghetti. So if that's what we end up having Sunday night, you know Mom chose it to guarantee that Hayden showed up."

"Spaghetti is my favorite food, too," Isla said. "Uncle Ash makes it for me."

"It's the one dish I manage to make without too much trouble."

"Well, you're one up from me," Heather said. "I'm afraid to say that I don't know much about cooking. I've been spoiled."

"Can't blame you for not cooking if you don't have to. I know I wouldn't. I'm just lucky that Isla will eat pretty much anything."

"I will!" Isla clapped her hands. "I love food!"

And yet, she still didn't eat that much. She had gained some weight since coming to live with him, but she was still a tiny little thing. The doctor had said to just feed her healthy food and let her eat until she was full.

"Well, we'd love to have you both join us for dinner before the program. And maybe I'll put in a word for spaghetti," Heather said with a wink.

"Can we go, Uncle Ash?"

Ash didn't love being put on the spot. But he could see that while Isla was excited, she was bracing herself for him to say no. If there was one thing he hated to do, it was to disappoint her.

"Yes, I suppose we can."

"Wonderful!" Heather smiled, her eyes sparkling. "I'll text you the address."

"We'll be there."

Chapter 11

Heather went into the living room to look out the front window. She worried that Ash would take one look at the house and keep right on driving. It would be naïve of her to not take into account Ash's feelings about the disparity in their levels of wealth.

She just needed him to come inside and spend time with them to see that they weren't all that different from him. Unfortunately, it was entirely possible that he wouldn't be able to look past the large house and other trappings in order to see that for himself.

"Is watching out the window anything like watching a pot?" Hayden asked.

She glanced over to see him making his way toward her, back on crutches, following his latest surgery. Whether this one would bring the relief they all hoped was still to be seen. Unfortunately, though, no matter how they tried to patch up the physical wounds that Hayden struggled with, it was the inner ones that seemed to be most resistant to healing.

"I don't know," she said as she turned back to the window. "I just hope they come."

"If they don't, it's their loss."

Heather wasn't sure that was entirely true. It felt like maybe it would be their loss as well. Some who shared their level of wealth tended to look down on those who weren't as well off, not considering that there were wonderful people in every income bracket.

She didn't doubt that there had been plenty of well-off people who had zoomed past her car on the highway that night she'd had her flat. Ash could have driven by as well, but he hadn't. To her, that showed his true character. He'd seen a need that he could help with, and he'd done just that.

"Are you going to be nice?" Heather asked Hayden as she continued to watch out the window. "Or is grumpy Hayden here tonight?"

"I plan to be mean and nasty," Hayden said, sarcasm strong in his words. He'd become a lot more sarcastic in the years since the accident.

"Well, at least they'll get a taste of the real you. Just don't scare them off."

"I'll try my best, but you know Hunter is better at schmoozing with people."

"You could be, too," Heather said. "You just need to put your mind to it."

A pair of headlights swept across the front of the house as a vehicle slowly approached. She watched as the truck came to a stop beside Hunter's SUV. Smiling, she made her way to the front door and pulled it open to see Ash helping Isla out of the back seat.

Cold air rushed in, but she didn't close the door as she waited for them to climb the steps.

"Hey, you two," she greeted them as they approached the door.

"Hi, Heather!" Isla exclaimed.

She stepped back to allow them to come into the foyer. After she closed the door, she said, "We can hang up your coats in the closet here."

Isla's eyes were huge as she stared around at the foyer and its decorations. Ash kept his focus on the little girl, helping her take off her jacket. When he was done, Heather took it from him and hung it up in the closet while he took off his own jacket and boots.

"Ash," Hunter said as he joined them in the foyer. "Welcome."

Ash shook Hunter's hand. "Thank you."

"Hey, Isla," Rachel sang out as she came skipping into the foyer. "You look beautiful!"

Heather was certain that the outfit Isla wore was one that Rachel had grown out of, but thankfully, the little girl didn't mention that.

"Come with me," Rachel said, holding out her hand. "Grandma has lots of Christmas trees."

Isla looked up at her uncle, and when Ash nodded, she took Rachel's hand and allowed her to lead her into the living room.

"We might as well follow them," Hunter said with a laugh.

As they joined the girls in the living room, Heather noticed that Ash was dressed in a pair of black jeans and a long-sleeve, dark green button-up shirt. His hair hung in long, loose curls, and while she might never have thought she'd find a man with longish hair attractive, clearly, she did.

Rachel was busy showing Isla her favorite decorations on the large tree in the living room. Isla's eyes were impossibly large, taking it all in.

"This is Hayden," Hunter said, drawing Heather's attention from the girls to see that Hayden had returned along with their mom. "And you met our mom at the Christmas party."

"I'm so glad you could come for dinner," her mom said with a friendly smile.

Hayden also greeted him, lifting his hand from his crutch to shake Ash's.

"Did you hurt yourself?" Isla asked, having abandoned the Christmas tree to stand next to Ash.

Ash stiffened at her question, but Heather wasn't worried. She'd discovered that Hayden actually tolerated those types of questions from children better than he did adults.

"Yep. I hurt my legs," Hayden said.

Isla's gaze traveled down his body, lingering on his crutches. "I hope you get better soon."

"Thanks. Me too."

Heather saw the tension leave Ash at Hayden's response. If he hung around enough, he'd realize that Hayden would never say or do anything to hurt Isla.

"Dinner is served, everyone," Carissa said as she came into the living room. "We don't want to be late for the service."

"Wonderful," her mom said, then waved in the direction of the dining room. "Let's eat!"

Heather held out her hand to Isla, and the little girl took it, then reached for Ash's. They followed the others out of the living room, through the foyer into the dining room.

The aroma in the air was delicious, but Heather had expected nothing less. Essie's spaghetti was amazing, and she was glad that she'd made it for them that night.

"Essie, this is Ash and his niece, Isla," Heather said as Essie came in from the kitchen, a basket of breadsticks in her hand.

Essie set it on the table and came to where they stood. "It is wonderful to meet you both."

"Essie is the most important person in our home," her mom said. "She keeps us all fed and cared for. We'd be lost without her."

Heather knew that people like Ash might think that Essie was just their employee, but while she might have started out that way, she was so much more than that now.

Ash shook her hand, and Isla accepted the hug that Essie offered. Essie had always showered them with love, and she had no problem doing it with new people. She and her husband, George, had never had children of their own, but they'd been like second parents to the triplets.

Once George had joined them, her mom directed everyone to seats, putting Isla between Heather and Ash. Hunter sat on the other side of Ash, and her mom sat next to Heather. The room was cozy, with a fire blazing in the fireplace along one wall. A smaller Christmas tree stood in the corner, and there were decorations on various surfaces.

For the first couple of years following the accident, the house had had one tree, and that was it. But in recent years, more and more of the decorations her dad had loved began to make their way out of storage once again. This year, her mom had reached new heights of decorating, and it was wonderful.

"Let's say a prayer of thanks for the food," Hunter said.

It surprised Heather to see Isla fold her hands and bow her head. Ash stared at Isla for a moment before he dipped his head. She wondered on Isla's response as Hunter prayed but then put it aside for the time being.

"Spaghetti," Isla breathed in awe as they passed the food around. "I love spaghetti."

"So do I," Hayden told her from across the table. "And Essie's is the best."

"I like Uncle Ash's," Isla said. "It's yummy."

"And also out of a jar," Ash murmured.

"Hey. You can get some tasty stuff out of a jar," Essie said. "I started off using jars."

"Jars?" Hayden pressed a hand to his chest. "I can't believe you'd admit that."

"Like you cared." Essie chuckled. "You and Hunter inhaled food with little thought of where it came from."

"We were growing boys," Hunter said. "And in our defense, your food always tasted amazing."

"If I still lived here and ate your food, I probably wouldn't be able to fit through any of the doorways since I don't get nearly enough exercise now," Hayden said.

"Well, I'm lucky to have such an appreciative audience to cook for."

As they ate, Hunter drew Ash into conversation. Since it wasn't business hours, Hunter didn't broach the proposal he and Ash had discussed. Instead, they were talking about motorcycles, something that Hunter had been passionate about as a teen, much to their mom's chagrin.

Their dad, however, had bought both Hunter and Hayden dirt bikes, and the three of them had gone to tracks to ride them. Eventually, they'd grown out of their passion for riding dirt bikes, but Hunter had gone on to buy himself a street bike in his early twenties.

It still sat in the family garage. But as far as Heather knew, Hunter hadn't ridden it since their dad's death. She'd never asked Hunter why he'd stopped riding, but she had a feeling it was a decision he'd made to put their mom's mind at ease.

Ash seemed to have above-average knowledge about motorcycles, though he said he didn't own one. Whether that was because he'd worked on them or been passionate about them the way Hunter was, Heather wasn't sure.

Her mom and Essie asked Isla about school and what she enjoyed doing. In between bites of spaghetti, she shared about how she loved art but hated reading. She talked about how Ash had learned to do her hair, which prompted a look in Heather's direction from her mom when Isla said that Heather had been there to teach him.

Heather hadn't mentioned what she was doing to anyone except Hunter, uncertain what her mom might say about it. What she might read into it. Heather was confused enough herself. She didn't need her mom to know just how much time she'd spent with Ash and Isla recently.

Of course, the fact that she'd wanted to invite them to the Christmas program probably spoke loudly enough to her mom.

"I get to sing in the program tonight," Rachel said.

"Really?" Isla sounded very impressed. "By yourself?"

"Yes. I'm singing a solo."

"That's so cool."

"Are you nervous, angel?" Essie asked.

"Nope! I've practiced lots, so I know the words really well."

Heather admired how confident Rachel was. She didn't think she would have been brave enough to sing a solo in front of a large congregation at her age.

"That's amazing," Essie said. "I can't wait to hear you sing."

Once they were done with the meal, they had some chocolate cake, which was Rachel's favorite, and then they got ready to leave for the church.

"I can go with you," Heather said to Ash. "To show you the way."

"Uh... sure. That would be great."

Her mom and Essie went with George, while Hayden went with Hunter, Carissa, and Rachel. It surprised Heather that Hayden was willing to go to the program as he tended to avoid large crowds. It probably had to do with the solo that Rachel was singing.

Hayden doted on Rachel, which made Heather happy and hopeful. It seemed that Hayden was happiest when Rachel was around. The little girl had brought light back into all their lives.

The past year since they'd met Carissa and Rachel had been a time for them to walk further away from their crushing grief and forward to a time when the memories of their dad would bring smiles and laughter instead of tears.

Once at his truck—which he'd come out and started a few minutes earlier—Ash opened the front and back passenger doors at the same time. Isla scrambled into the back seat while Heather pulled herself up into the front one.

The truck's interior was clean, and there was a light scent of air freshener with a hint of oil lingering within. Sitting there, she thought back to the night he'd rescued her, and she was happy that their paths had crossed.

"I can't wait to hear Rachel sing," Isla said from the back seat as they waited for Ash to join them in the truck.

"Me too." Heather turned as much as her seat belt allowed to face Isla. "I think it's going to be a fun program."

"Will Santa be there?"

Ash opened the door and settled behind the wheel, quickly shutting his door and closing out the cold. He glanced at her before putting the truck in reverse, though he waited for Hunter to pull out first.

"Not tonight. This time, they're talking about the more important reason we celebrate Christmas."

Rather than question it, Isla just nodded and said, "Jesus?"

"Yep." Like her praying at dinner, Isla's response surprised Heather and made her really curious about where she'd learned about Jesus and how to pray.

"And Rachel knows about Jesus too?"

"Yes, she does. She still likes Santa, but she also knows that this is more important." She turned her focus to the street in front of them. "Are you able to follow Hunter?"

"I should be able to," Ash said. "Doesn't appear there's too much traffic."

"Well, just let me know if you lose sight of him, and I'll give you directions."

Ash gave a nod. "I think I have an idea of where we're going."

"I hope you enjoy it," Heather said, now a bit worried that he might not. After all, he probably wasn't used to going to children's programs. "Does Isla have a Christmas program at school?"

"I'm not sure. I think I saw something about a winter concert."

"We're practicing songs," Isla said. "My teacher said we can invite our mom and dad and grandparents to come. Do you think Uncle Ash can come since I don't have a mom or dad?"

"I'm sure he could," Heather said, wondering why the school would have specified things that not all children had.

"Maybe you could come too," Isla said.

Ash said nothing in response to Isla's suggestion, leaving Heather to flounder a bit. "I'll... uh... talk to your uncle about it and see if it might work out."

She really hoped that it would, though she understood that Ash might not want that, and she wouldn't force him to acquiesce to Isla's request. He might be getting tired of her presence in their lives.

Chapter 12

Ash dropped Isla and Heather off at the church's main entrance, then went to find an empty spot in the parking lot next to the huge building. The lot was well-lit, and once he'd parked, he glanced around for Hunter but didn't see him.

He moved toward the portico-style entrance, pausing as cars drove past him to circle around and let out their passengers. When he finally reached the doors, he walked in and looked for Heather and Isla. They stood off to the right of the door, and he headed in their direction.

"We've already hung up our coats," Heather said as she gestured toward a room behind her.

She led him to where their coats were and waited as he hung his up. By the time they left the room, more people were milling about. Not wanting to lose Isla, Ash bent and lifted her into his arms. She hooked her arm around his neck, smiling as she looked out over the foyer, no doubt happy to have a higher vantage point.

"We can go into the sanctuary," Heather said. "Mom and Essie said they'd save us seats."

Ash followed her, moving carefully around people who were standing and talking with others. He couldn't remember the last time he'd been in a church. Attending church wasn't something his family had done, though his grandma on his dad's side had sometimes taken him and Gwen to her church as children. That church had been small and old, not at all like this very modern-looking building.

Heather led him down one of the aisles toward the front of the church. When she paused at a row, he saw that Eliza, Essie, Hayden, and George were already seated there. After a bit of shuffling around, Ash found himself seated at the end of the row with Isla between him and Heather.

Isla sat on the pew for a moment, but then asked to sit on his lap so that she could see more. Ash settled her on his knee, glad that he was on the end of the row because it would give her a better view of the stage. A piano was playing Christmas carols as people continued to file in. Hunter joined them soon after, followed a short time later by Carissa.

"Where's Rachel?" Isla asked.

Heather shifted a bit closer, her pressing against his. "She's with the rest of the kids. They're in rooms back behind the stage."

"Will I be able to see her?"

"You should. Carissa said that Rachel is standing on this side. Plus, they'll be projecting the program on those big screens," Heather said, pointing to large white screens at the front of the sanctuary.

Ash had to admit that he was curious about what was to come. However, he was also a bit nervous that he didn't know exactly what might be expected throughout the evening.

Soon, the sanctuary lights dimmed, and a man walked out onto the stage, stopping behind a microphone stand. His image was projected on the screens, showing him to be a middle-aged man with hair heavy streaked with gray.

"Welcome to our children's ministry Christmas program," he said, his smile broad and friendly. "They've all been practicing very hard to get ready for this evening. Before we let them out here, please join me for a word of prayer."

Ash bowed his head, though he kept an eye on Isla out of curiosity. She surprised him again by folding her hands and closing her eyes. Though she'd done that at the dinner table earlier, he'd thought she'd just followed what Rachel was doing.

They hadn't talked a lot about what had happened when she lived with her mom since Ash hadn't been sure she'd want to relive that time. What he knew about Gwen's life and subsequent death by overdose didn't mesh with Isla's familiarity with Jesus and praying.

Once the prayer was over, another man got up and led them in a Christmas carol as children filed out on the stage. Isla was practically vibrating with excitement as she watched what was happening on the stage.

These kids all looked quite little, and there was plenty of fidgeting and waving. A couple of women walked up on the stage with the kids and attempted to settle them down.

Soon, a little girl wearing a red dress stepped up to a mic that was set at a height that she could reach. She took a deep breath that was audible over the mic, then began to speak, her words clear and measured.

"For unto us a child is born, unto us a son is given, and the government shall be upon his shoulders, and his name shall be called Wonderful, Counsellor, the mighty God, the everlasting Father, the Prince of Peace." She took another deep breath. "Isaiah 9:6."

A song followed the recitation, then a narrator spoke as two figures—presumably Mary and Joseph—moved slowly across the stage toward what appeared to be a stable with large cut-outs of animals. It looked pretty good, Ash had to admit.

Isla spent the next hour captivated by what was happening on the stage, and Ash smiled at her excitement. When Rachel appeared to sing her part, Isla waved even though, with the lights down, Rachel wouldn't have been able to see her.

As he watched Isla, Ash found that he didn't care if it was pity or payment for him helping Heather. Whatever had prompted Heather to include Isla in their Christmas party at the hotel and this program at the church, Ash was grateful.

He still wasn't entirely sure how he felt about the Kings. It would be great if they really were a different sort of wealthy family. But even if they weren't, he'd take advantage of any opportunities they presented that would offer Isla the type of Christmas Ash couldn't—or didn't know how—to give her. Next year, hopefully, he'd be in a better position to give Isla a Christmas she'd enjoy—both financially and with the knowledge of how to make the holiday memorable for a child.

When the children's portion of the program was over, Ash pondered the things he'd heard. It would be easy to dismiss the performance as just a story told by children, but he couldn't. Clearly, the story of Jesus' birth was what Heather had been referring to when she said it was more important than Santa.

The man who'd opened the program climbed on the stage once the children had all filed off. He said a few words, further explaining what the children had shared through their program, which gave Ash even more to mull over.

After he said a prayer, the man dismissed them with an invitation to go to the fellowship hall for refreshments. Ash got to his feet when the others did, keeping Isla in his arms. The people in front of them had turned around and were speaking with Heather's mom, so he wasn't sure if they were ready to leave the row yet.

"Did you enjoy the program, Isla?" Heather asked.

"Yes! It was so great."

Heather smiled. "It was, wasn't it?" Then she looked at Ash. "Did you enjoy it?"

"I did," he said with a nod. He wasn't even just being polite. He really had enjoyed it, though clearly not as much as Isla had.

"We can go to the fellowship hall for a few minutes, if you're okay with staying a bit longer," Heather said. "Carissa and Hunter have gone already because that's where all the children have been taken."

Isla had school the next morning, but he couldn't find it in his heart to cut the evening short. "Sure, we can go for a little bit."

Isla grinned as he waited for the aisle to clear so he could exit the row. Once he did, Heather fell into step beside him as they followed others up the aisle to the exit. When they reached the foyer, Heather directed him to the fellowship hall, where plenty of children were running around.

"Where is Rachel?" Isla asked as she peered around the large room.

"I think they're over by the windows," Heather said.

Ash looked where she was pointing and saw Hunter and Carissa. As soon as they reached them, Isla asked him to put her down. When her feet touched the ground, she went to Rachel and gave her a hug. Rachel grinned and hugged her back.

"Did you guys get cookies already?" Heather asked Hunter.

"Not yet," Hunter said. "But now that you're here, we can take them to get some."

Isla and Rachel held hands as they walked to the closest table, where they let the girls choose two cookies each. The girls debated back and forth between the vast selection of cookies before they each picked two. Ash also grabbed a couple.

"I'm so glad that the two of you could make it," Heather said. "And that you enjoyed it."

"Thanks for inviting us." Ash looked at where Isla stood with Rachel. "Isla has enjoyed the evening a lot."

"I thought she might, but I hoped you would too."

"Can't say I ever remember being at a program like this, but I enjoyed it."

"Good." Heather smiled at him. "I wanted to talk to you about something else."

"Oh?" Ash crossed his arms as he eyed her warily. So far, she had been nothing but gracious and generous, but he kind of felt like somewhere along the line, there would be a catch.

"Do you plan to spend Christmas with your family?"

"You mean besides Isla?" Ash clarified.

"Yes."

"Then no," he said. "It'll just be the two of us."

"I'd love it if you would consider joining us for Christmas Eve and Christmas Day, if you have no other plans."

Ash regarded her for a moment, trying to figure out what her end game was. Christmas was a time for family to be together. Or maybe close friends. But strangers? People they'd known for only a few weeks? The invitation made little sense.

"Why?"

Heather didn't seem put off by his question, seeming to understand what he was asking. "Before my dad died, we'd often have people into our home who had nowhere else to go or no one else to celebrate with. Once he passed away, we kind of let that tradition slide away. It was hard enough being just the four of us without feeling like we had to act happy with people we didn't know very well."

Ash was sure that could be a challenge, though he hadn't experienced it for himself. Faking happiness wasn't something his family had ever bothered to do. By and large, holiday cheer had been absent in their gatherings.

"Last year, God put Carissa and Rachel in our path, and we knew that Dad would have wanted us to offer them a place to go for Christmas. It turned out to be the best Christmas we'd had since his passing. This year, I'd like it if you and Isla could join us. Isla already gets along well with Rachel, and I know Rachel would love to have her there on Christmas morning."

Ash figured that was probably true, and that, more than anything, tempted him to say yes right away. But he held his tongue.

"Anyway, you don't have to tell me right now," Heather said. "Just think about it."

"Okay." He appreciated that she wasn't putting pressure on him. The invitation was for more than just an hour or two, so he needed the time to think it over. "I'll let you know."

The rest of the family joined them then, and Hayden came to stand next to him. Ash waited for the man to say something, but apparently, Hayden was content to stay quiet as he leaned on his crutches. Given he wasn't one for a lot of talking himself, Ash didn't bother to break the silence.

"Why are you just standing over here?" Hunter asked.

"It's too noisy," Hayden said. "Quietest place is next to Ash."

"What are you?" Hunter asked. "A hundred years old? You used to be the noisiest of us all."

"Eh. Things change," Hayden said with a shrug, apparently not bothered by his brother's jabs.

"They sure do. Never thought I'd be considered the outgoing one of the two of us."

Ash found the relationship between the triplet siblings interesting. It certainly was different from what he'd had with Gwen. Of course, they hadn't really interacted much as adults. She'd taken off to live the life she thought she wanted not long after graduating.

He liked to think that they would have gotten along as adults, but she'd never let him into her life after that point. He hadn't even known that she'd left the Twin Cities for Chicago until he'd gotten the call about Isla.

His gaze went to where Isla and Rachel were dancing around to the upbeat Christmas music playing in the background. Even though Rachel was a little older than Isla, it didn't seem to matter to the friendship that was blossoming between them. After having Isla come home from school crying because some of the girls in her class were teasing her, it was a relief to see her playing happily with someone.

He could already imagine what Christmas would be like if they spent it with the King family. Isla would no doubt enjoy that more than if it were just the two of them.

Though Ash was sure he'd cave in the end, he was going to keep the invitation to himself for the time being. Telling Isla would only be asking for trouble because they still had a couple of weeks to go until Christmas. Things could still change.

Soon, the large room began to empty, with people gathering up their children and leaving. Carissa came over to where they stood, taking Hunter's hand when he held it out to her.

"We need to go soon," she said. "Rachel has school tomorrow."

"Here's hoping she unwinds on the way home because she doesn't look very tired at the moment."

Carissa looked over at the girls and smiled ruefully. "This is true."

Over the next several minutes, they managed to get the girls away from the cookies and into their winter wear.

"Will I see Heather this week?" Isla asked as Ash zipped up her jacket.

Ash glanced over to where Heather stood talking to Hayden. "Maybe."

"I hope she comes over again."

Ash wasn't sure what he hoped. Or maybe he was just in denial about it.

Chapter 13

Heather sorted through the stack of folders that HR had sent to her office. Not surprisingly, the number of people who were struggling had gone up over the past few weeks. Thanksgiving seemed to herald a difficult time emotionally and financially for many of their employees.

She wrestled a lot with deciding how to help the employees who had gone to HR with a need. The person in HR usually included a note with their recommendation, but she was the one who would make the final decision. If she was really stuck, she'd go to Hunter.

It had been something her dad had done himself during that time of year, often bringing the files home to discuss with her mom. Like him, she prayed a lot while she reviewed the files, knowing that amongst the genuine needs, there were some who tried to scam the company's generosity. She wanted to be able to discern the genuine ones.

Her cell rang as she flipped open the next file. Glad for a reprieve, Heather picked it up, pausing when she saw Ash's name on her screen.

"Hello?" she said, sitting back in her chair.

"Hi. Uh, it's Ash."

"Hey, Ash. How're you doing?"

"Good. I'm good. How about you?"

"I'm just fine. What can I do for you?"

"I'm calling for Isla." Ash cleared his throat. "She's been asking me to invite you to her school program."

"When is it?" Heather asked, so pleased that Isla wanted her there and that Ash had phoned to invite her.

"It's Friday afternoon at the school. I realize it's in the middle of the workday for you, so I understand if that means you can't make it."

"Well, one benefit of being my own boss means that I can leave during the day if I need to, so I'd love to come."

"Isla will be super happy to hear that," Ash said.

"Ah. She's such a sweetie. I'm glad that I can be there to see her perform. Should I meet you at the school?"

"If you'd like, you could come by the garage, and I'll drive. It's not too far away."

"Sure. That sounds perfect."

"Okay then. It starts at two, so I'd probably leave here a little after one-thirty."

"I shall be there by one-thirty then."

After they said goodbye, Heather set her phone down, a smile on her face. She had hoped that Ash might invite her to Isla's program, but she hadn't planned to press for it. Already, she kind of felt like she was inviting herself into their lives. But since he had initiated this invitation—at the behest of his niece—Heather hadn't hesitated to take him up on it.

Heather hadn't been able to hold out until Friday to see the pair again, so she'd dropped by after work on Tuesday for a bit. When Isla said nothing about her attending the program, Heather realized that Ash hadn't told her she'd be there yet.

Isla had mentioned it when Heather was leaving, saying how she wished Heather could be there. She'd just smiled and said she was sure that Isla was going to do a great job.

On Friday, Heather popped by Hunter's office to let him know she was gone for the rest of the day.

"Where're you going?" Hunter asked, not even bothering to pretend it wasn't any of his business.

"Ash asked me if I'd like to attend Isla's school program."

Hunter regarded her for a moment before he said, "You don't think you're maybe getting a little too involved in Isla's life?"

Crossing her arms, Heather glared at her brother. "Like you didn't get too involved in Rachel's life?"

"Well, no, because..."

Heather cupped her ear. "Because why?"

Hunter sighed. "Fine."

"Were you going to say that it was different because you and Carissa ended up engaged?"

"I guess," Hunter said with a frown.

"But when you first got involved in their lives, you weren't planning to ask Carissa to marry you."

"Are you interested in Ash romantically?"

Heather shrugged. "I really do like him, and of course, I think Isla is amazing. But I doubt he'd want anything to do with me romantically."

"Why is that?"

"Really? You don't know why he might not want to get involved with me?"

"Your money?"

"Yep. Even Carissa struggled with that. I'd imagine that Ash would have even more of an issue with it." Before Hunter could say anything more about it, Heather added, "But that's a discussion for another time. I've got to go. I told Ash I'd be there at one-thirty."

"I hope you have a good time," Hunter said. "We went to Rachel's program yesterday. Rachel didn't have a solo part—or any part—beyond standing in the second row."

"I don't think Isla has any part either, but I still want to be there for her."

"I get ya. Take pictures or videos. I'm sure Rachel would love to see Isla on stage."

"I will. I'll see you later."

Heather left Hunter's office and headed for the elevator. Thankfully, it was midday, so the traffic wasn't bad. When she walked into the garage a short time later, she found Ash at the desk where Isla usually sat. He looked up and gave her a quick smile as he got to his feet.

"Hi," she said. "Hopefully, I'm not late."

"Nope. You're fine."

She was used to mostly seeing him in a pair of coveralls and a ball cap when she came by after work. But right then, he wore a pair of dark jeans and a long-sleeve T-shirt. He grabbed his jacket from the back of the chair and shrugged it up onto his shoulders.

"Isla was beyond excited about the program today," Ash said as they walked out to his truck. "I just hope that she has fun."

"Why do you think she might not?" Heather asked once they were in the cab of his truck.

Ash started it up and pulled out of the parking lot. "Just worried that the other kids might ruin it for her. They haven't exactly been warm and welcoming to her."

"I'd ask if they had a reason, but there's no reason acceptable for hurting and bullying."

He sighed. "I want to protect her, but I guess taking on seven- and eight-year-olds wouldn't be appropriate."

Heather let out a huff of laughter. "Yeah. I think that probably would be frowned on. Even so, wanting to protect her is admirable."

Ash glanced at her but didn't reply to her comment. "Anyway, I just want this to be fun for her. She really enjoyed Rachel's Christmas program, and I want her to enjoy this too."

"Hunter said Rachel had her school program yesterday, but she didn't have a part beyond just singing with her class."

"Really? She did such a good job at the church program. I would have thought she'd have a solo singing part at the school too."

"I thought the same thing, but I guess not every kid can have a part. At least she had that solo at the church."

"I never had parts," Ash said. "But I was fine with that."

"I had a few parts, but I didn't really care if I got one or not. Hayden always enjoyed performing in front of an audience. Hunter hated being up on stage with a passion. He used to try so many ways to get out of programs when we were kids."

"Hayden doesn't come across as attention-seeking."

"No, he's changed a *lot* since the accident. Now, he avoids the spotlight."

"That's too bad," Ash said. "I can't imagine what he must be dealing with."

"None of us can, and we're around him a lot. Hunter, the most, since they live together."

"Hayden seems to get along well with Rachel."

Heather smiled. "Rachel is the one person who Hayden softens around. He adores her, and I think it's because she has such an easygoing approach to him and his injury. Or maybe it's because she hasn't known him any other way. When she met him, he already had crutches and visible scars. Of course, she's since realized that Hayden and Hunter are actually identical twins, so she knows Hayden used to look like Hunter."

"I didn't realize they were identical. Maybe it's their hair, too, as Hunter's is definitely more... business-like, while Hayden's is... well... more like mine."

Heather laughed. "Hayden's hair was already different from Hunter's before the accident. As soon as my mom couldn't drag him to the barber anymore, he let it grow out. Hunter has always liked a more conservative look."

"How did your dad feel about Hayden's long hair?"

"He didn't care. For him, Hayden's character was more important than his outward appearance. Dad was amazing in how he tried his hardest not to judge someone for anything but their character. I think he would really have liked you, and he would have adored Isla."

That got her another look, but otherwise, he didn't respond. She stood behind her statement because she absolutely believed that her dad would have liked the pair. She knew without a doubt that if he'd still been there, he would have been the one to invite Ash for Christmas.

When they reached the school, Ash found a parking spot, then they walked together to the entrance of the building. Once inside, there was a sign pointing to where the program was being held.

They weren't the only adults in the hallway as they made their way to the gym. Heather had a flashback to her own elementary years from the brightly colored posters on the walls and kids' laughter from the rooms as they passed them.

When they stepped into the gym, Ash paused, looking around.

"Do you know which side Isla is standing on?"

Ash shook his head. "I tried to ask her, but she couldn't tell me."

"So maybe we should sit in the middle?"

"Sure. I just want her to be able to see us. She was worried that I wouldn't be here." He hesitated. "I don't think her mom went to her school stuff."

"Then, by all means, let's sit front and center."

Thankfully, there weren't many people there yet, so they were able to find seats close to the front. Ash let her go into the row first, then took the seat on the aisle. The chairs were set close together, so their arms touched as they sat there.

"Hunter told me to be sure to take some video so Rachel can see it."

When someone sat down beside her, Heather looked over and smiled at the woman. That seemed to be enough to prompt the woman to initiate a conversation.

"What grade is your child in?" she asked, her gaze flicking to Ash for a moment, then back to Heather.

"Isla is in grade one," Heather said, deciding she didn't need to reveal her actual relationship to Isla.

"Oh, nice! My son is in grade two."

Heather was glad that she hadn't said that she had a daughter in grade one because then she'd be wanting to ask her why her child was mean to Isla.

"It's good that both you and your husband could be here," the woman said. "My husband couldn't get time off from his job."

"That's too bad." She heard Ash give a quiet cough, but she didn't turn to look at him. Heather wasn't sure that he was happy to be tied to her, but she also didn't think he'd have been happy if she'd shared his and Isla's situation with a stranger. Either way, she'd apologize to him later.

Thankfully, music began to play, keeping her from further conversation. Not long after, a woman stepped out to stand behind the microphone on the stage. She introduced herself as the principal and talked a bit about what had been going on at the school, then she called another woman up.

Over the next hour, different classes performed songs with enthusiastic actions. Heather couldn't help but smile at the antics of some of the children. But best of all was when Isla's class came out. The little girl had scanned the crowd, her smile beaming when she found Heather and Ash. She gave a little wave, which Heather happily returned.

Heather was glad that Isla seemed to enjoy being up there with her classmates. She sang all the words and did all the actions perfectly, from what Heather could tell, anyway.

When the program ended, the principal invited the parents or guardians to collect their child from their classroom, since they were dismissed for the day.

As they joined the others leaving the gym, Heather reached out and grabbed Ash's arm so that she didn't lose him in the press of people. He glanced back at her briefly but didn't pull away from her grasp.

Thankfully, Ash knew where he was going because Heather would have been lost trying to work her way through the crowd to find the door of Isla's class. There was already a cluster of parents around the door, so Ash maneuvered them off to the side.

The crowd eventually thinned, and soon Ash could step into the doorway. He greeted the teacher, who stood just inside the classroom. She was a middle-aged woman with a stern expression.

The look she gave Ash made Heather frown, but she didn't have time to say anything because Isla came flying over.

"Heather!" She flung herself at Heather, wrapping her arms around her. "You came to see me!"

"I did." Heather hugged the little girl, moving her out of the doorway, so they weren't blocking other parents. "You did a great job. You knew all the words and did the actions so well. I loved it!"

Isla gave her another hug, then turned to Ash. "Did you like it too, Uncle Ash?"

He picked her and kissed her forehead. "I did. Heather is right. You did a great job. I'm so proud of you."

Heather hadn't thought that the little girl's smile could get any bigger, but it did. It made Heather so glad that she had been able to make it.

"Why don't you get your things so we can go?" Ash suggested as he set her back on her feet.

Isla nodded, then skipped back into the classroom. The teacher approached Ash, and Heather braced herself for what was about to come out of the woman's mouth.

"I hope that you'll continue to work with Isla on her math and reading. She's still struggling and not at the level she should be at."

Ash nodded but didn't say anything else in response. Heather had a whole bunch she wanted to say, but it wasn't her place. She had no role in Isla's life that would allow her to talk to her teacher.

Thankfully, the woman had waited until Isla was out of hearing range before talking to Ash. Heather knew from experience that Isla was working hard, and she'd hate for the little girl to hear that her efforts weren't good enough.

"Can we go for supper?" Isla asked as they walked toward the exit a few minutes later.

"It's a little early for that," Ash told her. "Let's go back to the garage, and once I close it for the day, we can go for supper. How's that?"

"Can Heather come with us?"

Ash glanced at her, then said, "I'm sure Heather has to get back to work."

"Do you have to get back to work?" Isla asked, peering up at her as they walked toward the truck.

Heather wasn't sure what to say. Did Ash not want her to join them? "I actually don't."

"Then, if you'd like to go with us, you're more than welcome."

Ash sounded like he really meant it, so Heather smiled and said she'd love to join them.

Chapter 14

When they got back, Heather and Isla settled in the office while Ash went into the garage area. The man who worked for him part-time was doing an oil change on a car and straightened as Ash approached him.

"Fancy dude came by again," he said, wiping his hands on a rag. "Told him you weren't around."

Ash sighed and dragged a hand over his face. "Did he say what he wanted this time around?"

"He offered me a job." The man frowned. "Said I'd need a new one soon."

Ash eyed the man. "I'm not planning to close, but I'd understand if you'd rather work there."

"Whatever, man," he said with a huff of laughter. "I'm not going anywhere. I'd rather work for you any day of the week. You've been good to me."

Ash gripped the man's shoulder and squeezed it lightly. "I appreciate that."

"Yeah. I told the guy the next time he came, he'd better be bringing us a car to repair."

They shared a laugh, then the guy turned his attention back to the car. Ash pulled on a pair of coveralls and went to the other vehicle that would be picked up the next morning.

When the other man finished with his work, Ash thanked him for staying a bit later than usual.

"Anytime, man," he said. "You've helped me out often enough that I'm glad to be able to return the favor."

After the guy had left, Ash focused back on the car. As he worked, he thought again about the proposal Hunter had given him. It would be a huge help if he agreed to what Hunter wanted, but he wasn't sure how it benefited the man or his company.

It seemed a little one-sided in Ash's favor, and he didn't want to be indebted to anyone. Especially a wealthy man. The last thing he wanted was for someone else to have a say in his business, and he wasn't sure if agreeing to the deal meant giving Hunter the right to tell him how he should run the garage.

Still, he owed Hunter an answer soon, so he needed to spend more time going over the proposal. In the meantime, he had two people he needed to treat for supper.

"Ready to go?" Ash asked as he walked into the office after cleaning up.

It was a little earlier than he usually closed, but he wanted to get to the restaurant before it got busy with the supper rush. Also, Heather had already spent a good chunk of time with them, and he didn't want to keep her away from things she might still have to do that day.

"Yeah!" Isla clapped her hands. "I want pancakes!"

Her desire for breakfast for dinner severely limited the restaurants they could go to. But thankfully, the restaurant he'd planned to take them to served breakfast all day.

"Well, let's get you dressed," Ash said, then helped her into her jacket while Heather pulled hers on.

Once they were ready, Heather and Isla hurried for the truck while he set the alarm and locked the building up. It didn't take long to get to the restaurant, and Isla filled every second of the trip with excited chatter. Nothing had dimmed her joy over the program, and Ash was relieved that even though she hadn't had a speaking or singing part, she'd had fun.

At the restaurant, they were seated in a booth with Isla sliding in first, then insisting Heather sit next to her. When she glanced at him, Ash gave a nod and slid in the opposite side.

Once they were settled, Isla picked up the small menu that contained the children's options. "I want the chocolate chip pancakes with whipped cream. Lots of whipped cream."

Heather laughed, looking away from her own menu. "And do you think I should have pancakes, too?"

"Do you *like* pancakes? Uncle Ash likes them but only for breakfast."

When Heather looked at him, Ash lifted his menu to block out the two of them, causing the pair to giggle together.

"Well, I do like pancakes," Heather said when they stopped laughing. "But I'm probably going to have pancakes for breakfast tomorrow, so I'm going to order something else."

"Does Essie make you pancakes?" Isla asked.

"Yep. She makes the best pancakes."

"Uncle Ash makes good pancakes, too. Well, now he does. The first time he made them for us, he burnt them!"

"I prefer to think that they were just extra well done."

"Extra well done?" Heather laughed. "Nice one. I'm going to have to remember that."

"Do you burn food often?" Ash asked.

"Um...considering how much cooking I actually do, the rate at which I burn it is unreasonably high."

"Like one hundred percent?"

"Close." Heather grinned. "According to Essie, I'm as close to a hopeless case as she's ever seen."

"I'm gonna be a great cook," Isla announced. "I can already make toast and Pop-Tarts."

"Well, those are definitely important things to know how to make."

"I never burn them either."

"What's Uncle Ash's favorite Pop-Tart flavor?"

Ash choked on the sip of water he'd taken. He wanted to protest that he didn't eat Pop-Tarts. But since that would be a lie, he kept his mouth shut.

"He likes the blueberry ones with frosting on them. I like the chocolate ones. Which ones do you like?"

"It's been a long time since I last had a Pop-Tart, but I liked the chocolate ones too. Or, if Hunter and Hayden ate all of those, I also liked the strawberry ones. The boys wouldn't touch those."

Ash had a hard time picturing Heather eating Pop-Tarts. Their server appeared at the end of the table, notebook, and pencil poised to take their order.

"I'd like chocolate chip pancakes with lots of whipped cream, please," Isla announced before Ash had a chance to let the server know they weren't ready to order yet.

"Sure, I can get that for you, sweetie," the woman said with a smile. "What would you like to drink?"

"Chocolate milk, please."

The woman nodded and made a notation on her notepad before shifting her attention to Heather. "And for you?"

"I'll have the teriyaki chicken skillet."

The woman turned to Ash and smiled. "And you?"

"I'll have the fried chicken and mashed potatoes."

She wrote it down, then asked about the other side that came with his meal. Once she'd taken their orders, the woman left them alone.

"Heather showed me the video she took," Isla told him. "Did you see it?"

"I didn't need to see the video, princess. I was there."

"She said she would show it to Rachel. I hope she likes it."

The concern in Isla's voice tugged at Ash's heart. But before he could say anything to reassure her, Heather said, "I know she will."

Isla's smile returned. "I wish I could see her again."

Heather glanced at Ash, and he knew that it was because he had yet to respond to her invitation to spend Christmas with them.

Turning her attention back to Isla, Heather said, "Maybe we can arrange something during your school break. I'll talk to Carissa about it."

"Rachel is so nice. I wish all the girls in my class were like her."

Ash listened as Heather shared more about how they'd met Rachel and Carissa. He had to admit that the generosity of the King family baffled him a bit. Though he supposed that when you had a lot of money, it was easier to be generous. All he had were his time and talents.

He tried to be generous with those when he could be, but it had become harder with Isla in his life. In the past, he could put in much longer hours at the garage, doing some repairs at cost or for free for people he knew from the neighborhood who were struggling financially.

Since Isla had arrived, his opportunities to help had narrowed considerably. He'd stopped to help Heather because he'd suspected he'd be able to lend a hand without it taking much time.

There had been no thought in his head that their interaction would continue past that night, but he couldn't find it within himself to regret their ongoing contact. Mainly for Isla's sake. The little girl had opened up even more, blossoming under the warmth and care of Heather and her family.

"Here you go," their server announced as she appeared at the end of the table with a tray balanced on her hand.

She set the tray on a nearby table, then brought over a glass of chocolate milk and a plate stacked with pancakes and whipped cream. Once she'd set it in front of Isla, Ash could see that she'd taken the request for *lots of whipped cream* to heart.

"Oooooh." Isla grinned as she looked up at the server. "Thank you!"

"You're welcome."

The woman quickly set his and Heather's plates down as well, then said, "Is there anything else I can get you?"

Heather shook her head, and Ash said, "I think we're good. Thank you."

After the woman left them again, Isla said, "Can I say grace?"

After that meal with the Kings, Ash had broached the subject of her praying with Isla. She'd hesitated before telling him about a woman named Donna, who had lived next door to her and Gwen for a little while. Though she'd never mentioned Donna before, it quickly became clear that the woman had played a significant role in her life in the few months before Gwen had died.

The little girl had gone to church with Donna nearly every Sunday morning, usually after having spent the night with her. Ash had felt relieved to hear that Isla had been with her when Gwen had overdosed. He'd assumed that Isla had found her but had never wanted to bring up bad memories by asking her about it.

There had been no mention by the people who had met with him prior to Isla coming to live with him of her needing any counseling. He still wasn't sure if that was something he should be looking into for her. Unfortunately, he wasn't sure he could afford it.

Ash didn't want to focus on how he might be failing Isla right then, so he pushed those thoughts aside and told her she could pray.

Isla folded her hands together, then tucked them beneath her chin as she closed her eyes. "Dear Jesus, thank you for this food and all the whipped cream. Thank you that Uncle Ash and Heather could come to my program. In Jesus' name, amen."

"Amen," Heather echoed.

Isla didn't hesitate to dive into her stack of pancakes, humming her appreciation of them after she took her first bite. Though Isla rarely ate everything on her plate, pancakes tended to be the exception, so he hoped that would be the case that day.

"Is the garage open on Saturdays?" Heather asked.

"Usually just until noon if I have a lot of work, or if someone needs to pick up their vehicle. I used to always open on Saturday, but not so much now that I have Isla with me."

"What do you usually do on the weekends?"

Ash wasn't sure if she was asking to find out if they might be free for something or if she was just curious. "Nothing too exciting. Usually, we do some chores."

"I like to help with the laundry," Isla said as she picked up her glass and took a sip of the chocolate milk.

"Do you do it all?"

Isla laughed. "No. I put it in the washer, but Uncle Ash does all the other stuff. Then I help him fold it afterward."

"I bet Uncle Ash appreciates your help."

In truth, he really did. He wasn't a big fan of household chores, but with Isla helping him, it was a little more fun. She approached it all with a much better attitude than he did.

"He does. He says I'm a big help."

"You are," he agreed. "You also help with the dusting, sweeping, and vacuuming."

"And dishes," Isla added. "I like to wash the dishes sometimes."

Ash had a hard time imagining Heather doing dishes or dusting. But since she'd already surprised him a few times, he didn't vocalize his thoughts. Isla, on the other hand, had no such reluctance.

"Do you wash dishes and do laundry?" she asked, before shoving another forkful into her mouth.

"I do my own laundry," Heather said. "And I help Essie with dishes sometimes, though we do have a dishwasher, so most of the dishes get washed that way."

"Does Rachel do dishes and laundry?"

"I'm not sure about laundry, but I'm quite sure that she helps her mom with dishes."

"My mom didn't like to do dishes, so I did them a lot of times. Donna always let me help her too."

Heather looked at Ash, questions in her eyes.

"Donna was a friend of Gwen's. She often took care of Isla, and they'd go to church together."

"Oh, she sounds like she was important to you, Isla."

Isla nodded. "I love her."

"I think Donna viewed herself as a grandparent to Isla, given she didn't have any present in her life," Ash said by way of explanation.

Heather frowned. "Not even your parents?"

"No." Ash would have expanded on his answer if Isla hadn't been there, but he didn't want to go into the way his parents had treated Gwen with Isla present.

Heather seemed to understand that as she gave a nod, then turned her attention back to Isla. "I'm glad you had someone like Donna."

"Donna made me pancakes, and they were always yummy."

Ash tackled his food, relishing a meal that he hadn't had to make. He'd never managed to perfect fried chicken. In fact, the few times he'd tried, it hadn't even been edible. The inside had been raw, while the outside had been burnt. Definitely not something he'd been interested in eating.

He doubted that Heather frequented family-style chain restaurants, but she seemed to enjoy the food. Because of his interactions with Heather and her family, Ash was having to face his own prejudices and assumptions about the wealthy. Of course, he was also coming to think that perhaps the King family was the exception, not the norm.

He appreciated that Heather hadn't been pressuring him for an answer about Christmas, and also that Hunter hadn't been pressuring him about the proposal either.

There were moments when he couldn't quite believe what had transpired in the days since he'd stopped to help Heather. Would he do it again if he'd known what he was inviting into his life? For Isla's sake, absolutely.

He didn't like feeling as if he was a charity case, but he couldn't deny that the clothes that Heather had brought for Isla had meant the world to the little girl. And then there were the hair lessons. Those had changed things for him and Isla. He was gaining confidence in his ability to do Isla's hair, and she was happy to have better-looking hair when she went to school.

"I ate all my pancakes, Uncle Ash," Isla said with a grin.

"Good job, princess." He held out his fist, and she bumped it with her much smaller one.

"I finished all my food too," Heather said. "Do I get a fist bump?"

Her question caught Ash off-guard, and a laugh escaped him before he could stop it. "Sure."

When she held her fist out, he gave it a light tap with his, then watched as Heather turned to bump fists with Isla. His appreciation of how Heather treated Isla grew. And he had to admit that it drew him to her in a way he hadn't been to any other woman previously.

When he was younger, he'd focused on looks over personality. But with Heather, while she was, without a doubt, beautiful, that wasn't enough to interest him anymore. He had Isla to think of now. But seeing how Heather interacted with her, showing gentleness and affection, was a bigger draw than he'd ever experienced before.

Unfortunately, he had no idea what he was going to do about the emotions that had taken up residence in his heart.

Chapter 15

Later that evening, Heather settled into her bed, reflecting on the events of the day. The dinner had been unexpected, but she was glad that Ash had been willing to allow her to join them. She always enjoyed the time she spent with Isla.

But after it had been just her and Ash for the duration of the school program, she wondered about spending more time alone with him. Unfortunately, it would probably be a very quiet time, since Ash rarely seemed to want to say much whenever she was around.

Thankfully, Isla more than held up her end of the conversation, so Ash's silence wasn't as noticeable. Was it possible that he'd talk more if Isla wasn't around? There was no way to know unless they were alone together more.

Her text alert interrupted her thoughts. When she looked at the phone screen, she stared at it for a moment, surprised at the name there.

Ash: *I wanted to explain a bit more about Donna.*

She frowned at the words, though, because she didn't want him to feel he owed her any sort of explanation.

I'm happy to listen, but I don't want you to feel that you have to give me any sort of explanation.

The three dots indicating that he was responding popped up, then stopped, then started up again. Finally, after a couple of minutes, his response came through.

Ash: *I want you to know.*

Ash: *For Isla's sake.*

That response shouldn't have taken him so long to tap out, so Heather wondered why it had.

It sounds like Donna is important to Isla.

Ash: *She is. Thankfully, Isla was with Donna when Gwen overdosed. According to Isla, she usually spent Friday and Saturday nights with Donna. As well as any time my sister was high or drunk. Or "sick" as Isla put it.*

Heather read the words, a pit forming in her stomach at the idea of Isla being left alone with a mother strung out on drugs and/or alcohol. Would she have had food? Clean clothes? A safe place to sleep?

Ash: *Donna did the best she could for Isla, taking care of her when she wasn't working.*

I'm glad that she was there for Isla.

Ash: *That makes two of us.*

Heather wished they could talk instead of text, but it didn't surprise her that Ash was more comfortable communicating that way. At least he was talking to her apart from the time they spent together with Isla. It gave her hope that maybe they could forge a friendship that went beyond the little girl.

Has Isla seen Donna since coming to live with you?

Ash: *No. She's in Chicago. That's where Gwen and Isla lived.*

Has Isla asked to see her?

Ash: *No. She hadn't even mentioned Donna to me until recently.*

Heather wished that there was some way that she could facilitate a reunion between Isla and Donna, but it wasn't her place. At least Chicago wasn't on the other side of the country if Ash decided to do that himself. It was just a short flight from Minneapolis. Even driving, it wasn't super far away.

Ash: *I'd better go. Just wanted to let you know a bit more about Isla's history with Donna.*

Though she wasn't thrilled to end their conversation, Heather knew she should be thankful that she'd had that much interaction with him.

Thank you for sharing that with me. I hope you and Isla have a good weekend!

Ash: *You too. See you soon.*

Heather really hoped that was the case.

After they said goodnight, Heather looked back over their brief exchange. What was it about this man that drew her to him? Was it just Isla? Or would he have been as attractive to her all on his own?

No answers were forthcoming, and maybe there was a part of her that didn't need an answer—didn't want an answer. She wasn't sure that love could always be so easily dissected and explained. All she knew was that something in Ash spoke to something within her, and she wanted to embrace that.

But the question was... Did Ash feel anything like that for her? Only way she'd get that answer would be to ask him. Normally, she didn't back away from challenges, but she had to admit that this situation felt more high stakes than any other she'd faced.

Her heart was on the line.

The next afternoon, Heather followed Carissa into a local women's shelter, each of them carrying several large bags. Rachel was hanging out at the house with Essie and Heather's mom.

This was their first year helping the shelter. A few weeks earlier, Carissa had approached Heather to see if they could do anything to help the shelter and its occupants. Heather and Hunter decided to give them a sizable donation, but she and Carissa had wanted to do something more.

They'd come away from a meeting with the people running the shelter with several ideas of things to purchase for the women and children living there. Since they didn't have specific people to buy for, they'd chosen to put together gift bags that were geared toward women, younger kids, then older girls and boys.

Thankfully, Carissa was much like Heather in that she preferred to plan things out, so they'd spent several hours making up lists of things to buy. That had actually taken longer than physically purchasing the gifts. They'd been able to get a good chunk of them online, which had made things a whole lot easier.

Now they were there to drop everything off.

"Welcome!" the director of the shelter said as she came to where they stood just inside the door. "Here. Let me help you with those."

She took some of the bags, then led the way through a secure door into the back of the building. "We'll put them in the meeting room for now."

It took a couple more trips to empty the back of the SUV. Once they had everything in the meeting room, they began to unpack the bags. As they worked, Carissa told the director what they'd purchased and how they'd packaged it all up.

"I hope that we've done this in such a way that is fair and easy to distribute."

"It sounds like you've been meticulous with everything," the director said with a smile. "We sure appreciate your generosity."

"Thank you for allowing us to help," Heather said.

"Would you like to stay while we distribute the gifts?"

Carissa shook her head. "Thank you, but I think it might be better if we just remain anonymous."

The director glanced between them. "If you're certain?"

"We are," Heather assured her. "Just wish them Merry Christmas on our behalf."

"Thank you again." The woman walked them back out to the building entrance, then they said goodbye to her and went to the SUV where George was waiting for them.

As they settled into their seats, Carissa let out a long sigh. "I'm happy we did that, but I think we need to start a little ahead of time next year."

"I agree," Heather said. "A little more lead time would make it less stressful. But like you said, I'm glad we did it."

Heather leaned back in her seat, watching the city slip by as George drove them back to the house. She wondered what Ash and Isla were doing. He'd mentioned sometimes opening the shop on Saturday, but he hadn't said if he was opening it that day.

"Everything okay?" Carissa asked as she touched Heather's arm gently.

Heather turned to face her. "Hmmm?"

"You seem distracted."

"Oh. Well." Heather debated mentioning her thoughts about Isla and Ash. But she figured that, of anyone, Carissa might be the one to understand what Heather was feeling. "Just thinking of Isla. And Ash."

"Ahhh. I see."

Heather lifted her brows at that reply. "Do you?"

"He seems to be a very nice man and not bad looking, either," Carissa said with a broad smile. "And Isla is adorable."

"Yes, to all of that." Heather didn't think Carissa would buy it if she tried to deny the stuff about Ash.

"So, what's the deal?"

"Is there a deal? I'm not sure that there is. I mean, I've spent time with Isla, and she's so sweet."

"Rachel really likes her, though she did mention feeling sorry for her since she doesn't have a mom."

Heather's heart squeezed at the thought, remembering the conversation she'd had with Ash the night before. It sounded like even when Isla's mother had been alive, Isla still hadn't had a mom. At least not one who put her daughter's needs before her own.

"Considering what Isla has been through in her life, she's a remarkably happy child," Heather said.

"But it's more than just Isla, huh?"

"Yeah. I mean, I have a wonderful first impression of Ash. His stopping to help me out definitely cast him in a positive light. But then I met Isla and realized he was raising her on his own. Not many men would have done that for a child who wasn't theirs."

Carissa frowned. "There are men who wouldn't have done that even if the child *was* theirs."

Since Rachel's father hadn't wanted to be part of her life, Heather figured that Carissa knew what she was talking about.

"So, how are things with you and Ash?"

Heather sighed. "Me and Ash? There is no me and Ash. Not that I wouldn't like there to be. But I can't even begin to read him. I don't know if he's interested in me the way I'm interested in him."

"Ash might not even consider harboring an interest in you because he figures it would be useless."

"Useless?" Heather asked, even though she knew what Carissa meant.

Carissa gave her an exasperated look. "Well, I never considered for a moment that one of the reasons Hunter was helping us was because he was actually interested romantically in me. I just figured it was because he was a nice man. I actually tried to *not* feel anything for him, believing it would be useless."

"Because he had money, and you didn't?" Heather asked, not too worried about offending Carissa since they'd become super close over the past year.

"There were other things, but that was the big one."

"So you think Ash wouldn't even allow himself to consider a relationship because of that?"

"I can't say for certain, of course, but it may be a possibility." Carissa shrugged. "Or maybe you're just not his type."

Heather wanted to protest that, but what did she know? It could be that Ash preferred a woman who fit better into his world. Though Heather hadn't felt out of place when she'd spent time with Isla at the garage, maybe Ash didn't think she belonged there.

"I suppose I can't be every man's ideal woman."

Carissa laughed, bumping her shoulder against Heather's. "I think it actually speaks more highly of Ash that he isn't rushing to sweep you off your feet. He might be having a reaction to your wealth, but at least it's not to woo you, hoping to get his hands on your money."

"I've run into enough of those in my life," Heather said. "I'm able to spot them a mile away now. If I got a whiff of that from Ash, I'd be running in the opposite direction."

"So, what are you going to do about it?" Carissa asked.

"I don't know. Should I ask him out on a date? So far, I've been able to finagle time with him by inviting them to things or going to the garage to spend time there. I'm not spending time with Isla just to get to Ash, by the way. I truly do like the little girl."

"I know that," Carissa told her. "You would never use a child in that way. We just have to keep including them in things. Maybe he'll see you and the family in a different light. Maybe he'll see more of the things we all have in common than the differences that are more obvious."

"That would be the best-case scenario. I've invited them for Christmas, but he hasn't said one way or the other if they'll come."

"Why don't you ask him if they'll come tomorrow afternoon? Essie was talking about baking some cookies for Rachel to decorate. I'm sure that she'd love to have Isla there too."

Heather considered the idea, then nodded. "I know for sure that Isla would be on board with that. No clue about Ash, though."

"All you can do is ask," Carissa said. "You give him the option with no pressure. At least he's able to make the choice. I wasn't so fortunate."

"You mean because you got sick?"

"Felled by an infection."

"But hey, it all had a happy ending."

Carissa's smile was soft. "It certainly did. Only a few more weeks now."

"I still don't quite understand why you're getting married in the middle of winter," Heather said.

"Well, we'll enjoy our two-week honeymoon in Hawaii all the more."

"You should have had a destination wedding so we could have all had a break from winter."

"If we'd thought we could get Hayden there, we would have gone for that for sure."

Heather didn't even joke about giving Hayden grief for robbing them of an opportunity for a Hawaiian vacation in the middle of winter. She knew it would have been difficult for him to make the trip.

And maybe staying in Minneapolis wouldn't be such a bad thing. Especially if Ash and Isla were also around more.

Chapter 16

"Can we go to church, Uncle Ash?"

Ash looked down from the light fixture he was trying to screw a new light bulb into, lowering his arms as he stared at his niece. "You want to go to church?"

She nodded vigorously, her lopsided ponytails dancing. They hadn't been his best effort, but she hadn't wanted to sit still for him to do a better job that morning. Since they hadn't planned to leave the house, he'd figured it wasn't a big deal.

But church? Yeah, that was a bigger deal.

"Why do you want to go to church?" Ash asked as he turned his attention back to the light.

"I used to have fun when I went with Donna. We'd sing lots of songs, and they'd tell us stories. Sometimes we'd color pictures or do a craft."

"Do you think they do that at Rachel's church?"

"I bet they're doing Christmas stories and crafts now."

Ash finished screwing the light bulb in, then got down from the stepladder he'd been using. He flicked the switch to make sure it worked, then looked at Isla, who was gazing at him expectantly.

For a moment, he flashed back to when Gwen had been her age. Isla favored Gwen a lot, which meant that she also looked like him since he and Gwen had shared many of the same physical features, though Isla's hair was a darker brown and straighter than his.

He remembered Gwen standing just like Isla was, a hopeful expression on her face, asking one of their parents for something. Usually, it was permission to play with a friend or for the opportunity to paint or color. Like Isla, Gwen had loved art.

Too often, her requests had been rebuffed. Her hopes dashed all because it might have been an inconvenience to whichever parent she had asked. Ash's heart ached at the memory of the disappointment on Gwen's face as she'd walked away with slumped shoulders.

How might things have been different if she'd been given opportunities and support?

"I'll talk to Heather and see what she says about their church."

Isla's smile engulfed her face. Hope morphing into joy. "Really?"

"Really."

Isla flung her arms around his waist. "Oh, thank you."

Bending, Ash lifted her up in his arms, and she clung tightly to his neck. "Love you, princess."

"I love you too, Uncle Ash," she whispered in his ear.

Emotion choked Ash then. He'd never known that it was possible to love the way he loved Isla. And to receive her love in return was nothing short of a miracle.

After a moment, she loosened the hold she had on his neck, and he set her down.

"Thank you for the new light, too," she said as she looked up to where it glowed brightly.

"You're welcome."

She went over to the small desk he'd set up under the window and pulled out a coloring book and her box full of crayons that she'd received from the Christmas party. "I'm going to color for a while."

"Sounds good," he said, then he left her to her coloring. He had a phone call to make, or maybe he'd just send a text.

He found his phone where he'd left it on the kitchen counter earlier. Ash flipped it over in his hand a few times, debating if he should call Heather or just text her. His preference was to text, but maybe he needed to call to ask about this.

Wandering over to the window, Ash stared out at the small yard at the front of the house. He was happy that it wasn't snowing. The sun was shining, and he knew from checking the temperature earlier that it was a mild day, just below freezing. Maybe they'd go for a walk later.

Ash knew he was just trying to avoid making the call. Not that he didn't want to talk to Heather. It was that the idea of speaking with her made his heart pound just a little harder. If they did go to church the next day, he'd be seeing her again, and that appealed to him even more than talking to her on the phone, though he didn't want it to.

"Hello?" Heather answered the phone on the first ring, and for a moment, Ash was speechless. "Ash?"

"Uh, yeah. Sorry. Yeah. It's me." He wanted to slap his forehead at his stupid ramblings.

"Well, this is nice. I'm so glad you called."

Ash turned away from the window. "You are?"

"Yep. I enjoy talking to you."

Her response robbed him of words for a moment. "Oh. Well... uh... I enjoy talking to you too."

"I'm very happy to hear that." After a beat of silence, Heather said, "So, what did you want to talk about?"

Ash was relieved for the opportunity to get the conversation back on track and hopefully away from the awkwardness it had held so far on his part. He usually wasn't so awkward with his words, but there was something about Heather that made him struggle with all the words he wanted to say when he knew he shouldn't. "Church."

"Church? What about church?"

"Isla asked if we could go to church tomorrow, and she wants to go where Rachel goes. Is that the church where we were the other night?"

"Yep. We all attend that church."

"And they have something for children?"

"They certainly do. The children's programming runs at the same time as the main service. I think it's up to age twelve."

"What time does it start?"

"The service is at eleven, but it might be good to come a few minutes early so that we can get Isla to the kids' service with Rachel."

"Okay. And Isla can wear something like she wore for the Christmas program?" It seemed like a stupid question, but the last thing Ash wanted was for Isla to stand out because she wasn't dressed correctly.

"That would be fine. There isn't a dress code, and you'll see that there's a bit of everything. Rachel usually wears a dress, but if Isla prefers pants, that's fine too."

"I think she'd probably want to wear a dress."

"Then that would be perfectly fine." Heather hesitated. "I was actually going to text you about something."

"You were?"

"Yes. Essie has made a bunch of Christmas cookies, and she and Rachel were planning to decorate them tomorrow. Isla would be welcome to join them if you'd be okay with that. Maybe the two of you could come for dinner following the service, then they could decorate the cookies after that."

Ash wanted to say yes right away, knowing that Isla would love to spend more time with Rachel, doing something she enjoyed. But he felt like he should take the time to think it over.

"You don't have to let me know now," Heather said. "Tomorrow at the service would be fine."

"We'll join you," Ash said, the words rushing past his best intentions. "I know Isla would love that."

"Great! Maybe bring a change of clothes for Isla, so she doesn't get her church clothes messy when she decorates the cookies. I think that's what Carissa is planning to do for Rachel."

"That sounds good." So very good. Too good, really, considering how his heart warmed at the idea of spending more time with Heather. But it was Christmas, and Ash wanted this first Christmas with Isla to be filled with good memories for her.

"Why don't we meet near the room where we hung our coats the other night?" Heather suggested. "Whoever gets there first will just wait for the other."

"Okay. We'll be there."

"I'm really looking forward to seeing you and Isla again."

Ash heard the sincerity in her words, and it made him wonder things. "I'm looking forward to it as well."

Silence stretched between them for a moment, weighty and full of anticipation.

"Goodbye, Ash."

"Bye."

He ended the call, convinced that he was doing the right thing for Isla. But for him?

Every time he was around Heather, his attraction to her grew, and he needed to make a decision. Could he set aside his feelings regarding the wealthy and accept that Heather and her family really were different?

He knew part of his reticence had come from having to take Isla into account. But Heather treated her wonderfully, and Isla had blossomed even more thanks to the woman's care. So, with that concern taken out of the equation, he was left with the truth that he didn't want to acknowledge.

Never before had he been intimidated by someone, let alone a woman, the way he was with Heather. Or maybe... maybe he was intimidated by his response to her, knowing that he had nothing to offer her in the long run.

What would a woman of her wealth and stature want with a man whose hands were never completely free of stains and who could barely make ends meet? She was polished and poised. He was rough around the edges and not refined at all. As far as he could see, they had nothing in common, which would make a relationship difficult, if not impossible.

"Do I look nice?" Isla stood in front of the mirror he'd bought for her at a thrift store a couple of weeks earlier, turning side to side, her arms spread to the side.

"You look beautiful, princess."

He'd managed to iron most of the wrinkles from the long-sleeved shirt he'd found in the back of his closet and paired it with black jeans. If he was going to continue to hang out with the Kings and attend church regularly, he was going to need more dress shirts and at least one more pair of suitable pants.

He guided Isla away from the mirror and into her coat and boots. The entire drive to the church was taken up with Isla's chatter about Rachel and how she hoped the other kids would be nice. Ash hoped that too. From the moment she'd arrived at his home, she'd been searching for places to fit in.

Even now, he knew that while she felt comfortable with him, she was aware of the ways she was different from other children.

Even Rachel. Not every kid had two parents, but most, like Rachel, had at least one. Isla knew that she had none.

He hurt for her, knowing she was looking for similarities with the kids around her and only finding differences. He didn't think she was going to find a lot of similarities with the kids at church that day, but he hoped she found acceptance, regardless.

Once at the church, they found Heather waiting where she said she'd be, a big smile lighting up her face when she spotted them. Isla hurried ahead of Ash to wrap her arms around Heather.

"Hello there, sweetie," Heather said as she bent to kiss Isla's forehead. "How are you today?"

"I'm excited!" Isla grinned and did a little dance as she stood in front of Heather. "Is Rachel here?"

"She is. We'll find her after we hang up your coat." Heather looked at Ash and smiled. "Hi."

"Hey." Ash unzipped his jacket. "Thanks for waiting for us."

"I was happy to," she said, then turned back to help Isla out of her coat.

Within a couple of minutes, they'd hung their stuff up and were on their way to wherever the children met for their service. Isla clutched his hand tightly, and Ash felt a flutter of nerves at leaving her in a new place.

He hadn't felt that way when he'd taken her to her new school for the first time, but that had happened within days of her ending up in his care. Since then, his love for her had grown by leaps and bounds, as had the concern he felt for her.

"Hi, Rachel!" Isla said, letting go of Ash's hand to wave enthusiastically at the other girl.

Rachel returned the wave as she stood with Carissa and Hunter. "Hi, Isla."

As the little girls hugged, Ash shook the hand that Hunter held out to him.

"Good to see you again, Ash," Hunter said.

"You, too." Ash glanced at Isla as the girls moved toward the large doorway leading into the hall where they'd gone following the children's program. "Isla."

She turned back, then came over to where Ash stood. "Do I need to give them any information for Isla?"

"Yep," Carissa said. "Why don't you come with me, and we'll get her signed in?"

They moved as a group to a long table just outside the entrance of the hall. The woman seated at the table smiled when Carissa approached her. "Hi, Carissa."

"Good morning, Missy. I have someone here for the children's service."

"Oh, that's wonderful."

After he gave the information the woman requested, he managed to get a hug from Isla before she ran off with Rachel. Ash crossed his arms as he watched Rachel guide Isla to a seat, then speak to a woman who approached them.

"She'll be fine," Heather said, resting her hand on his arm. He looked down to find her regarding him with a soft smile. "Rachel will make sure that everything is okay, and if they need us, she knows how to reach her mom."

He nodded and looked back one more time at Isla, trying to be happy rather than worried. His protective instincts were at a level that he hadn't even known he was capable of.

With a sigh, Ash finally turned away, taking in the expressions of the other three there with him. All three seemed to understand what he was feeling, though Hunter's expression also held an edge of humor to it.

"It's a challenge being a father," Hunter said. "I'm not even officially Rachel's dad, and I already struggle with being worried and over-protective of her."

Being a father. The phrase hit him right in the heart. He hadn't been viewing himself as Isla's father, but the title felt right. At least to him. Isla would have no one else to call dad since Gwen hadn't listed anyone as father on her birth certificate.

Ash already felt like Isla was his daughter, but unless she asked for him to officially take on the role of father, he wouldn't mention anything to her about it.

Lowering his arms, he followed the others away from the hall. Carissa and Hunter moved ahead of them since there were too many people for them to walk four abreast. Heather's shoulder bumped into his as she moved closer to him to allow people to walk past them. He felt her hand wrap around his elbow, and he glanced at her for a moment, a bit surprised by how right... how natural it felt.

Strangely enough, he drew comfort from her presence, appreciating that she didn't seem to judge him for his reluctance to leave Isla since she cared for his little girl, too. Maybe they had something in common after all.

Chapter 17

Heather felt flutters of excitement as they made their way to the doors of the sanctuary. Until she'd seen him and Isla walking toward her, she hadn't been sure that they'd actually show up.

The relief had given way to happiness as she'd greeted the two of them. Having them there felt like a step in the right direction. That Ash had contacted her of his own accord about attending church had been a surprise but definitely a welcome one.

Now, she enjoyed walking at his side, even if it was just as a friend. She'd taken hold of his arm so as not to get separated as they walked among the large number of people in the foyer area. Like the last time she'd taken his arm, he hadn't pull away.

They followed Hunter and Carissa down the aisle to where their mom sat with Essie and George. Hayden wasn't there that day, but there was a possibility he might join them later in the afternoon. He hadn't committed to anything—he never did—but sometimes he surprised them by showing up anyway.

Once they reached the area where they usually sat, Hunter went into the pew first to sit by their mom, with Carissa following him. Ash waited for Heather to go in, then he sat on the end.

Sitting that near to him, Heather got a whiff of his cologne. It wasn't one of the expensive brands that she was familiar with, but it was pleasant, nonetheless. He had on a light gray, long-sleeve shirt with dark jeans, and he looked very nice. He could have worn anything, really, and not stood out. There were people in all different manner of dress, from jeans to suits and dresses.

Hunter was dressed much like Ash that day. He wasn't a fan of suits, and though he wore them for work quite often, he preferred just slacks, a dress shirt, and a tie at the office when he could get away with it.

Heather hoped that it made Ash more comfortable to see that Hunter wasn't dressed up. Though his questions about attire had been centered on Isla, she thought perhaps he was wondering for himself as well.

She wanted him to feel comfortable to come to the church again. If he felt out of place, she wasn't sure that he'd return, even if Isla wanted to. It encouraged Heather's heart that Isla was interested in attending church, so she didn't want to lose that because Ash didn't want to come.

Beyond that, she wanted Ash to come to a point where he wanted to attend church of his own accord. Where he wanted to have a personal relationship with God. If that was all that developed out of his interactions with their family, Heather would deal with her heartbreak, but it would be worth it.

The service was Christmas-themed, with a focus on the advent of hope. She noticed as they sang the familiar Christmas carols that Ash had a pleasant voice. It was a good time of year for someone unfamiliar with church to attend, as it was likely they would know the songs that were sung.

Ash sat still throughout the service, not shifting around on the seat as the pastor spoke. When they stood for the final song, Heather hoped it wouldn't be the last time they were together at a church service.

After they'd been dismissed, Ash stepped out of the pew, and Heather followed him. When she grabbed his arm once again, he glanced down at her.

"Don't want to lose you," she said with a quick smile.

The corner of his mouth tipped up briefly before Ash focused back on the people in front of them. It was slow going up the long aisle, then they made their way back to the hall where they'd left Isla and Rachel.

"Do we just wait here?" Ash asked.

"I'm not sure," Heather confessed. "Carissa and Hunter usually pick Rachel up. We can just wait until they get here."

It wasn't long before the other couple appeared, and Carissa said, "We pick the kids up from their group area."

"I usually wait out here to keep from adding to the crush," Hunter said. "Why don't you hang with me, Heather?"

She would have liked to go into the room, but she understood that wasn't ideal when there were so many children and parents.

As they waited, Hunter said, "So Ash and Isla are joining us for dinner?"

"Yep." She turned to frown at him. "You don't mind, do you?"

Hunter held up his hands. "Not at all. I've enjoyed the time I've spent with the guy."

"So have I."

He smirked at her words. "Yes. I'm sure you have."

"Is Hayden coming?"

"Not sure." Hunter pulled his phone out and tapped out a quick message. "I'll see what he says."

"We need more people there to eat cookies."

Hunter shuddered. "Can't we just tell them we need to save the cookies for Santa?"

"I'll let you try that," Heather said. "I dare you to stay strong against the disappointed looks when you refuse to eat their cookies."

"Okay. Fine. We'll eat their cookies."

Before she could respond, Carissa and Ash returned with the girls. Rachel looked happy, but Isla was absolutely beaming, and she had a paper clutched in her hand.

"Heather, I colored a Christmas picture," Isla exclaimed as they approached her and Hunter. "Do you want it?"

Heather took the paper and looked down at the carefully colored picture of the manger scene. She smiled at Isla. "You did a beautiful job, sweetheart. I'd love to keep it. Although maybe your uncle would like it."

"I'll color another one for Uncle Ash. This one is for you."

Heather's heart warmed at the simple gift. "Well, thank you very much, sweetheart."

Isla's smile still wreathed her entire face as she turned to her uncle. Ash quickly swung her up into his arms.

"Did you have a good time?"

"The absolute *best*!" She wrapped her arms around his neck, then pressed her cheek to his as she squeezed Ash. "Thank you for bringing me."

"You're welcome, princess. I'm glad you had fun."

"Are you ready for some lunch?" Heather asked. "You're coming, right?"

Ash nodded. "If it's still okay."

"It's definitely okay."

They moved as a group toward the coatroom, and once they had their coats on, they left the church.

"Can you come with us?" Isla asked, reaching out to put her hand on Heather's shoulder, since she was up in Ash's arms.

"That's up to your uncle," Heather told her, not wanting to assume she could hitch a ride with them. She'd planned to go with Hunter and Carissa since her mom and Essie had left with George immediately following the service.

"It's fine," Ash said with a nod.

"Then I shall be happy to join you."

Hunter gave her a knowing grin as they parted ways to go to their respective vehicles.

Isla spent most of the ride to the house talking about the children's service. Heather was happy to hear that she'd enjoyed it so much. Hopefully, that meant Ash would continue to bring Isla each Sunday.

Once they got to the house, they went in and found that her mom and Essie had gotten most of the dinner out of the oven. It smelled like they were having roast beef, which was one of Essie's best dishes. Although, honestly, Essie didn't have a bad dish.

Hunter engaged Ash in conversation as Carissa and Heather helped get dinner on the table. Isla and Rachel were sitting together in a large armchair in the living room, talking about some television show they both watched.

Hayden didn't show up for the dinner, though it sounded like he'd come once they were done eating. Him missing the meal usually meant that he was having a bad pain day. Heather was glad that he was at least planning to come at some point. Some time with him was better than nothing.

"Are you going to decorate cookies?" her mom asked once the meal was over, and they were clearing the table.

Heather shrugged. "I might. Or maybe I'll just supervise."

"I'm so pleased that Ash and Isla were able to join us."

Before Heather could respond, Hunter appeared with Ash behind him. "I'm going to go get Hayden, and Ash said he'd come along."

"Okay, darling," her mom said.

"We'll be back in a bit."

Heather met Ash's gaze for a moment before he turned to follow Hunter to the front door. She was glad to see that Ash was connecting with more members of the family. It gave her hope that he was willing to build a friendship with each of them.

Every time they were together, it made her want more, and she really wasn't sure what to do about it. If this was all just on her end, it was going to hurt.

But she wouldn't try to push him out of her life because he wasn't the only one to consider. Isla was forming connections and ties to them too, even if her uncle was more reticent. Because of the little girl, Heather wouldn't be the one to pull away or make things so awkward that Ash removed himself and Isla from their lives.

What was she supposed to do, though? Would Ash ever feel comfortable enough to ask her out on a date if he was interested? And if he didn't, what hope was there unless she made the first move?

"Patience, darling," her mom said as she slid an arm around Heather's waist. "You can't rush important things."

She wanted to, though. Ash was the first man that she found herself drawn to almost from their first meeting.

Heather sighed as she glanced at her mom. "I don't mind being patient if the end result is what I want. But if it's not going to work out, I'd rather know sooner than later."

Her mom chuckled. "I'm sure you're not alone in that desire, but life doesn't always work that way. Sometimes you wait with hope that ends in disappointment. The only thing that works is to trust God to bring about His will and to know that He will care for you regardless of what the end result is."

Heather thought of the past five years and the grief they'd all carried after her dad's passing. It still seemed wrong to believe that it had been God's will for her dad to die so tragically. However, the alternative was to believe that her dad's death had been a victory for Satan, and she refused to embrace that. So they carried on his legacy as best they could, and she knew that the advice her mom gave her would have been what her dad would have told her too.

She leaned her head against her mom's. "Love you, Momma. Thank you for the reminder."

"I only want happiness for you all of you, darling, and I pray that God guides both you and Ash. I would love to claim him and Isla officially as family."

"You just love getting instant grandchildren," Heather said with a laugh.

"I can't deny that is true." Her mom gave her a squeeze. "I just wish your dad was here to meet them. He would have adored both these girls."

Heather swallowed hard, emotion rushing over her. Whether or not Isla ever became a grandchild, her dad would have lavished her with love and would have spoiled her just like he would have spoiled Rachel.

When the girls returned, Isla wore a pair of jeans and a sweatshirt with a unicorn on it. Rachel was dressed similarly, and the two of them went right to the table where Carissa and Essie were setting out the cookies and decorating supplies.

"I've never decorated cookies until this Christmas," Isla said as she slid onto a chair at the table. "I think it's my favorite thing."

Given the little girl's artistic leaning, Heather wasn't surprised to hear that, and she couldn't wait to see what she did with the cookies that day.

Chapter 18

Ash wasn't sure why he'd agreed to go with Hunter to pick Hayden up. But when the guy asked if he wanted to ride along with him, he'd agreed. He'd thought Isla might object to him leaving her alone, but she'd told him goodbye without batting an eye.

"Do you have a girlfriend?" Hunter asked once they'd left the house.

Ash looked at him, surprised by the question. "Uh. No. Don't really have time for one."

"So, you're not interested in a relationship?"

"To be honest, I haven't given it a lot of thought since Isla came to live with me. She is my first priority."

"Being a single parent can definitely make dating more challenging. Carissa's top priority has always been Rachel. When Carissa became a priority for me, I made sure she knew that they were *both* important to me."

Ash wasn't entirely sure if Hunter was just relating his own story or if he was trying to get something else across.

"Isla has lived a life where she wasn't a priority for her mom. I will always do what I have to for her to know that she is important to me. I can't chance bringing someone into my life who might make her feel otherwise."

Hunter nodded. "That's understandable. Just make sure you're not blind to someone who might be as willing as you are to give Isla a place of importance in her life."

Was the man talking about Heather?

Ash didn't want to ask for fear that he might be reading something into what Hunter was saying. He certainly couldn't fault Heather for how she interacted with Isla. His conflicted feelings regarding Heather didn't center on how she treated Isla.

"I'm not," Ash said. "But sometimes there are things even beyond Isla that would make a relationship… challenging."

Hunter gave a laugh. "Most relationships face challenges."

When he'd been actively dating, Ash had often thought about his parents and their marriage. He didn't have a lot of examples of good relationships, but he'd known that he didn't want one like theirs. Nor did he want to be the type of parents they'd been.

They'd had high standards for him and Gwen during their growing-up years. But once they'd turned eighteen, their parents had cut them loose to live their own lives. And even though Ash had worked for his dad, he'd rarely, if ever, asked about Ash's life, and there had certainly been no family dinners like the Kings had.

He'd wondered if his parents had had kids simply because it had been expected of them, not because they'd actually wanted to have a family. While he'd managed to survive that type of upbringing, Gwen hadn't.

Isla may have come to him as an unexpected responsibility, but Ash was determined to make sure that she never felt that she was unwanted. Any woman would have to accept not just Isla but all the parts of his life, including a job that left him stained and dirty at the end of each day.

"Has Heather told you much about my dad's past?"

"No." Though Ash had to admit he was curious about the man who was missing from the King family.

"My dad was raised by a single mother who struggled to make ends meet. She worked hard to provide for them. Sometimes, though, it wasn't enough, and they didn't have food to eat, and they were even homeless for a while. My grandmother worked all kinds of jobs, from cleaning a bar to working as a maid in a budget hotel. No job was beneath her if it meant that she could provide food and shelter for my dad."

Ash tried to line that information up with what he knew of the Kings now. Clearly, things had changed somewhere along the line. "Did she win the lottery or something?"

Hunter chuckled. "Nope. She just instilled in my dad the necessity of hard work. He was also smart, and he used his intelligence to take advantage of every opportunity that came his way, from scholarships for school to grants for opening businesses. His focus wasn't on getting rich, however. He just wanted to take care of his family."

From where Ash sat, the man had done that and then some.

"But once his business began to flourish, he realized that he needed to do more. He understood that people didn't ask to struggle. That sometimes, it was circumstances beyond their control that put them in that position. It didn't make a person who could pay all their bills any better than the person who struggled to make ends meet. He never thought he was better than anyone else."

Hunter laughed, then added, "Well, that's not completely true. The people who want to sit around and be handed everything? Yeah, he thought he was better than them. Not because he was rich but because he was willing to work hard for what he had."

Even though he'd never met the King patriarch, Ash had to admire the man. If there was one thing that Ash wasn't afraid of, it was hard work. He'd done it every day since he was old enough to work. Though, admittedly, his efforts held more weight now since he had a little girl to take care of.

"Dad didn't just want us to work hard. He wanted us to admire the hard work of others, regardless of what it was they did."

Ash enjoyed hearing Hunter talk about his dad, and he wished that he could speak as highly of his own father. It was true that the man had been a believer in hard work as well. But from what Ash could remember, his dad had rarely looked beyond his own hard work to appreciate that diligence in others. The only time he noticed it was when the hard work of his employees didn't meet his standards, or if it inconvenienced him in some way.

There had been plenty of times as a kid when Ash had been willing to help shovel snow or mow the grass. But even though he'd tried his best to use the tools he'd been given to accomplish the tasks, he'd struggled sometimes. Instead of encouraging Ash or helping him with particularly difficult things like pulling the rope to start the mower, his father had berated him and told him to stop being so weak.

He might have eventually been able to do what he had to, but the struggles had often left him angry and in tears. But of course, tears were a no-no in his dad's world, even for a ten-year-old.

Ash had learned to work hard under his father's heavy hand, but he hadn't come to admire his father the way he could tell Hunter admired his.

"Anyway, I wanted you to know that about my dad and about us."

"Why does that matter?" Ash asked, realizing his bluntness might offend Hunter. Still, he needed to understand what the motivation was behind the conversation they were having.

Even though he could only see Hunter's profile, the man's grin was unmistakable. "Well, whether you want it or not, your niece has pretty much guaranteed that you're now part of our family."

Ash lifted his brows at that. "Uh... really?"

"Yep. Isla and Rachel will no doubt make sure that they can see each other frequently. Something also tells me that Heather wouldn't be averse to seeing Isla regularly." Hunter glanced at him as he pulled to a stop at a red light. "And you too."

"And me too what?"

Hunter turned to stare at him, an expression edging toward humor on his face. "Heather wouldn't be averse to seeing you regularly as well."

When a horn blared behind them, Hunter shifted his focus back to the road and accelerated through the intersection. It gave Ash a moment to consider Hunter's words.

"Anyway," Hunter said as he pulled up to the entrance of an underground parking garage. "Just know that you're always welcome in our family."

The conversation appeared to be over with that statement, and Ash breathed a sigh of relief because he really wasn't sure what an appropriate response was.

After Hunter called Hayden to let him know they were there, it wasn't long before the elevator door slid open, and Hayden made his way over to the SUV. Ash got out of the front seat as the other man neared the vehicle.

"I don't need to sit up front," Hayden told him.

"It's fine," Ash said. "I'm happy to sit back here."

Rather than argue, Hayden just nodded and maneuvered himself and his crutches into the front seat. Ash waited until he was settled before he climbed into the back, grateful for the spaciousness of Hunter's SUV. Otherwise, he would have been eating his kneecaps since both Hayden and Hunter needed their seats back nearly all the way. Since he was as tall as they were, Ash needed space as well.

"Am I going to be enduring a sugar overdose this afternoon?" Hayden asked as Hunter left the garage.

"You already know the answer to that," Hunter said with a laugh. "Not sure why you're subjecting yourself to that when you could have gotten out of it. Unlike Ash and me."

"Rachel texted me from Carissa's phone to ask me to come. She promised me cookies. How was I supposed to turn her down?"

"I'm sure you'll be wishing you had figured out the answer to that when your teeth are aching from the inch-thick icing on the cookies you'll be forced to consume."

"Has Ash been warned about what's coming?" Hayden asked.

"He knows that cookies are being decorated." Hunter glanced back at him. "Do you understand what that means?"

"Well, I figured it meant icing and sprinkles on cookies, but I'm getting the feeling that I've underestimated the amount of each involved."

Both men laughed at that, and Hunter said, "That, my friend, is probably true."

When they returned to the house, the cookie decorating was well underway, and Isla immediately called him over to see what she'd been doing. Ash dropped to his haunches beside her, bracing his arm across the back of her chair.

As he admired the cookies she'd decorated so far, he could see that she had worked on them in the same way that she colored in her coloring books. From his observations, she hadn't piled the icing on indiscriminately. She picked the icing colors to match the shapes of the cookies. He was particularly impressed by the Christmas trees, which had green frosting and then two types of sprinkles on them.

"The round ones are for the balls that hang on the tree, and the long sprinkles are for the lights." She smiled proudly at him, her eyes wide as she waited for his reaction.

Loving her as he did, there was only one reaction he could give, and thankfully, it was the truth. "They're all beautiful, princess."

Her smile grew even more as she turned her attention back to the cookies in front of her that still needed decorating. When Ash glanced around the table, his gaze met Heather's, and the smile she gave him was soft... almost affectionate. And while it warmed him, it also scared the life out of him.

Ash wasn't sure he knew how to be in a good relationship. Though he'd had relationships, none of them had worked out for one reason or another. And he definitely hadn't had a good example from his parents the way Heather and Hunter had.

Most of all, though, he felt like he'd already failed one woman. Gwen's death still weighed heavily on him, and he worried about not being able to give Isla what she needed. The last thing he needed was the responsibility of one more person, especially a woman like Heather, who deserved more than he could ever give her.

He really hoped that she'd be able to see how bad he'd be for her and instead focus her attention only on Isla. That would be the best thing for all of them.

Chapter 19

Heather leaned over to look at the cookie Isla was working on. "That's beautiful, sweetheart. Yours are even nicer than mine."

Isla laughed. "I love doing this. Is this the only time I can decorate cookies?"

"You mean at Christmas?"

She nodded. "Can I decorate at other times?"

"Yep. We can get different shapes and decorate for birthdays, Valentine's Day, and lots of other holidays."

"Oooh. I want to do that."

Heather hoped Ash would still let her hang around with Isla after the holidays were over. She glanced over Isla's head to where Ash sat on her other side. In that moment, she wished more than anything that she could read minds because she'd love to know what he was thinking.

But alas, mind-reading was not an option. And Ash's face gave nothing away. Could he read anything on hers? She certainly hadn't been trying to hide anything. But either she wasn't being obvious enough, or he just didn't care what he saw when he looked at her.

Heather had never had to work so hard for a guy's attention, and that stung her pride a bit, if she was being completely honest. If she'd given even half the attention to any another guy, they'd probably have been on several dates already.

It was the lack of reaction from Ash that made her think that it was more that he was not interested than him being oblivious.

She knew she needed to just let the situation go and be patient, like her mom had said. It was dominating her thoughts and affecting how she was viewing things when she should just be focused on the holiday.

"I want to do a snowflake with the glitter on it next," Isla said as she set the cookie she'd finished on the parchment that lay near the middle of the table. "Would you like that, Uncle Ash?"

"Definitely." He leaned over and kissed her head. "I can't wait to see how it looks."

"Can you make me cookies to decorate at home?"

Ash chuckled. "Sorry, sweetheart. I doubt I could make cookies like these without burning them."

"Do you know how to make cookies?" Isla asked, angling a look at Heather before focusing back on her snowflake.

"I'm afraid I don't."

"You know I'd teach you," Essie said. "Maybe I should teach the three of you."

"I would *love* that!" Isla exclaimed, then turned to Ash. "Can we do that?"

Ash glanced at Essie, then at Heather. "Uh... sure. I guess."

"Excellent," Essie said with a broad smile. "We probably don't need more cookies before Christmas, but maybe we can make some for New Year's."

"We're gonna learn to make cookies, Uncle Ash," Isla informed him, as if he wasn't sitting there listening to the conversation.

Ash smiled, and Heather soaked it in because while he was a handsome man regardless, when he smiled, it took things to a whole new level. At least for her. And it wasn't just the physical. It was the smiles he directed at Isla, loaded with love and affection, that hit her right in the heart.

"Maybe I should get Essie to teach me how to cook other things, too," Ash said, surprising Heather.

"That would be good," Isla agreed with a nod of her head as she got some white icing on a plastic knife. "She cooks yummy food."

"I could do that."

"Maybe you could do a class," Carissa suggested. "I'm sure that Heather and I would also like to learn how to cook some of the stuff you do."

"As long as it doesn't mean you won't show up for meals here."

"That's never going to happen," Heather assured her. "And not just because I live here."

"I'm fine to cook most the time," Carissa said. "But if I can eat a meal someone else made, I'm not going to turn it down."

"I just hope your lessons stick this time." Heather sighed. "We've been through this before."

Essie smiled and gave her a wink. "Perhaps all you need is the right incentive."

Heather laughed, glancing at Ash before leaning forward to grab another cookie to decorate. "One can only hope."

The idea of being able to cook for people was starting to hold more appeal. She hadn't felt like she'd needed that particular skill since she still lived at home, and there hadn't been any plans for her to move out. With Essie not letting people into her kitchen, being able to cook hadn't seemed necessary.

"I wanna learn to cook so I can make sure there's food to eat," Isla stated.

Her words had Heather looking over at Ash. He frowned at Isla as she focused on her cookie. It made Heather's heart hurt, knowing what had prompted that Isla's statement. That situation was in the past now, but Heather was sure that the effects of that time with her mom would linger for years to come.

She knew that Ash would do what he could to replace those memories and experiences with positive ones, and she very much wanted to be a part of that. Hopefully, the stuff Isla was able to do that Christmas would also help.

Ash still hadn't said whether they'd be there for Christmas Eve and Christmas Day, but after what Isla had said, Heather really hoped that he'd agree to join them.

~ * ~

"Can you tell me about what you learned in church?" Ash asked as Isla went through the motions of getting ready for bed.

She looked over at him from where she was carefully squeezing toothpaste onto her toothbrush. "When I went with Donna or today?"

He considered her question for a moment, then said, "All of it. Tell me what you've learned when you go to church."

She gripped her toothbrush in her small hand but didn't lift it to begin brushing. Even in profile, he could see that her brow was furrowed. He was just about ready to tell her not to worry about it when she started to talk.

"Today, cause it's almost Christmas, we talked about Jesus being born." She looked over at him, and Ash nodded to encourage her to continue. "Then before, at Easter, we talked about Jesus dying on the cross. It's not about rabbits and eggs."

Ash knew precious little about Christianity, and it was odd that he was learning about it from his little niece. And that sounded a little morbid to be teaching a six- or seven-year-old. "Why did He die on the cross?"

"For our sins," she told him. "So that we could go to Heaven and see God when we die."

Ash frowned, trying to figure out how that would work. Maybe Isla didn't really know what she was talking about.

"I know a Bible verse," Isla announced.

"You do?"

"Yep. We learned it in my Sunday school when I went with Donna."

"Can you say it to me?"

She nodded, her braids dancing with the motion. "For God so loved the world that He gave His only 'gotten Son, that whoever believes in Him should not... should not... perish but have 'erlasting life. John three-sixteen."

"Good job, princess," Ash said with a smile, even though he had no idea if she'd gotten all the words right.

The verse didn't clear up a lot of his questions, but he was still impressed by Isla's recitation of the verse. Given how much she despised reading, he would have thought that she would hate memorization too. But perhaps whoever had taught it to her had made it more fun.

Isla beamed at him, then began to brush her teeth. Ash went into her bedroom, lowering himself to sit on the edge of the bed to wait for her to finish up in the bathroom.

As he sat there, his thoughts were a jumbled mess. Each time he was around Heather or her family, he was left with more questions. And that night was no exception. But he knew that the questions he had about Christianity weren't going to be answered by his seven-year-old niece.

But should he go to Hunter or Heather with his questions?

On Tuesday night, Ash realized that he'd expected to hear from Heather, and there was a knot of disappointment inside him because he hadn't. He could see that Isla was disappointed as well, but she almost seemed more accepting of it than he was. That sadly spoke to how much disappointment she'd had in her life so far.

Logically, Ash knew that Heather had a life beyond helping him and Isla out. But disappointment wasn't always logical. If nothing else, however, it was a good reminder that he couldn't let people become important to them.

Isla stood with her arms folded on the counter, her chin resting on them. "Can I have a cookie?"

Ash dried his hands on a towel and picked up the container of cookies. He pried the lid off and then slid it toward to Isla. She grinned at him, taking her time picking out the cookie she wanted. Part of him wanted to tell her that every cookie was going to taste exactly the same, but he didn't. Just because he felt a little jaded, he didn't need to pass that on to her.

"I'm gonna eat one of Rachel's." She showed him a star that had a thick topping of yellow frosting on it. "Do you want one?"

Ash stared at the container for a moment before he gave in and sighed, leaning over to pick a cookie for himself. He took the one closest to him, happy to see it wasn't loaded with frosting.

"I'm eating one of yours." He showed her the tree, then took a bite. "It's delicious."

Isla giggled, then went to sit on a chair at the table. She took small bites of the cookie as she watched him finish cleaning up the kitchen.

"Do I have to go to school tomorrow?" Isla asked.

Ash paused in wiping down the counter. "Isn't your class having its Christmas party tomorrow?"

"Winter party," Isla corrected, her nose wrinkling. "And I don't care about that. I'd rather be at the garage with you."

It was bad enough that she already spent an hour or two there each weekday. He didn't want her to spend the whole day in the garage. That was going to be what happened over the Christmas break, regardless, but he didn't want it to be any more than it had to be.

He wished that she'd made even just one good friend in her class. Maybe then he'd have been able to find someone who'd be willing to babysit her during the days Isla was off school. He was willing to pay someone, but it had to be someone that he felt he could trust.

Unfortunately, there was no one like that in his life right then. That was undoubtedly a result of him not having much of a social life anymore

"You need to go to school this week," Ash finally said, hating to disappoint Isla. "You'll be at the garage every day over your Christmas break."

He thought she might argue with him. But instead, she just sat with slumped shoulders, her head bent forward. It was hard to see, but he really had no other options.

After he was done in the kitchen, they went to sit on the couch so that Isla could practice her reading. She still despised it, but at least she didn't complain about it too much. Though he wished he could give her a break over the Christmas holidays, Ash was pretty sure he was going to get a note from the teacher telling him that Isla needed to keep practicing even when she was out of school.

She'd just finished the second read-through of her story when his text alert went. His heart skipped a beat because there were only a couple of people who usually texted him. Hoping that it wasn't his employee texting to say he couldn't work the next day, Ash pulled his phone out to look at the message.

Heather: *Hey, Ash! Wondering if I could come by tomorrow afternoon and spend a little time with Isla.*

He shouldn't feel as excited about that as he did, but just reading those words made his heart beat faster in anticipation. If he was smart, he'd tell her no. But at that moment, he didn't care.

Sure. Isla would really like that.

So would he, but he wasn't going to say anything about that to her. He'd just be happy to have Heather spend time with Isla.

Heather: *Great! I'll be there around four-thirty.*

See you then.

Ash slid his phone back into his pocket, then glanced over at Isla to find her watching him with a wide, expectant gaze.

Though he knew that he probably shouldn't tell Isla that Heather was coming in case plans changed, he did anyway. Heather had proven true to her word so far. Plus, it would perk Isla up.

"She's coming tomorrow?" Isla asked, the book forgotten in her lap.

"Yes. After school."

"Yay! That will make my day better since I have to go to the stupid winter party."

Ash shook his head at her words. "Try to think about it more positively. Maybe you'll have a good time."

Isla crossed her arms. "Probably not."

"Well, at least you know you'll like some of the food there since you're taking two bags of your favorite chips."

"Nobody better eat them before I get some."

"Sweetheart, if someone eats all your chips, I'll buy another bag just for you."

"Okay."

"Now it's time to get ready for bed."

She handed him her book, then headed for the bedroom to start her nighttime routine. Ash took the book and put it with the rest of her things for the next day.

By the time he joined her, she was already in her pajamas and brushing her teeth. He was very grateful that she wasn't a child who objected to bedtime. If she'd fought him every night about going to bed, he wasn't sure what he would have done.

Within a few minutes, Isla was ready to sleep. Ash settled on the edge of her bed, reaching for the book that sat on the nightstand.

At the teacher's suggestion, he and Isla had gone to the library to find a book she might like to have him read to her. Apparently, the teacher felt that in addition to Isla herself reading, it would be beneficial to have someone read *to* her.

He understood that if they could find a story that engaged her, maybe her opinion of reading would change enough that she'd want to do it more herself. Though Ash was hopeful, he wasn't totally sold on the idea because Isla, while she was mainly cooperative, could also be stubborn.

Regardless, he opened the book about a pink horse with a multi-colored mane and began to read about the animal's adventures.

Chapter 20

Heather parked her car in the small lot in front of Ash's garage. After she got out, she retrieved a large basket from the back seat, then made her way to the door leading into the waiting area.

As soon as she stepped in, Isla's enthusiastic greeting had Heather smiling. She walked over to the desk and set the basket on it, careful to avoid the coloring book and crayons Isla was using.

"What's that?" Isla asked as she stood up, leaning close to the basket.

"I brought some supper."

"Really?" Isla's eyes sparkled as she looked up at her. "What did you bring?"

"I'm not entirely sure, to be honest," Heather said as she opened the lid. "Mom and Essie packed it for us."

"Is it like a picnic?"

"I guess it kind of is, only we're sitting at a desk." Heather thought that as long as she was hanging with Isla and Ash, she'd sit pretty much anywhere that was safe.

"Uncle Ash!" Isla called out. "We're havin' a picnic!"

Ash appeared in the doorway a minute later, wiping his hands on a cloth. He was wearing his usual dark blue coveralls with his ball cap on backward. His gaze went to the picnic basket, then met hers.

"What's this?"

"Essie and Mom sent supper along with me."

"We're gonna have a picnic on the desk," Isla informed him.

"Sounds like a plan," he said, though he didn't look completely convinced. "What's on the menu?"

"I'm not sure," Heather confessed. "George showed up right before I left the office with it and said Mom and Essie had packed it for us."

"Well, it should be tasty then," Ash said.

Heather crossed her arms and arched a brow at him. "Are you telling me it wouldn't be if I'd made it?"

When he mirrored her position and said, "Are you telling me that it would be?", she started laughing.

"Probably not," she admitted.

"Is your mom a good cook?"

"She's better than me. On the rare day that Essie has off, Mom will cook for us."

"Can we see what they put in the basket for us?" Isla leaned close and inhaled. "I'm hungry!"

"Didn't you eat at the party today?" Ash asked.

"Just the chips I took."

Ash shook his head. "They didn't have anything else you wanted?"

"I don't know," Isla said with a shrug. "I just wanted the chips. Oh. I also ate some carrots."

"Carrots and chips." Ash shook his head. "Well, I expect you to eat whatever Heather has brought."

"I will. Promise."

"Let me just get cleaned up," Ash said. "I'll be back in a couple of minutes."

Heather watched him go, questioning if coming had been a good idea. She'd told herself to just focus on Isla and not Ash, but clearly, that wasn't happening. The man demanded her attention without even trying.

As she lifted items out of the basket, Isla leaned close to peer at each one. Once the basket was empty, Heather set it on the floor. She peeled the lid off the top of the largest glass container and smiled.

"What's that?" Isla asked.

"It's called Shepherd's Pie."

"That doesn't look like a pie," Isla said. "And is it made out of shepherds?"

Heather laughed. "Nope. No shepherds. And you're right, it's not a pie like we're used to. It has ground beef and vegetables on the bottom and mashed potatoes on the top."

"I like mashed potatoes," Isla said, though she didn't appear convinced on the rest.

"I think you'll like it all. It's pretty tasty."

By the time Ash returned, they had everything set out and ready to eat.

"Something smells good," he said.

"It's shepherd's pie," Isla informed him. "But it's not made of shepherds."

Ash glanced at Heather, laughter in his eyes. "I can't tell you how glad I am to hear that."

"Have you had it before?" Isla asked.

"I think I have, but it's been a while. If I remember correctly, I liked it."

"You'll definitely like this," Heather said. "It's one of the comfort foods Essie likes to make."

They settled around the desk and began to dish up their plates. Before they began to eat, Ash asked Isla if she wanted to pray for the food. The little girl nodded, then folded her hands and bowed her head.

Heather did the same without looking at Ash. She was impressed—and grateful on Isla's behalf—that he was encouraging the little girl's faith. Her respect for him rose yet again, which was definitely the opposite of what she'd been hoping for. Not that she wanted to *lose* respect for him. She just didn't want more reasons to like the guy. Her heart had enough of those already.

"This is good," Isla said after she'd eaten a couple of bites. She had a spoon clutched in one hand and one of Essie's freshly made dinner rolls in her other.

"I agree with Isla," Ash said. "Another home run for Essie."

"I'll be sure to tell her. She'll be pleased."

As they ate, Isla told them about the party she'd had at school that day. Clearly, she hadn't been overly impressed by it. In fact, according to her, the only good thing about it had been the chips she'd eaten.

"I liked your party better," Isla said. "Decorating cookies was fun, and there was *Santa!*"

Heather smiled at her. "I liked that party too."

"We finally got a tree." Isla glanced at Ash. "But it's not very big."

"Unfortunately, we don't exactly have a lot of room for a tree, so we kind of had to go with a small one."

"I bet it still looks nice. Maybe you could send me a picture of it," Heather suggested.

"I don't have a phone," Isla said with a frown.

"I'm pretty sure your uncle will let you use his."

"You can take the pictures when we get home," Ash said.

Isla nodded, then went back to her meal.

"Did you have a busy day?" Ash asked.

Heather thought back over the hours before she'd come to the garage. "Yes. My work has ticked up since Thanksgiving."

"What do you do, exactly?" Ash asked.

Her heart sped up for a moment in response to Ash's interest in something about her. "I do a few different things, but my main focus is working alongside HR—human resources. My dad believed that employees whose needs were taken care of made better workers. To that end, we have an employee care department, which I'm the head of."

"What sorts of things do you do?"

"Well, we process requests for different needs. We have scholarship programs for the children of employees. People can request aid for medical expenses or referrals for mental health. We also look at requests for financial help."

"Is that a bit of a depressing job? I'm assuming most of the issues would be for people in somewhat dire straits."

Heather nodded. "Sometimes the situations people share about are heartbreaking. But knowing that we are helping them through those situations can help balance out the sadness. And there are positive things as well. Like the scholarships. We also send gift baskets and gift cards to people who get married or have babies. It's not all negative."

"What's caused the uptick since Thanksgiving?" Ash asked.

"Well, the holidays are difficult for a lot of people for different reasons. Sometimes people just don't have enough money for gifts. Other people realize they need some mental health help to make it through."

"Do you approve all the requests?"

"Most of them. If it's a fairly new employee, we usually pull their supervisor in just to get a few more details. The employee care department resources aren't supposed to be handouts, per se, but more hand-ups. We're a safety net to catch people who are struggling to hold on, but we're not there to walk beside them with an open wallet."

Ash nodded, his expression contemplative. "I mean no offense by this, but you all seem too good to be true."

Heather gave a laugh. "No offense taken. I can see how it would appear that way. The thing is, my dad was far from a perfect man, and none of the rest of us are perfect either. But we try to do what we can to have a positive impact on the world rather than a negative one. Our visibility is higher because we are doing it as a multi-million-dollar company. Lots of people help others, only their efforts aren't as widely seen because they're just individuals. That doesn't make what they do any less impactful."

"I suppose you're right."

"I'm definitely right," Heather said confidently. "Take yourself, for example."

Ash sat back in his chair, a frown on his face as he crossed his arms. "What about me?"

"I think I can safely say that the positive impact you've had on Isla's life is as significant as any impact we've had on any individual's life through our company. Don't discount what you've done because you don't have the resources of a big company. If more people were like you, the world would be a much better place."

"You and Hunter always seem to do that," Ash said, his frown having eased from his face, though his brow was still furrowed.

"Do what?"

"Try to put us all on the same level."

Now it was Heather's turn to frown. "Well, that's because, at the root of everything, we *are* all on the same level. God didn't create different levels of people. We may be born to different economic stations in life, but in God's eyes, we're all the same. It's our hearts that He looks at, not our color or gender or the size of our wallet."

Ash lowered his gaze to his plate. "I've never really given much thought to how God views me, to be honest. I only did what I did because it felt like the right thing to do."

"Not everyone would have done it, even if they knew it was the right thing. Plenty of people know what the right thing is and still choose not to do it because it inconveniences them. Or because it might cost them time, money, or energy that they don't want to give up."

Ash didn't respond right away, quietly eating the rest of the food on his plate. Heather once again wished she could read his mind, and part of her wanted to fill the silence. But if he was mulling things over in his mind, she didn't want to push him to talk.

"Good job, sweetie," Heather said to Isla when she noticed her empty plate. "Did you want more?"

Isla shook her head and poked at the container they'd determined held some of Essie's apple crumble. "I want room for the dessert."

Heather stacked their dirty dishes and put them back in the basket to be washed up at home.

The dessert wasn't as hot as it would have been if they'd been eating it at home, but she knew it would still taste good. After she'd dished some up for each of them, she let Isla put spoonfuls of the whipped cream that Essie had sent in another small bowl onto the top of each piece of apple crisp.

"This looks good," Ash said as Isla gave him a bowl. "Thank you."

"When is your last day of school?" Heather asked as they ate.

"Friday." Isla sighed.

"Don't they usually have the party on the last day of school?" Heather asked, trying to remember back to when she'd been in elementary school. It seemed it was an eternity ago.

"I'm not sure," Ash said. "Isla just brought a note home saying that there was going to be a party today and then assigned us something to bring. Thankfully, all Isla had to provide was two bags of chips."

"She doesn't have much time off before Christmas," Heather observed. "Like just three days?"

"Yep. She has more time off after the New Year."

"Do you have any plans for the Christmas break?"

Ash lifted his brows at her. "Work?"

Okay. So maybe that had been a dumb question on her part. "Sorry. I wasn't thinking."

He shrugged. "No reason you should."

Heather appreciated that he didn't point out that it was clear proof of the differences in their lives. In her mind had been the memories of her family traveling between Christmas and New Year's Day to some place they could spend time as just the five of them. Sometimes it would be a skiing vacation. Other times they'd go someplace warm. That had continued until her dad had passed away.

They hadn't been on a holiday like that since then, but maybe that should change.

"I get to spend the vacation here with Uncle Ash," Isla said. "I can't wait."

"I think that excitement might last a day," Ash remarked. "But I'm hoping that she proves me wrong."

Heather thought of the conversation she'd had with Carissa the night before, when the woman had told her that her last day of work at the restaurant was the twenty-third. An idea came to mind then, but she couldn't bring the subject up without talking first with Carissa.

Once they were done eating, Heather packed up the food, and Ash pitched in to help. After everything was put away, Heather turned her attention to Isla.

"Do you have homework?"

"Just reading." Isla sighed loudly.

"Do you have your book here? You can read to me before I go."

Isla hopped off the chair and went to where her backpack sat by the coats. As she retrieved her book, Heather glanced over at Ash.

"Hope that's okay."

"That's fine," he said. "Saves the fight at home. I still have to read to her before she goes to bed."

"You read to her?" Heather asked.

Ash nodded as he leaned back in his chair, stretching his long legs out and crossing them at the ankle. "The teacher said it would be beneficial if I read to her in addition to her reading to me."

"Huh. So what book did you choose to read to her?"

"I didn't choose the book," Ash said with a slight grin. "Nothing that would interest me would be age appropriate for her."

"He's reading about a pony whose tail is a bunch of pretty colors, and she gets teased because of it."

"Do you like it?" Heather asked. "Does Uncle Ash do a good job reading?"

Isla laughed. "I do like it, but Uncle Ash doesn't do the different voices really well, so sometimes I don't know who's talking."

When Heather looked back at Ash, he just shrugged. "I don't know what a pony with a multi-colored tail should sound like."

Heather loved that he was making an effort for Isla. Some men might not even attempt it, but Ash seemed determined to give his niece the best he could.

"You'll have to tell me all about it when you finish reading it," Heather said. "And I can't wait to hear what book you choose to read next."

Ash gave her a curious look but didn't say anything as Isla opened her book. As the little girl slowly read through the story,

Heather wished she could be there every night to listen to her. Already she could hear the progress she'd made, and Heather longed to be there to witness all the progress she made in life.

Maybe, if she didn't allow her feelings to make Ash wary or uncomfortable, he'd allow her to be part of their life, even as just a friend. It would definitely be better than nothing.

Chapter 21

Ash sat on the couch, his gaze on the small Christmas tree that sat on an end table in front of the window. Isla had insisted it was the best place for it, and Ash had no good reason to object. It had required a little rearranging of the living room, but that had been easy enough.

The Christmas music that Isla had wanted to listen to was still playing in the background. He hadn't turned the lights back on after she'd turned them off earlier, wanting only the strands on the tree to remain on. She had definitely been going after an atmosphere.

Even though she'd gone to bed awhile ago, Ash hadn't bothered to change anything. There was something strangely soothing about sitting in the dark with only the lights of the Christmas tree to illuminate the room.

Christmas was just four days away, and he still hadn't told the Kings they'd be with them for the holiday. He wasn't sure why he hadn't. There was no chance he'd change his mind.

The problem was, he just didn't know how to be a part of the celebrations the Kings were sure to have. Already, the times they'd spent with them had shown that they went all out for the holiday. Unlike his own family.

On Christmas Eve, they'd sometimes gone to church with his grandma, but that had stopped when she'd passed away. Other than that, they didn't do anything. His mom and dad would usually watch a Christmas show on television, but he and Gwen weren't required to hang out with them, so they hadn't.

On Christmas morning, there were no stockings. They'd have a simple breakfast, then open the one or two presents that his folks had gotten them. Christmas dinner was turkey or ham—whichever was cheaper—and once they were done eating, Christmas was over.

He knew that wouldn't be how it was at the Kings.

After all she'd been through so far in her life, Isla deserved this first Christmas after the death of her mom to be memorable. He wasn't sure how to do that by himself. Though he'd barely been able to get her a tree, he'd made sure to order her presents online since he couldn't get to the store without her with him.

Knowing it wasn't fair to leave Heather hanging with regards to Christmas, Ash leaned over and picked up his phone from the end table. Telling himself that he didn't want to interrupt anything Heather might be doing by calling, Ash opened a text screen.

Hi Heather. I'm sorry for not getting back to you sooner about Christmas.

He sent the message, then waited when he saw the three dots showing she was replying to him.

Heather: *Well, as long as you and Isla are coming, I'll forgive you.*

Ash gave a laugh as he read her response. *We are. I don't think Isla would ever forgive me if I said no.*

Heather: *You told her about it?*

Oh, definitely not. I've learned to not tell her about stuff like that. Even if I agree, I still have to listen to her talk about it endlessly.

Heather: *I was gonna say... I learned that from Rachel over the past year. Unless you want to be bugged like crazy, it's best to not mention it until it's five minutes from starting.*

Heather: *Anyway... I'm glad you're coming. We'll have Christmas Eve dinner around five-thirty, so feel free to come any time before that. Afterward, we'll go to church for the Christmas Eve service.*

Heather: *Then, on Christmas morning, we open stockings when we get up, then we have breakfast. After we eat, we open presents and just hang out until we have Christmas dinner later in the afternoon.*

As he read her messages, Ash realized that he'd been correct in assuming they'd have a busier Christmas than what he was used to.

I keep the garage open until four on Christmas Eve, so we'll come after that.

Heather: *No need to bring pjs. We'll have some for you. On Christmas Day, we're really casual. So just pack whatever is comfortable for the two of you.*

Ash hadn't been sure about staying the night, but clearly, Heather expected them to.

Heather: *We've got plenty of room, and if you're okay with it, Isla can share a bed with Rachel. I know Rachel would love to have someone closer to her own age to hang out with.*

There really was no way to refuse, though Ash couldn't remember the last time he'd slept anywhere but his own bed. Even as a youngster, he hadn't had sleepovers.

That would be fine. I'm sure Isla would love that as well.

Heather: *Sounds great! Can't wait to see you.*

Heather: *Both of you. Can't wait to see both of you.*

Since he was alone, Ash allowed a grin to form at her words. She hadn't exactly been subtle about the fact that she apparently enjoyed spending time with him. He still didn't have confidence that anything could work out between them romantically, but perhaps they could do a friendship.

Unless it was all or nothing for Heather. If she would only go for dating or nothing, then he'd probably have to walk away. He just wasn't sure how to start a conversation about that with her.

Hopefully, if he just continued on as he had been, she'd get the idea that all he was offering was friendship, without him having to put it into words. Because he was a coward, apparently, though he never would have thought that about himself prior to meeting Heather.

Ash waited until Christmas Eve to tell Isla where they were going, and the level of excitement she'd already had for Christmas skyrocketed. After he closed the garage for the day, they went back home and picked up the few things they'd packed for their stay, including the gifts he'd gotten her.

Christmas music played from his radio as they drove to the Kings' home, and Ash found himself embracing the spirit of the holiday in a way he never had before. Since it was dark already, the abundance of Christmas lights adorning the houses they passed made Isla oooh and ahhh.

They reached the Kings' home shortly after five, and Isla danced with excitement as they carried their bags up to the front door. He'd barely rang the bell when the door opened to reveal Heather standing there with a beautiful smile on her face. "Merry Christmas!"

She moved back to allow them to step into the foyer, then closed the door behind them. "I'm so glad you could make it."

She wore a dark red turtleneck sweater and a pair of black pants. Her dark hair was a shiny curtain over her shoulders that slid forward as she bent to hug Isla.

"Let's get your things off, then I'll show you where you can put your bags."

Ash took his jacket and boots off while Heather helped Isla with hers. After they put everything in the front closet, Heather led them up the wide stairs to the second floor.

"Is it okay if you sleep with Rachel?" Heather asked Isla.

"A sleepover with Rachel?" Isla clapped her hands. "Yay!"

"Well, here is the room she's staying in tonight." Heather led them into a medium-sized room with a queen-size bed. It was decorated in greens and pinks, and there was already a bag sitting at the foot of the bed.

Ash set Isla's bag down next to it, then followed Heather out of the room and down the hall to another bedroom. This one was decorated in grays and whites and also had a queen-size bed.

"Do you really have room for all of us?" Ash asked.

"Yep. We have enough bedrooms, plus Hunter and Hayden plan to stay on pull-out couches in the basement."

"Would it be better for Hayden to sleep here?" Ash didn't want the man to be uncomfortable. "I don't mind sleeping on a pull-out couch."

"He's fine. The couches are comfortable."

"I just don't want to put anyone out."

"You haven't. We're thrilled to have you here for the night." Heather smiled at him. "Are you ready to eat?"

"I am!" Isla exclaimed. "Is Rachel here already?"

"Yes. She's helping Essie set the table."

The three of them returned to the main floor and went into the kitchen, where they found everyone else. Essie put them to work, carrying the vast amount of food she'd prepared into the dining room.

Christmas music drifted through the house on speakers that Ash assumed were hidden in each room, as it was the same music in the kitchen and the dining room. There was a fire blazing in the dining room fireplace, and the room, along with the table, was festively decorated.

The whole place looked like Christmas had exploded all over it. He and Isla had had just the tree for decoration, while everywhere he turned in the Kings' house, there was some sort of decoration. There were even festive place cards with their names written on them.

Rachel showed Isla where they were sitting, and Ash found his name next to Isla's, with Heather on his other side.

Once everyone was seated, Hunter said a prayer for the food, then they filled their plates. Ash wasn't sure when the last time it was that he'd eaten so much. It was a full prime rib dinner that was probably the most delicious type of beef he'd ever eaten.

Dessert was apparently planned for after the Christmas Eve service, which was just as well since Ash was so stuffed, he felt like he could barely move.

When it was time to leave for the church, they piled into two SUVs. George drove one and Hunter drove the other. Isla went with Hunter, Carissa, Rachel, and Hayden, while Ash went with George, Essie, Eliza, and Heather. He sat in the front with George, though he felt bad that the women had to squeeze into the back seat. They didn't seem to care, happily singing along with the Christmas carols playing on the radio.

Once they were at the church, they stood together, waiting for George and Hunter to join them after parking the vehicles. When they went to sit down, Ash was on the aisle like previous services. Instead of sitting with him, though, Isla wanted to sit by Rachel. Heather scooted closer to Ash to allow Isla to sit on her other side next to Rachel. Even though Ash knew he shouldn't, he enjoyed feeling like they were part of the family and especially being close to Heather.

After several readings and songs, the church's pastor got up to stand behind the podium on the stage. He began to speak, his words engaging Ash's attention, raising again the questions he'd had after talking with Isla.

"Christmas is the start of a story, the beginning of a life-changing experience. When Mary gave birth to her son, Jesus, she also gave birth to our Savior. The person who would give His life in order to offer us the gift of eternal life. The true celebration of His birth comes when you accept the gift of eternal life that came to us through His death.

"From the moment of His birth, Jesus had one mission: to become the sacrificial lamb that would take away the sin of the world. Through His death and resurrection, Jesus offers us the gift of eternal life, if we would simply confess our sin and accept Him as Lord and Savior of our life.

"Today, if you haven't already accepted the gift of eternal life, I would ask you to consider what His birth, death, and resurrection mean for you. John 3:16 sums up what this holiday means for us. *For God so loved the world that He gave His only Son.* This refers to Jesus' birth, which is what we celebrate at Christmas. The verse continues with: *That whosoever believes in Him should not perish, but have everlasting life.* Don't just focus on His birth this Christmas, but look toward what it meant thirty-three years later when He died on the cross for our sins and rose again to offer us eternal life with Him in Heaven."

Ash recognized the verse the pastor quoted as the one that Isla had recited for him. Clearly, it was an important verse, and he mulled it over more as the pastor concluded his sermon, and the service ended with them singing *Silent Night.*

As they left the sanctuary, Isla and Rachel walked ahead of him, hand-in-hand, which made Ash happy. Isla needed a good friend, especially since she hadn't found one at school yet.

When they returned to the house, Hunter started up a fire in the living room, and with the lamps on the end tables casting only dimmed light in the room, it gave it a cozy feel. The Christmas tree stood tall in front of the windows with softly glowing white lights.

Heather, Essie, and Carissa disappeared as soon as they arrived at the house, but reappeared shortly with the dessert and coffee, setting everything down on the coffee table.

Ash settled into one corner of the loveseat. Hayden sat slumped in one of the armchairs, and Ash wasn't sure if he actually wanted to be there. He wondered how the guy managed when it was clear he was in a lot of pain.

Given how long it had been since he'd been injured, Ash wasn't sure why the man was still in pain. He would have thought that he'd have been able to get the treatment he needed to heal. Especially since they were so wealthy. If a man with his resources couldn't get the care he needed, what hope did others have?

They spent the next little while eating the assortment of goodies that Essie had prepared for dessert. Everything Ash tried was delicious, and he was glad they'd waited until after the service to eat it so he could really enjoy it. Once they'd decimated all the sweets, Essie and Eliza cleared it away while Heather and Carissa left the room, sharing conspiratorial looks.

When Heather and Carissa returned, their arms were full of bags, and they had big smiles on their faces. Ash watched them curiously, wondering what was to come. Hayden seemed to know, though, because he let out a groan as he watched his sister and Carissa set the bags on the coffee table. Even Hunter rolled his eyes, but he didn't say anything.

Chapter 22

Heather lifted one of the bags and peered inside, grinning when she saw which one it was. Pulling out the first item, she went to Hayden and dropped it in his lap.

"Your attire for tomorrow morning, brother dear," she declared.

"You're evil," Hayden muttered. "What are you going to do to me if I don't wear them?"

"I will sic Rachel and her disappointed puppy dog eyes on you."

"Fine." Hayden tucked the pajamas down next to his leg. "You play dirty."

"Only when I want to win." She patted his head, then turned to Ash. "And these are for you."

Ash stared at her, then at the item she held out to him. "What is it?"

"This a pair of Christmas pajamas. You need to wear them for tomorrow morning."

"Christmas pajamas?" His brow furrowed as he took the pajamas and looked at them. "Never realized they had such a thing."

"It's a tradition that Heather resurrected last year," Hunter told him. "It's easier to just go along with it."

"Yes, it most definitely is," Heather agreed. "Don't argue with me. Ever."

"I was just referring to the pajama battle," Hunter said.

"I know, but let's be honest. It's just a good practice overall."

Hayden and Hunter both laughed at that. Heather responded by dropping a pair of pajamas on Hunter's head.

"Do I get pajamas too?" Isla asked.

"You sure do." Carissa opened another of the bags and pulled out two smaller sets of folded clothing. She handed one to Isla and the other to Rachel.

Isla squealed in excitement, a marked difference from how the grown men had responded.

"See." Heather waved her hand at Isla. "That's how you *should* have responded."

"If I ever squeal like a little girl, just shoot me," Hayden said.

"I'd accept you squealing like a grown man."

"Never gonna happen."

"Where are my pajamas, darling?" her mom asked, no doubt wanting to distract Heather from her brothers.

"I've got yours here," Carissa said. "And the ones for Essie and George too."

Once all the pajamas were distributed, Heather settled onto the couch next to Ash. He hadn't unfolded the pajamas yet, so he hadn't seen how absolutely adorable they were. She was sure he'd have the same reaction as Hunter and Hayden, but he probably wouldn't be as annoying as them with their whining.

"Uh... thanks for including Isla and me in your pajama tradition."

Heather peered at him. "Are you being sarcastic?"

"No?"

She laughed. "It's fine. Hunter and Hayden aren't as excited about the pajamas as Isla and Rachel are, but they'll show up in them tomorrow. If you feel strongly about not wearing them, you don't have to. However, I should warn you that the only truly acceptable excuse is that they don't fit you."

"How did you know what size to get me?"

"You're about the same height and build as the boys, so I just used their size for yours."

"Why matching pajamas?" he asked. "I've never heard of that."

"Oh. Well, it makes for nice pictures on Christmas morning. Plus, it's just fun."

Heather picked up her mug of hot chocolate from where she'd put it on the end table earlier and took a sip. Being there with her family, as well as Ash and Isla, she felt a sense of peace and contentment.

But underneath the peace and contentment was still a layer of grief. Everyone there carried it in one form or another. Carissa had lost *both* her parents. Ash had lost his sister. Isla, her mom. Heather didn't think that grief tied them together, but it did give them common ground and an understanding of what loss could do to a person's life.

One thing Heather knew was that if her dad had still been with them, he would have loved the gathering that night. It made her sad that he hadn't lived to see Hunter get engaged to a woman who would bring the first grandchild into the family.

Isla came and crawled up between Heather and Ash on the couch. "Is Santa coming tonight?"

"I think he is," Heather said as she pulled the little girl in for a hug.

"We have to put out the cookies and milk," Rachel said. "Santa needs a snack."

"I almost forgot." Essie got to her feet. "Why don't you two come with me so we can get it all ready?"

The two girls went with Essie, each carrying their pajamas, and when they returned several minutes later, they had changed into them. Rachel had a glass of milk and a carrot while Isla held a plate with cookies in her hands. Heather grinned when she saw the thick layer of icing on the cookies.

Once the girls had set the items they carried on the end table closest to the fireplace, Isla climbed up beside Heather again. As she snuggled into her, Isla's gaze was on the fireplace, where flames glowed and danced. "Will they put the fire out so Santa doesn't get burned?"

Heather grinned at the question, so similar to Rachel's the previous year. "Oh, most definitely. Hunter will make sure the fire is completely out in time for Santa to come."

"And will he know where to find me?" she asked. "Since this isn't my real house?"

Heather pressed a kiss to the top of Isla's head. "He'll be able to find you. Don't worry about that. He found Rachel last year when she was staying here instead of their apartment."

"Really?" Isla turned to look over to where Rachel sat with Hunter and Carissa. "Santa found you?"

Rachel nodded. "Yep. He did."

Isla relaxed back into Heather. "I'm still not sure he's real."

Heather ran her hand over Isla's hair. "That's okay. You don't have to."

"There will still be presents?"

"Pretty sure there will be."

Isla seemed to be unwinding, staying slumped against Heather as she gazed toward the Christmas tree. There were no presents under the tree yet, and the stockings on the large wooden mantel were still empty. Once the kids were in bed, that would all change.

Heather was excited for that time. As a kid, she'd loved going to bed with the tree empty, then waking to find presents spilling out from underneath it. Even when she'd known that Santa wasn't real, she'd enjoyed that. She hoped that the excitement would be the same for Rachel and Isla.

Her gaze went to where Hayden sat, staring morosely at the fire. Heather wanted to help him feel better. But after five years of dealing with his moods, she knew that he was the only one who could change his current mindset. All she could do, which she did on a daily basis, was pray that God would work in Hayden's heart and that He would offer him a respite from the pain, both mental and physical.

Heather just hoped that, in time, Hayden could find some peace and hope for his future. And maybe, just maybe, he would one day find someone who loved him the way Carissa loved Hunter.

"Maybe I should put her to bed."

Ash's words had Heather shifting her gaze from Hayden to him, then she looked down at Isla. Her eyes had closed, and she looked to be asleep.

"I'm going to put Rachel to bed too," Carissa said.

"I'll carry her up for you," Hunter volunteered.

Ash got to his feet, then bent to lift Isla into his arms. Heather stood up as well and followed the other three upstairs to the room where the girls would be staying. Since they'd changed into their pajamas earlier, Hunter and Ash were able to lay them down once Heather and Carissa pulled back the comforter that covered the bed.

Heather turned on the nightlight in the corner of the room that Rachel used whenever she stayed at the house. Neither girl stirred as the four of them left the room.

Once they were out of the room, Heather grabbed Carissa's arm. "Time to go to work!"

Carissa grinned at her as they hurried down the hallway to the stairs. They had stockpiled all the gifts in her dad's office, and they'd wrapped them whenever they could find a few minutes when Rachel wasn't around. Heather had finished wrapping the last of them the night before.

"Where are we going, babe?" Hunter asked as he and Ash trailed behind them.

"It's time for Santa to arrive," Carissa told him. "Want to help carry presents?"

"Do I have to come down the chimney?"

Heather laughed as she pushed open the door to the office. "If we hadn't had a fire tonight, I might have made you put on a Santa costume and pose inside it."

"This is going to take all night," Hunter said when he saw the pile of presents. "Are any of them for me?"

"Mom made me buy presents for you guys too," Heather told him. "So don't worry. You won't have to cry tomorrow morning."

"Good. I'd hate to be reduced to tears while the girls happily open their millions of presents."

"Well, now you get to help carry them." Heather gestured for Ash to join her at the pile. "Here. Hold your arms out."

Ash did as she asked, then she began to stack presents on his outstretched arms, and Carissa did the same thing with Hunter. When their eyes were just barely visible above the gifts, Carissa and Heather grabbed the rope handles of several gift bags, then they all made their way back to the living room.

Their mom was still there with Essie, Hayden, and George, and the trio stopped talking and watched them carry the gifts in. Her mom and Essie got up and helped put the presents under the tree. Once they were in place, the four of them returned to the office for another load.

Heather realized that perhaps they'd gone overboard when she saw how the presents filled the space underneath the large tree and then spilled out around it. She couldn't find it within herself to feel bad about it, though. Most of the presents were for the girls, but there were also presents for all the adults. Considering there would be ten of them opening presents the following day, maybe that wasn't such an excessive amount.

Once the presents were all beneath the tree, she and Carissa turned their attention to the stockings. Conversation continued on behind them while the two of them sorted through the stocking stuffers and began to fill them. These things were more practical, but they'd had fun buying them, regardless.

By the time they were done, her mom, Essie, and George were ready to call it a night. Hayden followed shortly after, leaving Heather, Hunter, Carissa, and Ash in the living room.

The fire had died down to just embers, and with only the soft light from a couple of lamps and the Christmas tree lights, everything was calm and peaceful. Heather tucked her legs up on the couch as she settled into the corner of it.

"It feels weird to be on this side of things," Hunter mused.

"What side is that?" Carissa asked, looking up at him from where she was curled against him.

"The dad side. This used to be Dad's role. He and Mom would bring out all the presents once we were in bed. Now it's us."

Heather nodded. It hadn't really struck her while she'd been buying and wrapping the presents. But now, having set things up for the next morning, it really felt like they'd taken on their dad's role. It was a bittersweet moment.

The previous year, she'd missed her dad's way of making Christmas morning special for them. She'd tried to do what she could for Rachel. This year, however, with two kids to make the day special for, she still missed her dad, but she also felt closer to him. She knew he would have approved of what they'd done for the girls.

"Thank you for what you've done to make this holiday special for Isla," Ash said. "I wouldn't have even known where to start, to be honest. I barely managed to get her a Christmas tree."

Heather reached out to lay her hand on his arm for a moment. "I think Isla would have appreciated anything you did."

"From what she's said, her mom didn't go to any trouble for the holiday, which is probably because of our parents. They didn't put much effort into Christmas for us. Isla said that Donna would buy her a present, so at least she had something."

"I hope you enjoy tomorrow, too," Heather said.

Though her focus had been mainly on making the holiday special for Isla, she hadn't ignored Ash. There were plenty of presents for him under the tree, too. Hunter had helped her with ideas of what he might like. She could only hope that her brother hadn't steered her wrong.

"Just remember to wear your Christmas pajamas when you come downstairs tomorrow morning," Carissa said.

"Is there a fine if we don't?" Hunter asked.

"Not sure about a fine, but I'm sure Heather and I can come up with a punishment of some sort. Like making you actually eat the cookies the girls put out for Santa."

Hunter sighed, then pressed a kiss to the side of Carissa's head. "Fine. I'll wear the pajamas."

A wave of longing swept through Heather as she watched her brother and Carissa. She wanted that. She wanted a man who loved her the way Hunter loved Carissa.

And right then, she wished that man could be Ash.

Chapter 23

Ash looked at the pajamas that he'd laid out on the bed and frowned. He hadn't slept in them, preferring to wear what he wore to bed at home. Now he wasn't sure he wanted to wear them at all.

The top had the picture of an elf along with the words *Santa's Little Helper* on it, and while he'd felt a bit like that the night before, he wasn't sure he wanted to wear pajamas that proclaimed it. And then there were the pants that were going to make his legs look like candy canes. Would Hunter's and Hayden's be the same?

He crossed his arms as he stared at the pajamas, wondering how much trouble he'd get into if he didn't wear them. But then he imagined the disappointed look on Heather's face, and that had him sighing as he picked them up and went into the bathroom to take a quick shower and change. After he was dressed, he sat on the bed to pull on a pair of socks.

"Uncle Ash!" The door to his bedroom flew open, and Isla came running into the room. "We need to go see if Santa came." She flung herself at him, wrapping her arms around his neck. "Merry Christmas."

Ash pressed a kiss to the side of her head. "Merry Christmas, princess."

"Can we go down now?"

"Where's Rachel?" Ash asked as he got to his feet.

"She went to see if her mom was awake."

Ash had a feeling that Carissa and Heather were up already.

"I like your pajamas," Isla said, pointing at the elf. "Do you like mine?"

Ash took in the red, white, and green plaid pajamas that Isla wore that had a reindeer on the front of them. She also had on a pair of red socks and a headband that matched the plaid in the pajamas. "I do. You look beautiful."

She beamed at him. "Thank you! Rachel's are the same. We're twins!"

Ash took her hand and let Isla lead him from the room. Out in the hallway, he didn't hear anyone else, but he could smell food, so he figured that someone must be up. They walked down the stairs, where Rachel greeted them.

"Santa came, Isla," she said. "Come see."

Isla let go of his hand and raced after Rachel toward the living room. As he followed them, Ash hoped they were allowed to be in there.

"He ate some of the cookies and drank the milk," Isla said, awe in her voice. "Look at the presents. Did Santa bring them all?"

Ash entered the room in time to hear Heather say, "Not all of them. Just the ones with the North Pole wrapping paper."

Heather turned to him with a smile. "Merry Christmas, Ash."

"Merry Christmas," he said, noticing that she wore pajamas that also said *Santa's Little Helper* on them. The main difference between them was that the torso of his long-sleeve shirt was green, while hers was red.

"Look!" Rachel said, pointing at the fireplace. "The stockings are all full."

"You can open them if you'd like," Heather told them, heading over to where the stockings hung.

"We don't have to wait for everyone?" Rachel asked.

"Not for the stockings." Heather took down the stockings that had an *R* and an *I* on them. "Here you go."

The girls took the stockings and sat down on the thick carpet in front of the fireplace that already had a fire going in it. Ash settled on the loveseat, which gave him a good view of Isla as she pulled things out of her stocking.

He used his phone to take pictures of her, wanting to remember their first Christmas together. The joy on her face filled him with happiness. He needed nothing for himself that day. As long as Isla kept smiling, that was gift enough for him.

Christmas music once again played softly in the background, and when he glanced out the window beyond the Christmas tree, he could see snow drifting softly down. Usually, he didn't care a whole lot about ambiance, but Ash had to admit that the combination of everything gave him a very cozy, festive feeling.

Hunter and Carissa appeared, followed shortly after by Eliza, all wearing their Christmas pajamas. Christmas greetings were shared as they settled on chairs around the room. Heather retrieved stockings from the mantle and handed them out.

"How do I know this is *my* H and not yours or Hayden's?" Hunter asked when she handed him one.

"Well, Santa gave you two the same things in your stockings, and my H is a different color."

Ash watched as Heather approached him with a stocking. Smiling, she held it out to him.

"Thank you," he said. "You didn't have to do that."

"I didn't." She winked at him. "Santa did."

He couldn't help but smile in return. "Well, thank him for me."

"Thank *you* for wearing the pajamas."

"It was the least I could do. They're surprisingly comfortable."

"Don't forget your stocking, Heather," Carissa said. "Santa would want you to enjoy what he brought you too."

Heather laughed as she went and got the stocking with the red H on it. She settled on the couch next to Ash, lifting her legs to cross them as she peered inside her stocking.

Before he could look into his, Isla was scrambling up in his lap, her hands full of things.

"What have you got there, Princess?" he asked.

"I got stuff for my hair, and a Barbie doll, and some pretty socks."

Ash looked at the stuff she held out to him. "That's amazing."

"It is." She leaned against him for a moment, then slid off his lap to return to where Rachel still sat.

Curiosity got the better of him, and he began to pull things out of his stocking. Some things were wrapped, so he carefully removed the paper. Inside, he found a variety of practical things. A razor and blades. A toothbrush and toothpaste. A small bottle of cologne. A variety of men's skin products. Some socks. All of it from brands he'd never heard of, but that looked expensive.

Between the amazingly comfortable mattress he'd slept on the night before and all these items, he was going to be spoiled when he had to go back to his cheap stuff.

Essie and George appeared a few minutes later, and Heather immediately brought them their stockings as well. The only person who had yet to make an appearance was Hayden. No one mentioned that he wasn't there, but he saw Heather and Hunter exchange looks a couple of times.

Ash found himself relaxing and enjoying the morning. He hadn't been sure he'd get to that point, but there really was no need to be tense or uneasy. The King family had been so warm and welcoming, accepting them into their Christmas traditions and celebrations without hesitation.

Once they had all opened their stockings, Essie told them they had fifteen minutes until it was time for breakfast. Carissa, George, and Eliza went with her while Heather started to clean up the wrapping paper that had been around some items in each stocking.

"I'm going to check on Hayden," Hunter said.

"Make sure he's wearing his pajamas," Heather told him as he walked out of the room.

Ash had a feeling that even though Hunter had worn his pajamas, he wouldn't force his brother to do the same. He got to his feet to help Heather.

"Thank you for all the things you put in our stockings."

Heather smiled at him again. "If you don't like anything, blame Santa. For all the rest, Carissa and I will take the credit."

Ash couldn't help the chuckle that escaped. "I liked all of it."

Rachel and Isla were still talking over what they'd gotten in their stockings. If Isla was this enthused about a stocking, Ash couldn't imagine how she would be with the presents.

Ash held the black garbage bag as Heather stuffed the ripped wrapping paper into it, then they hung the empty stockings back on the fireplace mantle. Soon, the room was back to its original state.

"Why don't you take your stuff up to your room?" Heather told the girls. "You can play with it all again later."

The girls dutifully gathered up their things and went upstairs. When they came back down, everyone went into the dining room. Eliza instructed them on where to sit, and Ash found himself once again with Isla on one side and Heather on the other. They were just settling into their seats when Hunter returned with Hayden trailing behind him, his face drawn in pain as he moved with the help of his crutches.

Eliza went to Hayden and gave him a hug. "Merry Christmas, darling."

"Merry Christmas, Mom."

Surprisingly, even though he didn't wear a smile, he did wear the pajamas like Hunter and Ash had on. He settled onto a chair between his mom and Hunter.

Eliza looked around the table, her gaze lingering on each of them, a smile on her face. "I can't tell you how happy I am that each of you are here. I feel that God has brought us together, and I look forward to spending the rest of the day with all of you. Let's pray."

Ash bowed his head and listened as Eliza prayed, the sincerity of her words striking at his heart. In each of the people at the table, he'd seen that same sincerity. They lived their lives with an openness and joy that Ash envied. Well, except for Hayden, but given his circumstances, that was understandable.

Isla's arrival in his life had brought about some changes in how he approached the world. He definitely had a bigger protective streak than previously. But he also felt like his heart had grown, expanding with the love he felt for Isla.

She'd brought softness and love to his life, and he realized, looking around the table as they ate, that her doing that had prepared him for this. He didn't think he would have been as open to the Kings' presence in his life if she hadn't already touched his heart.

There was a little bit of everything for breakfast. Fruit. Bacon. Sausage. Scrambled eggs. And the most delicious cinnamon rolls he'd ever eaten. Also, the coffee... It was better than anything he'd had before. Maybe there was something to be said for buying more expensive grounds. Not that he was going to do that, but he was definitely going to enjoy the coffee—among other things—while he was there.

Once they were done with breakfast, everyone pitched in to clean up. Eliza had said that there would be no opening presents until the food was put away and the dishes cleaned up.

After everything was done to Essie's satisfaction, they all returned to the living room, the adults settling into seats while the girls took up positions on the floor once again.

"Hunter, do you want to play Santa's little helper?" Heather asked.

Hunter rolled his eyes but got to his feet, abandoning his seat beside Carissa. "Let's go."

"We'll wait for all the presents to be distributed before we open them, okay?" Heather said before handing Hunter the first present.

Ash used his phone to take pictures of Isla and the ever-growing pile of presents in front of her. With every present that Hunter handed her, her eyes got bigger. At one point, she looked over at him with a slightly shocked look on her face.

Sensing that she was getting overwhelmed, Ash went to her. She raised her arms to him, and Ash lifted her up. She clung to him with her face pressed into his neck. He returned to the couch where he'd been sitting and just held her as she took shuddering breaths.

"It's okay, princess," Ash said softly, rubbing her back.

Glancing around, he saw concern on the faces of the people there. Hunter and Heather each stood with a present in their hands, watching them.

"I think she got a little overwhelmed by it all," Ash told them. "This is her first time having a Christmas like this."

Eliza wiped at her eyes and gave him a gentle smile. "She's a special little girl. I'm glad we could do this for her."

By the time they had passed all the presents out, Isla had shifted around so that she could see, but she hadn't returned to her stack of presents yet.

"Can we open now?" Rachel asked, running her hands over the presents in front of her as if trying to figure out which one to open first.

"Yep," Heather said. "Go for it."

"Do you want to go open your presents?" Ash asked Isla.

She nodded, then slid from his lap to join Rachel. After staring at her stack for a couple of moments, Isla reached out and picked up the one closest to her.

Though he had presents of his own, Ash focused on Isla, taking more pictures of her as she opened the gifts Heather and Carissa had bought for her.

"You need to open your presents too," Heather said as she dropped down on the couch beside him.

Ash turned to look at the woman. Her eyes were shining with happiness, and he felt his heart thump in response to the smile she gave him.

"Did you open yours?" he asked.

He felt a little bad that he hadn't bought any presents for them, but he hadn't had a clue what to get them. Anything he could afford for them, they could have bought themselves.

"I did. That picture from Isla was perfect."

"I'm glad you liked it. She had a lot of fun making it."

He watched as Isla opened a present that had her staring. When he realized what it was, he could only stare himself. Even if she wasn't sure what the gift was, he knew. There had been times he'd wished that he could afford a tablet for her, but it had always been way out of his budget.

Getting to her feet, Isla brought the gift to him. "What's this, Uncle Ash?"

Ash lifted her onto his lap and took the box from her. "This is a tablet."

"You can do lots of stuff on it," Heather said. "Even coloring and drawing."

"Maybe you'd be the better one to show her what it does," Ash said, holding the box out to Heather. "I'm afraid my knowledge is limited to my phone."

"Sure." She smiled at him as Isla scooted off his lap to sit between him and Heather.

Ash wanted to protest the expense of the gift, but he wouldn't do it right then. Instead, he listened as Heather explained things about the tablet.

"We bought the same tablet brand as your phone, so you'll be able to download apps for her. Also, we've included a gift card for the app store so you can buy her apps that she might enjoy."

Their generosity overwhelmed Ash. Isla didn't understand the expense of the gift the way he did, but already he could see that it was going to be a favorite item for her.

"You need to open your gifts, man," Hayden murmured from the armchair near Ash. "Everyone else is already done."

After seeing what they'd bought for Isla, Ash was a little worried about what his own pile of gifts might contain. Hunter and Hayden seemed to have ended up with clothing and books. Hopefully, that was all his included as well.

Chapter 24

While Ash tackled his pile of gifts, Heather showed Isla what she could do on the tablet. He had no idea what to expect, but he was sure that it would be more than he'd ever received before in his life.

Thankfully, as he began to make his way through the gifts, he found practical items. The new winter jacket looked to be thick and warm. As did the pair of gloves and knit cap that matched the jacket. The boots he opened next were unexpected and yet something else that he could really use. And whoever had bought them had gotten the size right on.

In addition to all the winter wear, someone had also bought him a pair of brand-name sunglasses and a leather jacket that would look great with the jeans he usually wore. They were both things he never—in a million years—would have purchased for himself.

He might have bought himself a new jacket or new-to-him jacket, since that was practical and necessary. A leather jacket and brand-name sunglasses were not. Still, he knew he'd wear both of them and be thankful.

After that came a couple of pairs of jeans, several T-shirts that felt amazingly soft, a pair of coveralls, and some thick socks. All of it were things he'd use, and even though he still thought it was all too much, he was grateful.

The final gift had him pausing, however, given the size of the box. He glanced at Heather before he began to unwrap the paper with Santas on it. She was watching him with a big smile on her face, which didn't bode well for what he thought might be in the box. She looked far too pleased.

His heart pounded as he worked the paper from the box, and as soon as he saw the name on it, he paused. As his grip tightened on the box, the paper crinkled beneath his fingers.

"This is too much," Ash said as he continued to stare down at the phone. "I mean, thank you. But really, I can't accept this."

"I understand why you feel that way," Eliza said, her voice gentle. "But it brings us joy to share what we have with others. I pray each day that God gives us opportunities to pass on what He's given us. It would be wrong to not share when we have so much. God opens many doors in many ways. You crossing paths with Heather has just allowed us to give a bit more to you and Isla. And being able to do that is a blessing to us as well."

Ash shifted his gaze to stare at the woman, letting her words sink in. She seemed sincere as she spoke. He hadn't thought about what they might get out of the generosity they'd showered on him and Isla.

"Thank you," Ash said, not sure how to refuse the gifts in the light of her words. "I appreciate all you've done for us."

"I hope that we'll continue to see lots of you two, even after the holidays," Eliza said. "You are always welcome in our home."

Looking down at the phone, Ash swallowed against the emotion that filled him. It still all felt like too much, but their acceptance of him and Isla was what meant the most to him.

"You just need to swap out your SIM card," Hunter said. "And the phone should be ready to go."

"Here," Hayden said, holding out his hand. "I can do it if you want."

Ash readily gave him his old phone along with the new one, grateful that he didn't have to figure it out. When it came to technological things, he could squeak by with the limited knowledge he had, especially for things like phones. But Hayden's help was definitely welcome.

He mainly used technology when he worked on the cars in his garage. There was no getting around the advances in how the newer cars were made, so he kept up to date with the machines he needed to use. It was where most of the money he made went, since he wouldn't be able to work on the majority of cars beyond simple oil changes without that technology.

They spent the next little while relaxing in the living room, with Hayden spending the time explaining things about the new phone to Ash. Isla had gone back to where she and Rachel had opened their presents. Together, the girls looked over the things they'd received, clearly happy with everything.

Ash still had a hard time believing what all he and Isla had been given. What surprised him the most was that everything was so well-suited to him. He hadn't had a chance to look over everything Isla had opened, but it looked like her gifts had been well chosen, too.

Something told him that he had Heather to thank for all of that. She was the only one who'd spent enough time with him to know what he might like. Gifts aside, just the idea of her taking the time to think about what he'd like really touched Ash. It made him wish that he'd been able to buy her gifts.

But where Heather had been able to figure out what he could use, Ash didn't know what he could have gotten for her. She'd probably been able to just look at him and see what he needed because of how worn his things were. Because everything she wore was pristine, not to mention expensive, he didn't have the same benefit.

The fact that he couldn't give Heather anywhere near what she'd given him reinforced just how different their lives were. Eliza seemed to feel that he and Isla had some sort of place in her family's life, but that didn't necessarily mean she would want him to date her only daughter.

"Was everything the right size?" Heather asked. "If not, I can go with you to get stuff exchanged."

"I think it will all be fine. Thank you very much for everything."

Heather beamed at him. "You're welcome. This has become one of my favorite Christmases since my dad died. Last year was fun too, since Carissa and Rachel were with us. But this year, it's double the kids and double the fun." She reached over and gave his forearm a light squeeze. "And, of course, you've made it special too."

"I've enjoyed being here, and I think it's clear that Isla has loved it."

"And it's not over yet," Heather said. "Just wait for dinner. You won't be able to move afterward. The turkey isn't the only thing that ends up stuffed on Christmas in this house."

"I can't remember the last time I had a full turkey dinner, so this is going to be memorable."

Heather relaxed back into the couch, crossing her arms and legs. "I hope you plan to stay another night because you're not going to want to go anywhere when the turkey coma kicks in."

"I hadn't planned to..."

"Is the garage open tomorrow?"

Ash shook his head. "I figured I'd spend the day with Isla."

"Then stay here with us," Heather said. "We can go ice skating, or if it's too cold, we can just hang out inside, playing games and watching movies. Isla would have a blast. And hopefully, you would too."

Ash was quite certain that they would, but he wasn't sure that was a good thing. The more he and Isla enjoyed the time they spent with the Kings, the harder it would be for them to go back to their own boring life that pretty much only consisted of work and school.

But because of their dull life, Ash wanted Isla to have experiences that he couldn't give her. She'd smiled and laughed more in the days since they'd met Heather than she had since she'd come to live with Ash. It was as if the worry and sadness she'd carried home from school each day—not to mention the fear and wariness she'd arrived with—had lessened considerably, and he wanted things to stay that way as long as possible.

"Okay. We'll stay," he said.

"Wonderful!"

Ash had a hard time believing that she was really that excited about them staying, though her beaming smile seemed to be genuine.

Hunter got up to add another log on the fire, while Heather turned her attention to the girls. She and Carissa helped them gather up their things, and soon they were heading out of the room. Ash figured he should take his presents up to his room as well, so he carefully stacked everything and carried it upstairs.

As he came down the stairs, he spotted Hunter, and without thinking it through, Ash said, "Can I talk to you?"

Hunter's brows rose, then he nodded. "We can go to my dad's office."

Ash fell in step beside him as they walked down the hallway that led to the room where they'd gotten the presents the night before. He hadn't paid much attention to it then, but now he looked around curiously.

It was a spacious room with a wall of windows, and the other walls were covered in built-in shelves that held tons of books. There was a large desk with an equally large chair behind it, but Hunter ignored that and led the way to a leather couch in front of the windows.

After they were settled on opposite ends of the couch, Hunter said, "You doing okay?"

Ash gave a huff of laughter. "A tad overwhelmed, if I'm honest."

"Honesty is always good," Hunter said with a smile. "I hope that you're overwhelmed in the best possible way."

He considered Hunter's words, then nodded. "Yes. You could say that. I think that's true for Isla, too. Thank you for helping to make this first Christmas without her mom so special."

"Rachel has been quite excited to have someone her age around," Hunter said. "She really likes Isla."

"I'm glad to hear that. Isla has struggled to make friends at her school since she came to live with me. She arrived a few weeks into the school year, and it seemed that all the friendships were formed. There was no room for her in any of them."

Hunter frowned. "I'm sorry to hear that."

"I haven't known how to help her deal with it, to be honest. My first instinct was to knock heads, but I figured that probably wasn't acceptable."

Hunter laughed. "Yeah. I understand that urge. I never realized how protective I could be until Rachel came into my life. I'd do anything to make sure that she was safe and happy."

Ash nodded, glad to know that the other man understood what he was feeling when it came to parenting a little girl. "I want the best for Isla too, which is kind of what I wanted to talk to you about."

"You have a parenting question?" Hunter asked, his brows drawing together. "I'm not sure I have much to offer as yet."

"Not really, though I'm sure you know more than I do at the moment." Ash paused, uncertain how to voice what he needed. "I found out recently that Isla used to attend church regularly. A neighbor used to take care of her when my sister was... incapacitated, and Donna would take her to church with her."

"That's wonderful," Hunter said.

"I want to take her to church since it seems to be something that she wants."

"Is that why you came last week?"

Ash nodded. "I'd like to continue to take her there, especially since she already knows Rachel."

"Rachel seems to really enjoy the children's program, so I'm sure it would be a good place for Isla too."

"I want... I *need* to understand more."

"About the church or about Christianity?"

"Both, I suppose, but more about what it all means." Ash rubbed his hands against his thighs, wishing he knew what to ask to start the conversation.

Thankfully, Hunter didn't seem to need him to ask anything. He started to talk, expanding on what the pastor had talked about at the service. Ash listened, trying to figure out how he could be that important to God.

Why would God care enough about him... a simple mechanic? He didn't have as much trouble believing that God could care about Isla. But him? He'd never been important to anyone. It seemed so far-fetched that with all the wonderful people in the world, God would offer this gift to him.

"He loves you, Ash. He knows you by name, and He *cares* about you. The gift of eternal life is offered to everyone... *everyone*. Including you. We all have worth and value in God's eyes, and He wants us to be with Him in heaven."

Ash looked up from his hands to meet Hunter's gaze. He could see the earnestness of the man's words reflected in his expression. And alongside that was compassion.

"I want that," Ash said, forcing the words past vocal cords that were tight with emotion.

He wasn't sure what was causing the emotion. All he knew was that he'd been presented with a truth he'd never heard before, and he wanted it in his life, for himself. He wanted it to be something that Isla continued to believe. It felt like the most important decision he could make, not just for himself, but for her, too. She would need him to be someone who guided her in her spiritual life, and he couldn't do that if he didn't embrace it for himself.

When Hunter shared how he could accept the gift of eternal life, Ash didn't hesitate to bow his head with the man and pray, confessing his sins and asking God to come into his heart. He had no problem turning his life over to God, willing to do what was necessary to live in such a way to show that God was in his life.

After the prayer, Hunter stood up and pulled him into a tight hug. When he released Ash, he said, "I can't tell you what a gift it's been to be with you as you made this decision in your life. This doesn't mean your life will be perfect, but it does mean you'll never be alone. God will always be with you."

Ash hadn't been looking for a perfect life, but he liked the idea of never being alone. Of being able to pray the way he'd heard the Kings pray. And though it hadn't been the reason he'd decided to become a Christian, Ash couldn't help but think how it was something he'd have in common with the Kings.

He liked that thought.

Chapter 25

Heather went back downstairs after changing out of her pajamas into a pair of black leggings, an oversized Christmas sweater and thick socks. The two girls had stayed in the room, playing with the dolls they'd unwrapped earlier. She headed into the living room, stopping at the entrance when she saw it was empty.

Turning around, she headed to the kitchen. There she found her mom and Essie along with Carissa, but there was no sign of Hunter or Ash. Hayden wasn't there either, but she had a feeling that he'd retreated to the basement. Probably to play some video games or to watch a movie on the large television in the room where he and Hunter were sleeping.

"Do you know where Ash and Hunter are?" she asked as she slid onto a stool at the counter.

"Nope," Carissa said. "I haven't seen them since I came back downstairs."

Heather frowned, wondering where they could have gone. Though she wanted to go look for them, she stayed put, taking the cup of coffee her mom slid across the island to her. Sooner or later, they'd show up because she was pretty sure that they hadn't left the house.

She sipped at her coffee, listening as her mom, Carissa, and Essie talked about the upcoming dinner. They weren't asking her for any advice because her cooking skills were non-existent. Carissa's, on the other, had been approved by Essie, so she could participate in meal preparation.

Heather wasn't bothered by being excluded. But if she ever hoped to move out on her own, she needed to learn how to cook. Hopefully, Essie's classes with her, Ash, and Isla worked out, and she actually learned how to cook at least a few meals. It was more important to her than it ever had been before.

Though her feelings for Ash seemed to be futile, Heather found that she was surprisingly content. The sharp and overwhelming grief that had filled so many previous Christmases had dulled to a gentle ache. An ache that Heather didn't want to go away.

Though she was grateful to be at the point of being able to focus on the happier times with her dad, she never wanted to get beyond missing him. There were still so many milestones ahead where his absence would be acutely felt, starting with Carissa and Hunter's wedding in a few short weeks.

She knew that Carissa would feel a double whammy of grief at that event, since both her parents would be absent. At least Hunter still had their mom, as well as Essie and George. Still, their dad would be as keenly missed as Carissa's parents.

The murmur of male voices interrupted her musings just moments before Hunter and Ash appeared in the doorway of the kitchen. Ash had changed out of his Christmas pajamas into jeans and a long-sleeve T-shirt. Hunter also wore jeans but with a sweater.

Hunter was grinning, and even Ash had a rare smile on his face. Heather watched them over the rim of her mug, trying to ignore the way her heart fluttered at the sight of Ash.

Hunter slung his arm around Ash's shoulders. "Ash came to talk to me a little while ago, and I was so privileged to be able to share the Gospel with him and be at his side when he gave his heart to God."

"Oh, Ash," her mom said as she approached him. "That is such wonderful news."

As she reached out to give him a hug, Hunter lowered his arm. Her mom was small compared to Ash, but Heather knew she was hugging him with all the strength in her body.

Absorbing what Hunter had announced, Heather watched her mom reach up to cup Ash's face in her hands. It was a wonderful revelation that Ash had pursued that conversation with Hunter, and she was so happy for both Ash and Isla.

Her own salvation had come at an early age, so she didn't know what it was like to live her life without the assurance of eternal life. It pleased her to know that Isla would now be raised in a home that gave importance to that.

Heather knew that this would have made her dad so happy. Even as much as he had loved Christmas, he had loved God more. To him, having someone accept Jesus on Christmas Day would have been the most amazing thing ever.

Once her mom let go of Ash, Heather set her mug down and slid off her stool to go to him. His blue gaze landed on her, and a small smile tipped up one side of his mouth.

"I'm so happy for you, Ash," Heather said, crossing her arms to keep from throwing them around him. Her mom could get away with that, but she wasn't sure that she could. "That's such wonderful news."

Ash nodded. "I'm glad that Hunter was willing to answer my questions and explain things to me. I never knew... never imagined..." He gave a shrug. "It's all so new to me."

"You're very brave to ask questions about the things you don't understand. Not everyone would do that."

"Honestly, I might not have, but for two things," Ash said, his brow furrowed. "Most important was Isla. But the other thing that factored into it was knowing that none of you would mock me for not understanding."

"No, we definitely wouldn't do that. This is too important." Heather paused. "Well, not that we would mock anyone for anything."

"Hayden would probably mock us for something," Hunter muttered.

Heather gave a wave of her hand. "He's our brother. That's what you boys do."

A quick grin crossed Ash's face. "I used to wish I'd had a brother, but now I'm kind of glad I never did."

"I don't blame you. The two I have have done their best to gang up on me over the years."

"Only because we love you," Hunter said as he put his arm around her shoulders and pressed a kiss to her head.

"Perhaps you could have loved me a little less," she said as she gently elbowed him in the ribs.

"Ah, but where's the fun in that?"

"You all need to take your sibling love out of the kitchen," Essie said with shooing motions.

"Are you sure you don't need help?" Heather asked, even though she knew what the answer would be.

Essie gave her a look and made more shooing motions. "I know where to find you if I need you."

They left the kitchen and headed back to the living room. The fire had burned down, so Hunter put another log on it, then sat down next to Carissa on the love seat. Heather took the end of the couch closest to the fire, and Ash sat down next to her, which wasn't necessarily a good thing since her stupid feelings liked to read into everything.

They hadn't been there long when the girls appeared, each of them carrying a coloring book, and Isla had the bucket of crayons she'd received as one of her gifts. Isla put the crayons on the coffee table, then crawled up onto the couch between Heather and Ash.

"Want to help me pick a picture to color?" Isla asked as she flipped the book open on her lap.

Heather leaned close. "There are lots of pictures in this one."

"Yeah," Isla said, tilting her head to grin at Heather. "I love it."

As they flipped through the book looking for the perfect picture for her to color, Heather felt her affection for the little girl grow. She hadn't thought a lot about having kids. Though she'd known her parents wanted grandchildren, her dad had encouraged them to focus on their education. In her mind, children would come eventually, but she'd wanted to be settled in her job at the company first.

After her dad's death, grief had kind of squashed any desire for a relationship or having kids. It hadn't been until the previous year when they'd met Rachel and Carissa that she'd begun to think of the future with a family of her own.

Too bad that the first person to make her consider it more seriously was a man who kept his feelings locked down so tightly that she had no idea how he might feel about her.

"I think I'll color this one," Isla said, pointing to the picture of a pony with wings. "Do you like it?"

"I do, and I'll like it even more when you've colored it."

"Do you like this one, Uncle Ash?" Isla asked, leaning against him as she set the book on his lap.

"Yep. What colors are you going to use for the pony?"

"Pink and purple. Maybe yellow."

"I bet it will be beautiful."

Heather had discovered that her new favorite thing was watching Ash interact with Isla. The guy might be reserved in his interactions with people in general, but he was never that way with his niece. And from what she'd heard about Isla's life so far, the little girl deserved someone who made sure that she knew she was loved and cared for.

"Okay. I'm going to color it now." She slid off the couch and went to join Rachel at the coffee table.

"She seems quite artistic," Heather said. "Is that something that runs in your family?"

Ash looked over at her. "Gwen used to enjoy drawing stuff. I was more of a doodler."

"I can't draw at all, though I do enjoy coloring. Those adult coloring books can be good for relaxing."

"Maybe I should get one of those," Ash said. "So when Isla wants me to color with her, I can color something besides unicorns and ponies. Are there ones with cars?"

"I have no idea."

But if there was, she was absolutely going to buy it for him. Too bad he hadn't shared this *before* she'd bought Christmas presents for him. But there was nothing saying that she couldn't buy it for him... just because.

"Thank you for buying her a bunch more things to feed her coloring addition."

Heather laughed. "I can't tell if you're being sarcastic or not."

His mouth quirked up on one side. "I'm not. I think she had limited access to that kind of stuff at Gwen's. If it's something she enjoys, I absolutely don't mind her having excessive amounts of crayons and coloring books."

"You're a good man, Ash. I hope you know that."

A flush crept up his cheeks, and his gaze moved to where Isla knelt coloring. "I try to do my best for her. She also makes it easy. I think I've loved her from the moment I set eyes on her, even if I didn't realize it at first."

"So you believe in love at first sight?" Heather asked.

Hunter coughed, but Heather ignored him.

"Uh... I guess I do. At least in a situation like with Isla."

"I don't know if I believe in love at first sight, since I prefer that a man's actions define them rather than their looks. There are plenty of handsome men wandering around who don't behave admirably."

Ash looked at her as he nodded. "That's what I want to teach Isla. To strive harder to be beautiful inside than outside."

"Sometimes it's hard to look past the outward trappings to see who a person really is." Heather continued to ignore Hunter as she tried in a not-so-subtle way to encourage Ash to look past her wealth to see that she was just like any other woman.

Ash had returned his attention to Isla, his expression as hard to read as ever. She wondered if she really was just barking up the wrong tree. That as much as she longed to be part of their lives, maybe it just wasn't meant to be in the way she wanted.

She knew that she could be the one to make the first move, but she really needed Ash to decide he was willing to look past the differences in their lives and embrace the things they had in common. It wouldn't work if he was just giving in to her, even if he did have feelings for her. He had to want to be with her enough to push everything else aside.

So far, nothing he'd said or done showed that he wanted that.

How long did she wait, her emotions pinging back and forth? One minute, wanting to hang around with Ash and Isla in hopes that he might come around. The next, wanting to distance herself so that she wouldn't get hurt.

The worst part of it all was that beyond what she felt for Ash, she'd grown so attached to Isla—too attached, maybe. And from what she could see, Isla had grown attached to her, too.

Her festive mood started to dim, even as her mom and Hayden joined them in the living room, and conversation picked up. Heather didn't want to be pulled back into the depressed mood that had been since her dad's death. This Christmas was supposed to be a time of joy and love.

"Want to color a picture in my book, Auntie?"

"Sure." Heather moved to sit with the girls, eager for something fun to focus on. "Why don't you choose one for me?"

After a bit of consideration, Rachel gave her a picture of two kids flying a kite. Under the direction of the girls, she picked crayons and began to color, listening as her mom and Carissa discussed the upcoming plans for the wedding.

She was looking forward to it, especially since it wasn't going to be a high-stress event, with only a few close friends and family present. Once upon a time, she'd believed that the best wedding was a huge wedding. But as she'd watched Hunter and Carissa plan their low-key one, she'd changed her mind, deciding that perhaps that would be the sort of wedding she'd like to have, too.

Of course, she had to find a groom first.

When Essie called for them to come help get dinner on the table, everyone jumped in to carry the food from the kitchen to the dining room. It all smelled tantalizing, and it proved to be as delicious as any Essie had ever made. Even Hayden seemed to be enjoying himself. That was such a good thing, and Heather wished it could be that way all the time.

Once the dinner was over, her mom made Essie and George join her in the living room, leaving the rest of them to clear the table, put the food away, and clean everything up.

"Glad Essie finally let us help her," Ash said. "I'm not used to having someone wait on me."

"I get that," Carissa told him. "I had to learn that Essie doesn't do what she does because it's a job or because she gets paid. She does it because she enjoys it. She considers it a labor of love. Just remember that, and you won't feel like she's waiting on you."

"And as you've seen, the kitchen is her domain," Hayden said as he stood at the dishwasher, loading the dishes Hunter placed in front of him. "And she'll let us help when she wants it."

"This is definitely a better meal than we would have had at home," Ash said. "I'm very thankful for everything about the past couple of days."

"You're staying until tomorrow, right?" Hunter asked. "We have an outdoor skating rink. Dad used to have one set up for us every winter when we were younger, and I decided to do it again for the first time in ages."

"Neither of us have skates."

"No worries," Carissa said. "We have a large assortment that should include sizes for you and Isla."

Heather and Carissa had actually bought extra skates when they'd realized Ash and Isla would be there with them, guessing at their sizes.

Ash looked at her, their gazes meeting and holding for a long moment before he turned his attention back to Hunter. "I think Isla would enjoy that."

"I don't know how to skate, Uncle Ash," Isla said, from where she sat at the counter with Rachel. "Do you?"

Ash nodded. "I played hockey when I was in high school."

"So you can teach me?" Isla asked.

"Yep. I can."

"You'll have fun," Rachel told her.

Though she was glad for Isla's sake that they were staying an extra day, Heather wasn't sure it was good for her. But what was one more day in close proximity to Ash? She could always start trying to get over him after Christmas when he and Isla had gone home.

Chapter 26

Ash helped Isla zip up her jacket, then tugged her knit cap down over her hair. He smiled as she did a little dance, glad that the weather was nice enough that they could go skating.

They'd had a substantial breakfast, and now they were in the mudroom at the back of the house getting ready to go to the rink. The two girls were the first ones out the door, with Hunter right behind them, carrying a large box with all the skates. Carissa followed after him.

Heather was still pulling on her boots, and Ash didn't want to just walk out and leave her behind, so he hung around, tugging on his gloves. She was dressed in a pair of fitted jeans and a puffy jacket that ended at her waist. Her hair was braided in a single braid that hung out from under the knit cap she wore.

"You don't have to wait for me," she said, glancing up at him before grabbing her other boot.

"I don't mind." And he really didn't. Whether he should or shouldn't was still up for internal debate.

When she straightened, she looked at him. "Guess it's time to skate."

"Yep. It's been a few years, so I hope I haven't forgotten how."

They stepped out onto the wide back porch, then made their way down the steps to the deck. All of it was cleared of snow, as was the path they walked on, leading them away from the house.

The day was somewhat cloudy, and there was a slight chance of snow, but at least it was warm-ish. The temperature was hovering a bit below freezing, which meant nothing was melting, but they also wouldn't freeze to death on the ice.

The path cut through an opening in a cluster of evergreen trees, leaving Ash feeling that he was stepping out of one part of the world and into another. They left behind the landscaped space of the large backyard for a less structured area. Not too far beyond the trees was the rink.

"Wow," Ash said as they continued along the path. "I wasn't expecting... this."

Heather laughed. "My dad rarely did anything by half-measures. He wanted us to be able to use this any time of the day or night, which is why we have lights out here too."

"That's just amazing. Nothing like the backyard rinks I saw growing up." They'd never had one because their dad had said it was a waste of time and money. And considering he wasn't going to play pro-hockey, nor was Gwen going to be a figure skater, maybe it would have been.

"Hunter set this up to cater to us adults, I think. We definitely aren't kids anymore, impervious to the cold and spending all our time on the ice."

When they reached the rink, Ash saw what she meant. There was a covered section along one side that had a bench inside of it, along with a wood-burning stove.

Hunter had set the box down on the bench, and Carissa and the girls were pulling skates out of it. Heather joined them, taking a set of skates that Carissa held out.

"I think these should fit you," Heather said as she handed the skates to him.

"Thanks." After checking the size, he was pretty sure she was right. "Isla, bring your skates here, and I'll help you put them on."

Isla skipped over to where he sat, a pair of pink and white skates in her hands. Heather came over as well and worked on one of Isla's skates while Ash focused on the other. The two girls chatted while they waited for them to finish.

It didn't take long to get Isla's skates laced up and tied, then Ash took her over to the ice where Hunter stood with Rachel, who was gripping the handles of a skating aid. Hunter helped Isla onto the ice to the other skating aid, and Rachel showed her how to grip the edges and push it along the ice.

Ash watched her for a moment before turning back to deal with his own skates. Heather was still working on her first one, trying to tighten her skates with her nicely manicured nails.

"Here. Let me help you," he offered.

She straightened and looked at him, her brow furrowing a bit. Without waiting for her to respond, he knelt on one knee and tightened the laces of the skate she'd already put on. As he worked, she took off her other boot and slid her foot into the second skate.

He looked up to find her watching him. "Tight enough?"

After wiggling her ankle from side to side, she nodded. He tied it off, then went to work on the other one.

"You're good at that," she said after he tied off the second skate.

"I've had plenty of practice," he told her as he settled onto the bench beside her and went to work on his own. "Used to tie my own skates as well as Gwen's."

"I hadn't been on skates in several years and probably wouldn't have gotten on them now, except Rachel convinced me to."

"And did it all come back to you?" Ash asked as he tightened the laces on his first skate.

"I was a bit wobbly," she said with a laugh. "Hung onto the boards for the first couple of laps around the rink. How long has it been for you?"

Ash did some quick calculations. "Probably over a decade."

"Well, I won't judge you if you're a bit unsteady."

He gave a laugh. "Thanks."

"Lookit me, Uncle Ash!" Isla called from the ice as she slowly moved past where they sat. "I'm skating!"

Ash straightened so he could see her better. "Good job, princess."

Once she had moved on, he quickly finished lacing his second skate. Heather got up and moved to the opening in the boards, where she stepped onto the ice. It wasn't long before she was gliding smoothly after the girls.

Hunter watched her for a moment before he got off the ice and sat down on the bench beside Carissa. She'd gotten as far as putting the skates on but hadn't laced them up yet. He lifted her foot onto his lap and began to work the laces.

"I hope I don't break any bones," she muttered.

"You say that every time, love, and you haven't yet," Hunter said.

"It would be just my luck that with the wedding two weeks away that I'd break my leg or arm."

"I'd still marry you, even if you had to come down the aisle on crutches."

"You'd better," she said with a laugh. "Since you keep convincing me to get up on skates."

Ash watched them for a moment, taking in their interactions with each other. He enjoyed seeing them together. They shared their affection easily, and it made being around them comfortable. And it was clear that Hunter didn't just love Carissa, he also doted on Rachel. Through Hunter, he could see that it was important to be with someone who wanted to provide that sort of environment for a child. Who understood how important it was.

It seemed that the whole King family understood that importance. They were so loving with Rachel, which made sense, since she was basically a member of the family already. What was so impressive was that they also showered that love on Isla.

As Isla came around again, Ash joined her on the ice, taking a few tentative strokes before gaining some confidence. He didn't really want to land on his butt, though he was sure Isla would find it funny. His pride, however, wouldn't be as impressed.

He'd done just one lap around the ice when upbeat Christmas music began to play, spilling out from speakers hidden around the rink. The girls were singing along with the lyrics at the top of their lungs, clearly enjoying themselves.

"Take my hand, Uncle Ash," Isla called out to him.

Ash immediately headed in her direction, taking the hand she held out. She let go of the skating aid with her other hand and almost plopped over on her face. Heather came up behind her and took her other hand. Together, the three of them slowly moved around the rink.

The last three days had been surreal for Ash. Kind of like a vacation—something he hadn't been on in a long time—so he was relishing this break for him and Isla. The peace inside him was new, and he wasn't sure if it was from being with the Kings or from the decision he'd made following his conversation with Hunter. Probably a bit of both.

"I'm so happy!!!" Isla yelled it out at the top of her lungs.

Ash couldn't help but chuckle at her words. He heard Heather laugh and glanced over at her. The smile on Heather's face was filled with joy that was reflected in Ash's heart.

When her gaze met his, Ash felt his heart skip a beat. Stopping to help Heather that night on the highway had changed the trajectory of his and Isla's lives. Was it possible that there was more change to come?

He rarely thought too much about his emotions, but as he skated around the rink with Isla and Heather, Ash embraced the fact that he was happy. Well and truly happy. The joy that bubbled inside him was a foreign feeling, but he never wanted it to go away. And he wanted that for Isla, too.

Heather was a beautiful, intelligent, and sweet woman. Way better than him, that's for sure. But for some reason, his heart had warmed to her even though he'd fought against it. And though he had no idea why, he got the feeling that she was interested in him.

Unfortunately, there was no way to know for sure without putting himself out there. He would need to get over his hang-ups regarding her wealth. He'd gotten to where he could accept that the Kings were different from the recent experiences he'd had with wealthy people.

But what he struggled with the most was the practicality of dating someone who could buy his business several times over without it even making a dent in their bank account. How could he take Heather on a date when all he could afford were chain restaurants? And what sort of gifts could he buy her for things like birthdays and Christmases?

Because of Isla, he couldn't date just for the sake of dating. He had to consider where dating a woman might lead. And as far as he could see, with Heather, it wouldn't lead to anything but heartache when she decided she didn't want to be with a man who owned a struggling garage and couldn't treat her the way she deserved to be treated.

With that thought, the joy he'd felt dimmed. Thankfully, Isla was still enjoying herself, and they stayed out on the ice until it was time for lunch.

Once they were done eating, Ash knew it was time for them to leave. He had to work the next day, so he wanted to do a few things around the house while he had the time.

"Would you like to drop Isla off this week to spend the day with Rachel until school starts again?" Carissa asked after the girls had gone off to pack up Isla's things. "I've taken the week off, so it wouldn't be a problem to have Isla with us."

Ash was tempted because the alternative was for Isla to spend hours in the office at the garage. He glanced at Heather, who was stacking plates from their meal. She didn't say anything, just met his gaze, then turned her attention back to the dirty dishes.

He didn't need her to give her thoughts on Carissa's suggestion, because he was sure she'd tell him to go for it. Isla would also want to spend that time with Rachel.

"I'd have to drop her off around seven-thirty," he said. "Since I open the garage at eight."

"That's fine. I can even give her breakfast."

"I hate to take advantage of you." It felt like they'd done so much for the two of them already.

"You'd be doing me a favor," Carissa said. "Having someone for Rachel to play with would be nice. She won't be as bored, and I'll be able to get more stuff done."

He studied her for a moment, then watched as Heather left the room. The Kings were able to make it appear like he was doing them a favor while they were actually doing one for him. It made it seem like things were more equal between them, even though there was still such inequity in their positions in life.

"If you're sure."

"Oh, I'm very sure. It will be great."

"I know Isla will be happy to spend time with Rachel instead of sitting at the garage."

"And Rachel will enjoy having someone to play with. She gets bored hanging out with just me. Sometimes Heather helps break up that boredom, but usually, it's just her and me."

"Sounds good. I'll bring her by tomorrow morning. I usually close the garage at five, so I wouldn't be back to get her until five-thirty."

"That's fine. Sometimes we come here in the afternoons, so if we do, I'll let you know."

Heather came back into the dining room just as the girls reappeared. Ash had packed his things that morning, so he just had to grab it all—much more stuff than he'd arrived with.

"Do we have to go, Uncle Ash?" Isla asked as she leaned against him. "I like it here."

So did Ash, but he knew they needed to get back to their real life. "You'll see Rachel tomorrow."

Her eyes lit up. "Really?"

"Yep. Instead of hanging out with me at the garage, I'm going to take you to Rachel's house so you can spend the day with her."

"I'm so glad!" Isla danced around, and Rachel joined in, the two of them hugging each other.

Ash smiled, then excused himself to get his things. When he came back downstairs, everyone had gathered in the foyer to say goodbye to them.

"Thank you for everything," Ash said as he stood in front of Eliza. "It's been an amazing Christmas for both Isla and me."

Eliza reached out and gripped his arms, looking up at him from her diminutive height. "I don't want you to think that you were the only one blessed by spending this time together. You and Isla have brought us much joy and love, especially since we had the privilege of being part of you giving your heart to God."

At her urging, he bent so she could kiss his cheek and give him a hug. He couldn't remember the last time his mom had said something like that to him, let alone offered any type of affection.

When he straightened, Eliza gave him a fierce look. "We'll be seeing you again. You're as good as family now."

Ash swallowed hard against the emotion building inside him. Did they really view him and Isla as family? Was it really that easy for them?

"We'll be around."

Hunter shook his hand. "We still need to get together and talk about the proposal."

Ash nodded. "Yep. Let me know when it's convenient for you."

When he turned toward Heather, she gave him a small smile. "Thank you for all you've done for Isla." He cleared his throat. "And for me. I appreciate it more than you'll ever know."

Heather crossed her arms, hugging herself. "I'm glad you could spend Christmas with us. It was very special."

Words flooded into Ash's mind, but he managed to keep them from spilling out of his mouth. Instead, he said, "It was special for us too. I've never had a Christmas like this one, and I'm glad that Isla's first Christmas with me also included all of you. We'll never forget this."

"I'm glad." Another gentle smile. "Don't be a stranger."

He hesitated, then said, "We won't be."

Isla threw her arms around Heather. "I love you."

The woman lowered her hands to run them over Isla's hair. "I love you too."

The exchange punched him in the gut. Heather gave her love to Isla so freely, and Ash couldn't help but wonder if she could love him that way, despite their differences.

It was a question that plagued him as they left the mansion and returned to their much more modest home. Unfortunately, there was no clear answer.

Chapter 27

Though Heather purposely avoided seeing Ash over the next few days, Isla was a different story. Each day, Isla was there with them as she and Carissa did last-minute things for the wedding. But before that event could take place, they had the New Year's Eve party.

"Did Ash say if they were going to come?" Heather asked when Hunter revealed that he'd invited Ash and Isla to the party.

It technically wasn't a party for kids, but the previous year, they'd included Rachel, and it had worked out fine. They had once again reserved a suite in the hotel where the party was taking place. They could take Rachel—and Isla, if she came—to the room, if they needed a break from the festivities.

Hunter shrugged. "It seemed like he was actually considering it."

That surprised Heather, but it also gave her hope—which, unfortunately, was what she'd been trying to kill by keeping her distance from him. "What's he going to do for clothes?"

"I told him I had a suit I could loan him."

"You're not *exactly* the same size," Heather pointed out. Ash had probably an inch in height, and he was a bit wider in the shoulders than Hunter or Hayden. That might not matter in casual clothes, but it absolutely did in a suit.

"I know that." Hunter grinned. "I figured you could help me pick out a suit to pass on to him."

Heather let out a huff of laughter. "Sneaky. So I guess we're going shopping today?"

"Yep. And Carissa is picking out an outfit for Isla."

Did Ash's acceptance of the invitation mean he was coming to accept that the differences in their lives weren't so significant?

She really didn't want to get her hopes up *again*. So far, she'd just been setting herself up for disappointment, and she wasn't terribly keen to experience that yet again. Maybe she should just hang out in the room with the girls and watch movies while eating room service.

"So, did Ash take you up on the proposal?"

"After we made a few changes to it, he agreed," Hunter said. "However, he let me know that he's sort of been... under attack, if you will, by a new garage in the area."

Heather frowned. "Really? In what way?"

"The owner has been coming around, offering Ash's one employee a job. Plus, they've been undercutting his prices. Basically doing what they can to drive him out of business."

"Well, that's horrible." She understood that was the way a lot of businesses operated. Still, her dad had absolutely refused to do that sort of thing.

He'd talked with competitors who were struggling, offering to buy them out if they wanted or go into partnership with them, making sure, either way, that people didn't lose their jobs. He had never aggressively gone after another business.

"I've done a bit of research on the company."

"Do we know them?" Heather asked with a frown, knowing that if they were headquartered in Minnesota, it was likely that they did.

"Yeah." The name he gave made Heather scowl even more. "I plan to pay them a visit to let them know that we're working with Ash now."

"Does Ash know that you're going to talk to them?"

Hunter sighed. "I wasn't sure if that would be a good idea."

"You've got to be honest with him," Heather said. "If Ash feels that you don't think he can fight his own battles, this partnership won't succeed."

"It's not that I don't think he could. I just don't feel that the playing field is even between them."

Heather laughed. "The playing field isn't even between you and Keith Harrington either."

"Maybe not," Hunter agreed. "But we're closer to being even than Keith and Ash are. I feel like Ash's business is kind of hanging on by a thread. He's a smart man, and I think he'd be even more successful if he'd taken some business courses. He had good questions for me and even made a few suggestions."

"So you're definitely going to work with him?"

"Yep. And I'm looking forward to it. I already have some people in mind to start things off."

"People from work who want a career change?"

Hunter shook his head. "No. Although if that was the case with anyone, I would support them. There are a couple people at work I've spoken to who have relatives who might be interested in what we're hoping to do."

"Maybe introduce them to Ash at the party," she suggested.

"If they're there, I will."

"In the meantime, let's go shopping." They still weren't going to get a perfect fit on a suit, but at least anything they got would fit better than one of Hunter's suits.

~ * ~

Ash tugged at the sleeves of the suit coat. It surprised him how well it fit, considering he and Hunter weren't exactly the same size. He tried to remember the last time he'd worn a suit and came up with... never. There'd just been no reason for him to wear one.

Isla had been spinning around in her fancy dress ever since he'd helped her put it on earlier. Thankfully, all he'd had to do with her hair was brush it straight and put the headband on. He wasn't sure how she was going to last the night, but Hunter had assured him they had a room at the hotel where they could take the girls if they got tired.

He was still convinced that he'd temporarily lost his mind when he'd told Hunter he'd attend the party. Part of the blame belonged to Isla. Rachel had told her all about the party since she'd attended the previous year and planned to go again that year. That meant that Isla had begged and begged to go as well.

Ash hadn't planned to ask for an invitation to the party just to appease Isla. However, when Hunter asked him if they'd like to go, Ash had known he was going to say yes.

"Heather's gonna be there too, right?" Isla asked as she spun around again.

"Yes, she is." It felt like forever since he'd last seen her, and he felt a bit parched for the sight of her. He'd never felt like that for someone before.

He'd missed her, but since she hadn't come around, it seemed that she hadn't missed him. It made him think that she'd only been coming around because of Isla. Had he misinterpreted her interactions with him? It wouldn't surprise him if he had. After all, he'd had a hard time believing she'd ever be interested in him. Guess he'd been right.

Pushing aside those thoughts, Ash smoothed his hand down his tie and stared at himself in Isla's full-length mirror. Maybe he should have gotten a haircut.

Too late for that now, though. Ash resisted the urge to run his fingers through it since he'd taken a little extra time after washing it to put some product in the curls so that they didn't look quite so out of control. He usually wore a ball cap to keep it contained, but he was pretty sure that wouldn't fly at this sort of party.

"Let's go so I can see Heather and Rachel," Isla said, tugging on his hand.

Turning from the mirror, he smiled down at her. "Okay then. Let's get our jackets on."

Isla skipped out of her room and down the short hall to the living room. The coat Isla chose out of the front closet was one that Rachel had passed on to her. It was a black wool coat that was long enough to cover her dress and had two rows of large silver buttons down the front.

Hunter had brought a long coat for him along with the suit because Ash's more casual jacket wouldn't look quite right, apparently. He pulled it on along with gloves in deference to the cold that had settled over the Twin Cities in the past couple of days. They'd had a stretch of five days following Christmas when the weather had been beautiful. Mild with no snow. That had ended overnight a couple of nights ago when the temperatures had plummeted because of a cold front moving in from Canada.

Ash looked out the front window, checking to see if the car Hunter had said he'd send for them had arrived yet. He'd protested the luxury, but Hunter had insisted.

When the car pulled up, he was glad to see that it wasn't an actual limo, though he was sure that Isla would have been delighted with that.

"Time to go," Ash said as he opened the door.

Isla skipped out onto the small porch, then stopped to wait while he locked up the house. Before long, they were seated in the car and on their way to the party.

Isla chattered non-stop the entire way to the hotel, which Ash didn't mind because it sort of helped to keep his mind off his worries about how the evening would go. Though he'd been aware from the moment he accepted Hunter's invitation that he was going to be out of his depth, he'd managed to ignore the thought until that day. Now it wouldn't leave him alone.

Once the car deposited them at the entrance to the hotel, Ash took Isla's hand and led her inside, where people waited to direct them to the ballroom where the party was taking place.

"Isla!" Rachel came flying over to meet them as they stepped into the ballroom. Her dress was similar to the one Isla wore, and the two looked adorable as they hugged.

Hunter and Carissa followed behind Rachel and greeted him with smiles. Ash tried to keep from looking for Heather, but that seemed a nearly impossible effort.

"Glad the two of you could make it," Carissa said. "Isla looks so cute, and you look very dapper."

"Thanks to Hunter," Ash said, not afraid to give that credit to him. "This is definitely not my normal style."

"Honestly, it's not mine either." Hunter looked down at himself. "I'd rather never have to wear a suit."

"The only suit I care about you wearing is the one we've decided on for the wedding."

Hunter grinned. "I guess if I have to."

Carissa leaned into Hunter as he slid his arm around her.

"Well, come join us at our table," Hunter said, then the pair turned and led the way through the room to one that sat near tall windows off to the side.

The table was set with ten places on a black tablecloth. There was a centerpiece with white and silver candles and roses in a tall vase on a small silver cloth. It was all very elegant looking, reinforcing the feeling that this wasn't where he belonged.

"Heather!" Rachel and Isla called her name in unison.

Ash turned to see Heather coming toward them with her mom, Essie, and George. She wore a form-fitting dark blue dress with a wide neckline, long sleeves, and a full skirt. It reminded him of pictures he'd seen of actresses from years gone by. Her hair was up, and long, sparkly earrings dangled from her ears. She looked elegant and refined, as did her mom.

The only person missing—unsurprisingly—was Hayden. Ash wished he was there, as he really enjoyed the interactions he had with the man. Though he never voluntarily spoke about his pain, it colored many of his actions and reactions, but Ash had nothing but admiration for the man.

"Ash, I'm so glad you could make it," Eliza said as she approached him, opening her arms to give him a hug.

A light cloud of perfume enveloped Ash as she held him close. "Thank you for inviting us."

She stepped back and smiled up at him. "You're like family. Of course, you should be here."

Ash let the words wash over him as she turned to hug Isla. Unlike her mom, Heather's greeting was a bit more reserved. Though she smiled at him, she didn't approach him like she had before. He felt like he'd lost something precious, and he didn't know how or why. Or if he could get it back.

"We're going to make the rounds," Hunter said. "Can you keep an eye on Rachel?"

As he watched Hunter and Carissa walk away, Ash was glad he didn't have to go with them.

"Let's sit down," Essie said, setting a hand on each of the girls' shoulders.

Naturally, they wanted to sit beside each other, so Ash waited until they were settled before taking the chair next to Isla. There were ten seats at the table, but the Kings, plus he and Isla, only added up to nine. Did Heather have a date that hadn't shown up yet? And oh, did that idea make his stomach feel sick.

She settled down across the table, and it was George who took the seat beside Ash. The older man struck up a conversation with him about one of the Kings' cars that he wanted some work done on it.

They continued to talk about cars while the girls chatted with each other and Essie. People periodically stopped by to talk to Heather, greeting the rest of them with a smile. Ash regarded them with curiosity since he'd been expecting a much more obvious show of wealth from the people there.

"Who is this party for exactly?" Ash asked George. When Hunter had invited him, Ash had assumed it was for friends and business associates of the King family.

George glanced at the guests milling around the room, some standing in small groups talking. "This is for all the employees who work locally."

"All the employees?"

"Yep. From the managers who work directly with Hunter and Heather all the way to the people who clean the offices after hours."

Huh. Ash looked at the people there with new eyes, seeing several men who looked about as comfortable in their suits as he did in his, tugging at the necks of their dress shirts.

"It looks like people enjoy being here."

"Yep. Along with the Christmas party for the children, it's a much-anticipated event."

Something relaxed inside Ash as he realized that he wasn't as out of place as he'd imagined he would be. Now, if he could just figure out how to talk to Heather.

A short time later, someone spoke into a microphone, encouraging people to find their seats. Carissa returned to the table while Hunter and Eliza climbed onto the small platform on one side of the room where the DJ was set up. Eliza spoke first and welcomed people to the evening, thanking them for coming, then Hunter took the mic, adding his greeting to his mom's before he said a prayer for the meal.

Once Eliza and Hunter joined them at the table, servers dressed in white shirts and black pants flooded into the room with large trays holding plates of food. Ash would have thought they'd serve their table first, but they were actually among the last to get their first course.

The wait was definitely worth it as the soup was tasty. Ash didn't remember ever eating a meal with more than a main course and a dessert. This multi-course meal was yet another new experience. And what a time to experience it, as each of the courses was delicious. Isla's eyes got bigger as each course arrived, and several times, she looked at Ash after they set food in front of her as if to ask his permission to eat it.

Music played in the background during the meal, just enough to keep the room from being echo-y. After dessert and coffee, the music increased a bit in volume, and people began to wander out onto the empty space in the center of the room to dance.

Heather took Isla and Rachel out onto the dancefloor, but no one else at their table moved. Ash watched Heather smile at the girls as they kept to the edge of the floor closest to their table. Once again, Isla was experiencing something new that brought a smile to her face. He didn't think he'd ever tire of seeing that.

By the time she came back to the table, he could see that she was tiring a bit. She crawled up into his lap, resting against his chest as he wrapped his arms around her. He wondered if maybe they should head home, even though it was still a couple of hours until midnight.

"I can take the girls up to the suite," Heather said.

"Would you like to go upstairs, Rachel?" Carissa asked her daughter.

"We can watch a movie?"

"Yep. And you can change into the special pajamas we brought."

Heather got up, and Rachel slid off her seat. Ash went to set Isla on her feet to go with Rachel, but she hung on to him.

"Guess I'm coming too," Ash said as he got up with her in his arms.

The four of them left the ballroom, the music and murmur of conversation fading away as they headed for the elevator. Rachel pressed the button to call it. Then, once they were inside the elevator, Isla leaned away from Ash so that she could press the button for the floor they were headed to.

After climbing quite a few floors, they stepped out of the elevator. Heather led the way along a thickly carpeted hallway to a door with a gold number on it. She fished a keycard from a hidden pocket in her full skirt and swiped it over the lock on the door, then pushed it open.

Ash looked around as he carried Isla into the room. He didn't know why he continually underestimated things when the Kings arranged them. Instead of a hotel room with a queen-size bed, a small table off to the side, and a television sitting on a dresser, they walked into a room that looked like it belonged in the Kings' home.

Isla squirmed in his arms, so Ash bent to set her on her feet. She hurried over to join Rachel, who was looking through a bag on the coffee table.

Ash turned his attention to Heather, their gazes meeting for a moment. There was an ocean of words pressing against his vocal cords, but he didn't know how to let them out. But he knew if he wanted to have a chance with this wonderful woman, he needed to get his thoughts sorted out and verbalize them.

Chapter 28

Heather looked away from Ash and went to where the girls were. She helped them pull out the pajamas that Carissa had picked out for them to change into if they wanted to. Even though Rachel hadn't needed the suite the previous year, they thought it was more likely that the girls would want to hang out together that night.

"These are beautiful!" Isla said as Heather held out the pair they'd gotten for her.

Both pajamas were the one-piece style and made of soft, fluffy material. They had hoods with iridescent unicorn horns on them. Isla's pajamas were pink, and Rachel's were purple.

"Why don't you get changed into them?" Heather suggested. "Then we can put on a movie for you to watch."

They'd come by the suite earlier and left their coats, and while they'd been there, Rachel had done some exploring. Because she knew where stuff was, she led Isla through the door to the bedroom.

"I'd better go help them with their zippers." Picking up the bag, Heather took a couple of steps, then glanced back at Ash. "I'll stay with the girls. You can go back down if you'd like."

"Actually, I think I'd rather hang out up here."

Heather nodded, not really that surprised by his response. "I'll be back in a couple of minutes."

She found the girls in the bedroom and quickly helped them get out of their dresses. It didn't take them too long to take off their tights and pull on their pajamas. Isla was so thrilled that she ran out to show Ash as soon as Heather had zipped her up.

Heather found the fuzzy socks that Rachel had picked out for them and handed them to the girls. The room was a bit on the cool side, so she thought they'd enjoy being cozy while watching the movie.

"You look beautiful, princess," Ash said as he knelt on one knee in front of Isla. "I bet you're nice and warm."

She hugged herself. "Yes, I am!"

"Let's get the movie started," Heather said.

"We're gonna watch in the bedroom," Rachel told Isla. "On the big bed."

The girls skipped back into the bedroom, with Heather following more slowly. Hunter and Rachel had figured out what movie they wanted to watch, and he'd set it up on his laptop, which he'd hooked up to the large television on the wall opposite the bed.

It didn't take long for Heather to get the movie started. The girls propped themselves up against pillows next to each other in the middle of the bed, anticipation on their faces.

Heather looked over and saw that Ash had joined them. He'd removed his suit coat and now leaned against the doorjamb with his arms crossed. They might have put him in a gorgeous suit, but there was no hiding the rugged appeal of the man. Even though she knew she shouldn't have feelings about it one way or another, she was glad he hadn't gotten a haircut.

Five days of not seeing him had done absolutely *nothing* to help her get over her growing feelings for him. Though honestly, she hadn't really expected that to be the case. Maybe in the new year, she'd be able to gain the distance she needed in order to let her feelings settle into those of a friend rather than something more.

"You don't have to stay in here with us, Auntie," Rachel said. "We'll be fine."

A corner of Ash's mouth tipped up at Rachel's words, making butterflies come to life in Heather's stomach. That reaction made her not want to go out into the suite's living room to hang with Ash. It was too bad he hadn't gone back down. Though honestly, it didn't surprise her he hadn't wanted to.

Ash disappeared from the doorway, and Heather let out a sigh before she followed him, resolved to spending the next hour or so with him. She couldn't exactly kick him out of the suite. Her mom had taught her better than that.

In the living room, Ash stood at the floor-to-ceiling windows that ran along one wall, his hands in his pockets. She took a deep breath, then walked over to the windows, coming to a stop an arm's length away from him.

"I don't think I've ever seen the city from this height." Ash glanced over at her. "It's beautiful."

Heather looked out at the lights spread out below them. The tableau was even more impressive because of the addition of the Christmas lights that so many homes and buildings still had on them.

"There will probably be some fireworks as we get closer to midnight," Heather said.

He turned to face her more fully for a moment. "I bet Isla would love to see that. I'm not sure if she's ever seen fireworks."

"Hopefully, there will be some displays on this side of the building."

"Do you have to be back downstairs at midnight?" Ash asked.

"No. I told Hunter and Carissa I'd stay up here with the girls unless they asked specifically to be downstairs for the countdown."

"Will they be upset if I'm not there?"

Heather shook her head. "Not at all."

They stood looking out the window for a couple of minutes before Ash said, "I would have thought you'd have a date for the evening."

"Really? Why?"

He shrugged. "It just seems like the sort of event one would bring a date to."

"I would never bring someone I wasn't serious about to something like this."

"I guess I'm just surprised you don't have someone like that in your life."

Heather wanted to talk about her dating failures about as much as she wanted a root canal. But, just like a dental procedure, sometimes it happened anyway. "I haven't had the best of luck finding guys who weren't focused on my money."

"There aren't any rich guys around?"

"There are, and I've even dated a couple," Heather said. "But equal wealth isn't exactly the top quality I'm looking for in a boyfriend."

"Getting beyond the idea of how rich you are is probably a challenge for a lot of guys."

"It's not that I don't understand that. I get that to a lot of the world, the wealth my family has means we're very out of touch with the struggles of the average person." Heather wrapped her arms across her waist. "I'd be stupid to say that our wealth hasn't made our lives easier. We don't have to worry about paying our bills or how we're going to put food on the table."

"Yes. That's a struggle for a lot of people," Ash agreed.

Heather stared at the city lights, their definition blurring. "But what people don't see is that there are still things that money can't protect us from. Money didn't save my dad, and it certainly hasn't eased the grief we've felt over the past five years without him. We didn't even get a chance to throw a bunch of money at the hospital to get the best care possible for my dad. And with Hayden, even being able to buy the best care possible for him hasn't meant he hasn't been in physical pain, never mind the mental pain."

She turned to look at him. "Don't you think that we would have given up all our wealth if it meant we could have kept our dad with us or spared Hayden the pain he's had to endure? Sometimes having wealth makes dealing with that kind of stuff more difficult because, in those moments, you learn exactly how little your money protects you from the worst pain in life. The loss of a loved one."

"Death is the great equalizer, I suppose." Ash cleared his throat. "I know part of my struggle with it all is just not believing that you look at my life... at me... and don't see inferiority."

"What?" Heather frowned at him. "We would never view you as inferior. You're an amazing man, and I'm not the only one who thinks that. I know you've heard us talk about our dad and his mother. Dad would absolutely reprimand us for thinking that someone who worked hard for a living was inferior to us."

"I know. Hunter's explained that to me. None of you have ever made me feel that way. It's my own issues that keep getting in the way. You do realize that not all rich people are like you, though, right?"

Heather sighed. "Yeah. I know. It's why it's been difficult to build friendships, never mind relationships, with our peers, if you will. I'm so glad that Carissa came into our lives. She's become the friend I always wanted and never had."

"I had friends in high school and some in the years after. But when my dad sold me the business, I ended up working so many hours that I didn't have the time or the desire, honestly, to spend my evenings drinking at a bar. Friends all kind of faded away."

"Well, I think you could count Hayden and Hunter as friends now. I know they view you that way."

Ash nodded and looked back out the window. "I never imagined finding myself with people like all of you in my life. I can't figure out what I did to deserve it."

"I choose to look at it more as God blessing us," Heather said.

From talking to Hunter over the past week, she knew that he'd had conversations with Ash about all this. There really wasn't much more to say. Either Ash could accept the differences in their lives and have a good relationship with them—in whatever form that might take. Or their wealth could always be the thing that stood in the way of them being able to forge a genuine friendship with him.

"I missed you this past week."

Ash's gruffly spoken words sucked the air out of Heather's lung for a moment. "Me? You missed *me*?"

"Yeah. I mean, Isla saw you every day, so I heard plenty about you." He shifted his weight and stared out the window. "But I kinda missed talking to you myself."

The love she'd been trying to kill off blazed alongside renewed hope at his confession. "I've missed you too."

"I thought maybe you preferred Isla's company to mine," he said. "Not that I'd blame you. She's amazing."

"Yes. She is," Heather agreed, trying to keep a huge smile from taking over her face. She still wasn't one hundred percent sure where this was going. He'd just said he didn't have friends, so maybe that's what he missed about her. "But as I said earlier, so are you."

He laid a hand that had some stains on it over his heart. "It scares me."

"What scares you?" She wasn't going to assume *anything* when it came to this man of few words.

"The thought of letting you become important to me. If I screw stuff up—because that almost feels like a guarantee—Isla and I will lose something incredible."

"*I* become important?" Heather asked. "Or my family?"

"All of you are already important to Isla and me." Ash lifted a finger and ran it around the inside of his collar as if it was choking him, though he met her gaze. "But I meant you."

"Well, if it helps any, you are already important to me."

His brow furrowed. "So why haven't I seen you this week?"

Though she had an overwhelming urge to brush off his question, Heather decided to be honest. "Because I'd convinced myself that I needed to get over my feelings for you. It seemed like you weren't interested in anything but friendship with me."

"Oh." His frown didn't ease at her words. "And did you?"

"Did I what?"

"Did you get over your feelings?"

"Nope. And up until a few minutes ago, I wasn't happy about that, I'll be honest."

Ash ran his hand over his mouth, scratching at his scuff. "Do you believe that... uh... love would be enough to make things work?"

"Not if the people involved aren't devoted to doing the hard work."

"Hard work?"

"Being understanding of each other's differences. Talking through issues before they get out of control. Spending quality time together even when schedules are busy."

"And if the couple are very different and from very different worlds?"

Heather wished she could give Ash the assurances he seemed to need, but it wasn't possible. He wasn't wrong to be concerned about their differences. At the end of the day, only he could determine how much work he'd be willing to put into a relationship. He could likely find a woman better suited to his lifestyle, probably making a relationship easier.

She didn't want him to find someone else, but she also didn't want him to go into a relationship with her filled with doubts about it. If he didn't have confidence in his ability to do the work, it was better that they find out now.

The thing was, she was quite certain that if he decided to pursue a relationship, he'd commit to it. From almost the moment they'd met, she'd seen that he wasn't a man to take his commitments lightly. In the time she'd known him, he'd been willing to step outside his comfort zone several times for Isla's sake.

"Differences can make things challenging, but not impossible. Again, it all depends on if you feel the relationship is worth the work."

Ash nodded, seeming to consider her words as he kept his gaze on her. "I can't give up my garage."

Though she was glad that they were now getting more personal, Heather frowned at him. "I'd never ask you to. Carissa has continued to work her job at the restaurant where she's a server. And after she and Hunter are married, she plans to go back to nursing school. Hunter only wants her to be happy. And he's learned—we've all learned—that we can't be the ones to determine what makes another person happy."

"You don't care that my garage isn't hugely successful?" He held up his hands. "That these will probably always be a little dirty and not nicely manicured?"

Heather reached her hands out, threading her fingers through his as she gazed into his beautiful blue eyes. "Those are not the things about you that matter to me. But they are a part of who you are, so I accept them."

She saw the moment when he understood what that meant for him and what it needed to mean for her.

"Just like I need to accept that your wealth is a part of who you are."

She gave him a rueful smile. "I'm afraid so."

"If we uh... date, will you let me pay, and will you be disappointed if they're not fancy events?"

"I would want our dates to be things we both enjoy. We just need to talk about these things, Ash. Never stop talking to me."

A corner of Ash's mouth tipped up as he gently squeezed her fingers. "I'm not sure if you've noticed, but I'm not a real chatterbox."

Heather laughed. "I *have* noticed that. But as long as you're talking to me about the important stuff, I won't expect you to make endless amounts of small talk."

Ash lowered their joined hands and tugged her a little closer, making her tip her head back to look into his eyes. His expression was serious as he regarded her.

"Always be upfront about stuff with me. I'm not great at picking up on subtle things. If I've done something... if you're upset with me about something... just tell me. I never want to hurt you, but if I do, you need to let me know."

"I can do that." If she could ask him to talk to her when that might go against his nature, she would do her best to be upfront about things when that wasn't always something she did well.

Ash pulled her close, wrapping his arms around her. Heather sank against him, resting her cheek on his chest. She inhaled his scent, which she recognized as the cologne she'd given him at Christmas. Lacking was the smell of the garage that he sometimes carried with him.

"Will your family be okay with us dating?" Ash asked, his voice rumbling in his chest beneath her cheek.

"Yes," Heather said without lifting her head. "They all think you're a good man."

"Have you known me long enough to be able to say that for sure?"

Heather moved back enough so she could look at him again. "Our first interaction was you helping me when you didn't have to. And the fact that Isla loves and trusts you goes a long way toward supporting my belief that yes, you're a good man."

"Having Isla in my life has made me want to be a better man," he said. "You make me want to be better, too. And I want to learn more about God and how that fits into my life."

Heather was glad to hear that because she knew it would only benefit him and Isla. And of course, it would benefit them as a couple too. She had a feeling that Hunter would take Ash under his wing and be a spiritual mentor for him.

"I pray that God uses each of us to make the other a better person." Ash could give her a perspective on life that she'd never had before, and she knew that would be good for her.

They stood in silence for a few minutes, with only the muffled sound of the movie in the background, then Ash led her over to the couch that faced the window.

Ash sat down on one end of the couch, drawing her down beside him. She wished she'd packed some clothes to change into, but she did her best to get comfortable in her dress, pulling her legs up and tucking the full skirt around them. For his part, Ash had loosened his tie and undone the top button of his shirt.

For the next hour, as they sat holding hands, Ash haltingly shared about his growing-up years and his relationship with his sister and parents, which had led to him gaining custody of Isla. In turn, Heather told him about when they'd heard the news of her dad's death and how they'd tried to carry on in those dark days, stepping into roles they hadn't anticipated being in without his guidance for years to come.

Even in that short conversation, she learned so much about what had molded Ash into the man he'd become. It was encouraging to see that he was choosing to move beyond the examples he'd grown up with in order to provide Isla with the love and nurturing she needed.

"You're such a good dad," she told him. "I admire that about you."

"I never really thought much about having kids, but now I can't imagine my life without Isla." He paused then said, "I hope she'll want to call me dad someday."

Heather squeezed his hand. "I think if you asked her if she'd like to call you dad, she would absolutely want that. Are you going to adopt her?"

"Yep. As soon as I can get it all sorted out, I want her to be legally mine."

"Auntie, the movie's done," Rachel announced as she and Isla came out of the bedroom.

"Wow." Isla drifted toward the window and stood close to the glass, looking out at the lights. "That's so pretty."

"It's like we're on a cloud," Rachel said as she joined her. "Looking down on the world."

Ash found the remote for the television and turned it on, looking for a channel with some New Year's Eve programming. There were only about ten minutes left until the ball dropped to usher in a new year.

"Did you want to stay up here?" she asked Ash as they watched the girls.

"Yes, I think so," Ash said. "Unless you'd rather go back down."

She shook her head. "I'd prefer to stay here with you and the girls."

With that decided, she got up to find her purse. After pulling her phone out, she sent a quick text to Hunter to let him know that they'd be staying in the room with the girls. He sent back a thumbs up.

"What's that?" Isla asked as a flash lit up the sky.

Ash stood up, and they joined the girls by the window. The girls bounced on their toes as they watched the spectacular display, oohing and ahhing over the colorful explosions. Behind them, the announcers on the television began hyping people up for the countdown in just a couple of minutes.

When Ash put his arm around her shoulder as they stood behind the girls, Heather leaned into him, feeling a sense of peace and anticipation fill her. She thanked God for bringing her and Ash to this point, even though she'd had some doubts and had gotten to where she'd accepted that nothing would happen between them.

It was a good reminder that while she might have thoughts on how things should unfold, God might have a different path for her to walk to reach the destination she wanted. Though she might have wished they could have started dating almost right away, they'd still ended up on the same page. She was definitely going to embrace the *better late than never* motto for their journey so far.

"Ten, nine, eight." The voice of the commentator grabbed her attention.

As the count neared one, the fireworks display went crazy, and the girls squealed in excitement. When it hit one, Heather looked at Ash and saw that he was smiling down at her. The affection on his face made her feel like her heart would burst.

But instead of giving voice to those feelings just yet, she said, "Happy New Year, Ash."

"Happy New Year." He bent his head and brushed a kiss on her cheek. "I can't wait to see what this year holds."

"Me too."

"Happy New Year, Auntie!" Rachel turned to give her a hug while Isla hugged Ash.

"Should we go downstairs so we can tell the others Happy New Year?"

Rachel nodded, then ran to the bag to pull out two pairs of fluffy slippers. "Isla, come put these on so our socks don't get dirty."

Isla seemed a bit confused by the idea of going downstairs in her pajamas, but Ash assured her that it was fine. Once the girls had their slippers on, they left the room. Heather was excited about sharing her news with her family because she knew they'd be happy for her and Ash.

Epilogue

Ash looked around the room, searching for Carissa or Heather to see what they wanted him to do next. He had arrived at the church just before five to help set up for the wedding and to be there for the rehearsal.

Carissa and Hunter—at Rachel's request—had asked if Isla could be a flower girl. They'd gotten their hands on a matching dress to Rachel's, and Isla was over the moon.

The chairs had all been set up in the rows as directed by Hunter. They were having less than fifty people, which seemed like a very small wedding for people in the Kings' sphere. The room they were setting up was a small hall with large arched windows that looked out over the snowy landscape beside the church.

"We need to put these over each of the chairs," Heather said as she approached him with a smile and an armful of navy fabric in her arms.

Ash couldn't stop himself from moving closer to her. She was like a magnet to him these days, but he wasn't complaining. And she wasn't either. "Over the chairs? What's wrong with how they are?"

She lifted one and held it up. "The chairs are the wrong color."

Heather draped the cover over a nearby chair, then stepped closer to him. She slid an arm around him to rest her hand on his back and her head on his chest. "You'll have it all figured out by the end of the wedding."

He smiled... something he'd done a lot of over the past week. "I don't suppose it matters much if I do figure it out. I'll probably forget it in a week, since it's not information I'll need very often."

"True," she said with a laugh.

As she leaned against him, Ash reveled in her closeness. Since he hadn't been raised in a home with free-flowing physical affection, he was soaking up everything that Isla and Heather offered him. And he'd been trying to be better about initiating it himself, thinking that if it was something they gave him, perhaps it was what they also wanted to receive.

Ash ran his hand up and down Heather's back, enjoying the brief interlude, since he knew it was going to end all too soon. But despite being tired from having worked a full day at the garage, there was nowhere else he'd rather be.

The past week had been different from any he'd ever had before, though it felt a bit like the time following Isla's arrival. Both had brought changes he hadn't known he needed, but he was definitely on board with. He'd chosen to focus on Heather without allowing her wealth to influence how he perceived her. Because of that, he'd been able to see more clearly who she truly was.

From the start, she'd tried to show him that, but his view of her had been clouded so often by his inability to see past her wealth. Everything she'd done, he'd questioned her motives because he couldn't believe that a rich woman like her would actually want to be with someone like him.

But over the past week, he'd seen her joyful with laughter and sad with grief. Genuine emotions that hadn't been brought about by anything connected to her money. Ash was just happy that he'd been a part of those moments because it had caused the feelings he had for her to grow even stronger, sending roots deep into his heart.

He'd never felt about a woman the way he felt about Heather, and Ash prayed that the feelings he had for her never dimmed but only grew stronger as time passed.

"Okay. Back to work," Heather said as she gave a light tap to his chest, then went up on her toes to brush a kiss across his cheek. "These chairs aren't going to cover themselves."

They worked together to slip the covers over each of the chairs. Ash did the cover, then Heather put a stretchy sage green fabric that had a silver ring gathering it together in a shape of a bow around the upper part of the chair.

"Everything going okay?" Hunter asked as he clapped Ash on his shoulder.

"You tell me." Ash gestured to the chairs. "I don't have a clue."

Hunter laughed. "I have no clue either, man. I'm just doing what they tell me."

"Sounds like a good plan for married life."

"I would have to agree with you." Hunter's gaze went to where Carissa and Heather had set out some boxes on the table they'd been using to organize the decorations. "Guess we'd better see what they need done next."

Next was apparently lacing tiny lights through the arch that stood in front of the large windows. After that, Heather and Carissa wove strands of dark blue and burgundy ribbon, along with some greenery.

They'd just finished that when Ash heard voices and turned to see that Eliza had arrived with George, Essie, and the girls in tow.

When Isla spotted him, she raced toward him and jumped up, trusting that he'd catch her... which he did.

"I'm gonna be so pretty tomorrow," Isla told him with a beaming smile.

He dropped a kiss to the top of her head. "You're so pretty today, princess."

She put her hands on his cheeks, then leaned forward and popped a kiss on his nose. "I have to practice tonight."

"Yep. You listen to what Carissa and Heather tell you and do your best."

"I will. Promise."

When she wriggled, Ash put her down and watched as she headed to where Rachel stood with Carissa. He noticed Hayden had arrived as well and made his way over to him.

"How's it going?" Ash asked, well aware it was a bit of a loaded question. Hayden rarely, if ever, gave anything but a stock *Fine* in response, and he stayed true to form that day as well.

Looking around, he said, "Seems a lot of fuss to say I do."

By now, Ash was used to Hayden's acerbic comments, and he knew that they were more an indication of his pain level than his true feelings about what was going on. He didn't take him to task over it because he understood the man. Plus, it wasn't his place.

"Don't tell Rachel and Isla that or they might give you their disappointed looks. They think this is all amazing."

"Yeah. Wouldn't want that to happen." Hayden sighed. "Lucky you don't have to wear a suit tomorrow."

"I don't have to, but I will be anyway."

Hayden frowned. "But why, man?"

"I figured that your sister would probably like it if I did."

Hayden rolled his eyes. "Dating for a week and already whipped."

Ash chuckled. "I look at it as trying my best to make Heather happy."

"And what about her making you happy?" Hayden asked.

"I figure she was trying to make me happy by not asking me to wear a suit."

"Should've stuck to that, man."

Ash shrugged. "Wearing a suit is a small price to pay."

Thankfully, he could wear the one he'd used for the New Year's Eve party. Heather had given him a tie to use, which she probably assumed that he'd just wear with a dress shirt and dress pants. He did plan to do that, but also with the suit coat.

"I'm never getting married," Hayden muttered as Heather headed in their direction.

"Never say never," Ash replied.

The other man shot him an incredulous look, but he didn't have a chance to reply before Heather reached them.

"Ready for the rehearsal?" Heather asked him. "The pastor just arrived, so we'll get going right away."

Hayden gave a single nod, then sighed before making his way to the front of the room where he sat down on one of the chairs.

Frowning, Heather turned to him. "What sort of mood is he in?"

"Probably about an eight out of ten on his sarcastic scale."

Since he'd shared his perception of Hayden's communication cues, Heather understood what he was talking about.

"Hopefully, the rehearsal goes quickly so he's not on his feet too much."

Heather took his hand and led him over to where Eliza stood with a man Ash recognized from the services he'd attended. He'd never met him before, but it looked like that was about to change.

After Eliza had introduced him to the pastor, they all migrated to where the arch was. Since Ash wasn't part of the wedding, he stayed out of the way as the pastor took charge of things.

He was prepared to step in if Isla wasn't listening, but he needn't have worried. She and Rachel followed directions like a dream, and even Hayden did everything he was told without any sarcastic comments.

They did two run-throughs and called it good. Then they were off to an upscale restaurant for their rehearsal dinner in a private room. Ash sat beside Heather at the table, still marveling that he'd actually gotten his act together enough to put aside his reservations and just go for it with her. He had no regrets, and even though it had been just a week, he had great hope for how things would go for them.

Once they were done with another multi-course meal and awaiting coffee and dessert, Ash put his arm around the back of Heather's chair. She angled herself toward him and gave him a smile.

"Thanks for helping out today," she said. "I know it's probably not your idea of a good time on a Friday night."

He grinned. "Given what my Friday nights are usually like, this is great."

"Well, I'm happy you're here."

"I wouldn't want to be anywhere else."

~ * ~

Heather blinked back tears as she watched Carissa walk down the aisle on George's arm, discovering to her dismay that even though she and her mom had shed a lot of tears over the past few days, there were still more to fall. She had hoped that if they had allowed their grief over those who won't be with them for the wedding to freely flow before the big day, that at the ceremony, they could focus on the joy of Hunter and Carissa's marriage.

That wasn't what had happened.

Carissa had struggled with her emotions as she'd gotten ready, her loss double that day since she was missing both her parents. Though they still had their mom there, their dad had looked forward to the day when each of them would have gotten married.

His absence was like a chasm, and her mom had shed tears as she'd walked down the aisle on Hunter's arm.

And now Heather could see her sitting in the front row with Essie and George, the three of them quietly crying. She gripped the stems of her bouquet more tightly, hoping she wouldn't have to unwind the tissues she'd wrapped there.

She moved her gaze to the one person she was pretty sure wouldn't be crying that day. Except when she looked at Ash, he was watching her with concern on his face. That threatened to bring more tears to her eyes, but she still tried to offer him a reassuring smile. It must have been good enough since his expression softened, and he winked at her.

Her smile in response to that felt more natural, even though grief still lingered around the edges. She clung to her love for Ash as she listened to Hunter and Carissa say their vows, wondering if such a ceremony was in her future. Their paths might have only crossed six weeks ago, and they might only have been together for a week, but when she looked at Ash, all she saw was a man she admired and loved. Maybe it had been love at first sight after all.

When the ceremony ended, the heavy emotion seemed to lift as upbeat music accompanied Carissa and Hunter as they walked from the arch to the back of the room once the pastor had pronounced them married. Isla and Rachel skipped after them in their sage green dresses with navy satin sashes. Heather's dress, as well as the ties and pocket squares in their suit, were burgundy.

She and Hayden moved more slowly behind the girls, but soon they too were at the back of the room with Hunter and Carissa. Heather gave her best friend and new sister-in-law a tight hug, then moved on to do the same with Hunter.

It wasn't long before Ash had found her, and he wrapped her in his arms without any hesitation. Heather clung to him, grateful for his presence there that day.

"You look so beautiful," he murmured.

Plenty of men had told her that over the years, but the words had never meant as much as they did coming from Ash. She shifted her head back so that she could look into his eyes. "Thank you. And I must say that you look handsome as well. Though, honestly, I think you're handsome in a pair of jeans and a T-shirt."

"Hayden told me I was dumb for wearing a suit when I didn't have to."

Heather laughed. "I'm not surprised. He tried to convince Hunter that he should get married in jeans."

Before they could continue that conversation, they were being directed to leave for the limos waiting out front of the church. They had a short time for pictures at an indoor garden, then they'd be off to the reception.

When Carissa had insisted on doing the wedding all by herself, Heather couldn't really understand why. But in the end, it had been lovely, and Heather had felt a sense of satisfaction when it had all come together.

For the reception, however, Hunter had insisted that Carissa let professionals carry the weight of it. So aside from the two of them deciding on the menu, they'd done nothing else to prepare for it, which meant that now they could just relax and enjoy it.

They'd chosen to have it at a mansion that had been converted into a wedding venue. Because of the small number of guests, they had been able to use the conservatory of the mansion, which was a beautiful space with lots of greenery and windows. Though they were only using the conservatory, Hunter had rented out the entire venue, so they wouldn't have to share it with anyone that night.

The drive to the mansion was relaxing, and Heather leaned against Ash, listening as Isla and Rachel chatted together about everything related to the wedding so far. She had a feeling they would be thrilled when they got to their destination.

"This is... wow..." Ash said as they pulled up in front of the mansion to park under the portico.

As she climbed from the limo with Ash's help, the air felt colder than it had earlier, but she was sure that was down to the sun having set. Ash kept her hand in his as they followed Isla and Rachel up the stairs to the wide front door. Heather might live in a mansion, but this one was more historical than theirs, which made it even more beautiful.

Guests arrived shortly after they did, and soon the reception was underway. Even though it was an expensive venue with expensive food, it was still relaxing since everyone there was close to their family.

Once the main meal was over, there was a break for people to mingle with others there who might not have been seated with them.

"Can we wander through the building?" Ash asked.

"The main floor," she said as they got to their feet. "You want to look around?"

He nodded and offered her his hand. Heather took it without hesitation. She knew he was conscious of the condition of his hands, but the stains or the roughness of his skin never bothered her. In fact, she appreciated the reminder that he was a man who worked hard with his hands.

Heather enjoyed getting a look at the rest of the public spaces of the mansion. They ended up in the living room, where flames danced in a fireplace along one wall.

"I've never been to a wedding like this," Ash said as they wandered close to the large windows that looked out over the front of the mansion.

That didn't surprise Heather, but still she asked, "In what way?"

"It just seemed to have such a focus on building a strong marriage and making sure God was part of it. Very different from the one and only wedding I've been to."

"You've only been to one wedding?"

Ash nodded. "I've had friends in relationships over the years, but the only wedding I remember going to was when I was about twenty. A friend of mine got his girlfriend pregnant, and they decided to get married. That lasted about a year before the woman kicked my friend to the curb. So yeah, this is quite different."

"I know it was important to Hunter and Carissa that the ceremony reflected their love for each other and for God. They spent time with the pastor in the weeks leading up to the wedding, and the message he gave was based on those conversations."

"I worry that I won't be as good as I want to be in our relationship. I didn't have a good example with my parents the way you did with yours."

Heather leaned against his shoulder. "I think you'll be just fine. But I know that Hunter would be more than happy to talk to you about any concerns you have. And I want you to feel comfortable about sharing that stuff with me too."

Ash turned to face her more fully, his expression serious and yet loaded with emotion. Heather lifted a hand to his cheek, feeling the roughness of his scruff against her palm.

"I didn't know it was possible to feel about someone the way I do about you," Ash said, his voice low. "And so quickly."

Heather felt his words settle into her heart, matching up with her own feelings. "My dad told us that his greatest wish was that if it was God's will for us to marry, that we'd find a love like he had with my mom. I don't know exactly how love felt for them, but I saw how they were with each other, and that's how I want to be with you."

With brow furrowed, Ash regarded her, and Heather held her breath. She needed him to figure out for himself how he felt about her. If she told him that she loved him, it was possible that he would say it back to her. But would it be because he felt he should, or because that was how he really felt?

It was a conundrum that she wasn't sure how to overcome. She had confidence in her own feelings. She'd been in love before, but it had never felt as strong or certain as what she felt for Ash. Maybe it was because she knew for once that he was with her despite her money, not because of it.

"I love you, Heather," he said. "Though I have to say that it absolutely scares me to death because I don't want to hurt you or do anything to mess things up."

"Are you scared enough to want to end things?" She was quite sure that he didn't want that, but she wanted to settle that in his own mind.

"No." He reinforced that response with a shake of his head. "I refuse to allow my fear to rob me of what I think is one of the most precious things I've ever had in my life. I was scared about things with Isla, too. Fear is a great motivator, though, and I plan to have it motivate me to be the best I can be for you and for her."

That was the realization she'd hoped he'd come to. Her own realization about accepting scary things had been her dad's death. Life was too short to let fear hold her back. As long as Ash was willing to take the risk, so was she.

"I love you too, Ash." She smiled at him. "You and me... we're going to figure this out together. I have no doubt about that."

His expression softened, and a smile tipped up the corner of his mouth in a way she always found super attractive. He wrapped his arms around her, and she lifted her chin. When he bent his head down, Heather placed her hands behind his neck and went up on her toes to meet him for their first real kiss.

The press of his lips against hers felt like a declaration... a promise... and she would forever remember that moment for the joy and love that filled her.

~*~*~ *THE END* ~*~*~

ABOUT THE AUTHOR

Kimberly Rae Jordan is a USA Today bestselling author of Christian romances. Many years ago, her love of reading Christian romance morphed into a desire to write stories of love, faith, and family, and thus began a journey that would lead her to places Kimberly never imagined she'd go.

In addition to being a writer, she is also a wife and mother, which means Kimberly spends her days straddling the line between real life in a house on the prairies of Canada and the imaginary world her characters live in. Though caring for her husband and four kids and working on her stories takes up a large portion of her day, Kimberly also enjoys reading and looking at craft ideas that she will likely never attempt to make.

As she continues to pen heartwarming stories of love, faith, and family, Kimberly hopes that readers of all ages will enjoy the journeys her characters take in each book. She has no plan to stop writing the stories God places on her heart and looks forward to where her journey will take her in the years to come.

Printed in Great Britain
by Amazon